THE COMING OF ELI

The Early Years

CHAPTER 1

The Journal

A watertight iron box sat atop the table, basking in the glow of a single candle as the young lad opened it with eager anticipation. The instructions of his mother's final request were clear, it was time he learned the truth about his life. Inside the musty container sat a thick hard covered journal, the type used aboard ships as a log. Carefully emerging it out, the 11-year-old Eli began to read it with heart pounding concentration. Within the front cover was written: "Elizabeth Griffin, born February 16, 1724, in Pyle, Wales". But in a different handwriting was: "Died August 2, 1741". Eli & Noah recognized that it was Colleen's handwriting. Pausing a moment to peer closer, the youth continued on. His mind began to en vision the history as it unfolded.

He learned that Elizabeth was the elder of 2 sisters. Her father, Nicolas, & mother Maybelle were farmers who worked the land they lived on for the owner, a wealthy Englishman named Lord Ervin. He was a distant cousin through marriage to the royal family and not well received at court due to his excessive drinking, gambling, & philandering. Years before, he was granted a meager post as an overseer to the sea trade out of the growing port of Bristol. A position Ervin was suited for since his only positive characteristic was his ability to barter and trade. Eventually he established several profitable trade routes throughout the Americas, Africa & the Caribbean.

In the summer of 1738 Ervin traveled to Pyle to oversee his vast properties throughout Wales. For several months he had been displeased with the harvest outputs from numerous farms including the Griffin farm. When he arrived his eye immediately focused more on the 14-year-old Elizabeth then the business at hand. She had blossomed into a fetching little lass; her long auburn hair and sparkling hazel eyes was a perfect complement to a petite budding figure. Ervin's imagination raced as he struggled to conceal it from her family. As Nicolas pleaded his case about the poor weather being the main cause of the lack luster harvest, Ervin sat there calculating his move. He proposed that young Elizabeth escort him back to Ervin Estate where she would be employed as a house maid. Even though Nicolas objected to the proposition he had no choice but to accept it or be thrown off the land.

Noah was astounded as the tale unfolded. He placed a comforting hand on the shoulder of young Eli as they read on together. Noah Studman was a tall burly seaman of 35 plus years. Dutch by birth, he was an experienced sailor and first mated on several ships before settling in Charleston almost 8 years before. He and Colleen struck up a close friendship as Eli slowly grew up before their eyes. For the last 3 years Eli was crewing on Noah's small fishing boat and learning all the jolly dutchman knew about the sea. Some would say Noah gave up the open sea life due to his fancy for Eli's Mother and the quick learning youth, but Noah would deny it.

They read on, "At first, I was mixed with feelings of joy & sorrow. I would have the chance to truly help my family with this new position but being taking from them hurts me deeply". Wrote the innocent lass.

"The first 2 years at the estate was good. I mostly took care of his wife, Lady Winslow and their 2 sons. The elder, Ervin II was close to my age with the other boy, Reginal 2 years younger". She mentioned their spoiled ways, and at times very spiteful characteristics toward anyone below their class. Typical snobbish attitudes for members of the royal family, no matter how down the line they were. It was clear to Elizabeth that the entire family had an air of aloof about them, especially Lord Ervin.

"It was in late December of 1739 when word came of the loss of my family. I was informed they had perished at the hands of bandits who had ravaged the area farmers". She went on to express her deepest sorrow and remorse for the only family she had. Noah couldn't help but feel there was much more behind this tragic loss. Long chats with Colleen over the years enlightened the wise dutchman to the plight Elizabeth & Colleen faced. As for Eli, he began to sense the emotion in the words he read. He was only 11, yet his mind was far beyond his years.

Lord Ervin's growing profit for the family company (Royal Shipping Line) was about to excel him into the good graces of King George II. For almost 5 years he has finagled & bartered the small sea trade company into several thriving shipping routes. Increasing the size of the company ships almost 10-fold with routes regularly hit along the eastern American coastline and throughout the growing Caribbean islands, with the occasional trip to West Africa for slaves. On the verge of his overdue public recognition by the royal family, bad news hit the Lord hard.

Elizabeth privately informed him that she was with child. Late night forced visits to her darken chamber eventually brought her to this unwanted condition. Her only solus was she never had to see his face as he would repeatedly ravage her from behind. Quick thinking, he told the pregnant lass to keep this strictly to herself. He would take care of everything with complete discretion and comfort. A day or so later he told Elizabeth that arrangements were being made to have her moved to a private cottage in the country and setup with enough money and assistance to have her baby.

A few weeks later, Ervin left on his usual tour of his farms in Wales. He had sent word to a former employee, Horace McLeary, who lived in northern Scotland, to meet with him in Wales to "Discuss some very Important & secretive work to be done". Once they met, the shady Scotsman was let in on a plan to dispose of the pregnant orphan teen. He and his wife Colleen had a small cottage a few miles from the Scottish seaport. Horace was instructed to lull Elizabeth into comfort and then eliminate her. Colleen was unaware of the death plot and naturally became a pawn in this unspeakable plot.

Colleen was a meek minded woman in her late 20s. She had that plain farmer look with a sturdy round built. Her marriage to Horace 10 years before was an arranged one. This was a normal practice for its time when the father was pressed for money. And even though she knew of her shady husband's misgivings she had little choice but to stay with him. He was widely known in the village to be a drunk and philanderer, especially with the loose women. Colleen bore the physical & emotional scares with quiet contempt, just biding her time.

Upon his return to Bristol, Ervin told Elizabeth she would be taken in comfort to the Northern Scottish village and completely looked after once she had her child. And before the lass showed any physical signs of her situation, she was taken by boat to her new home. It was during the weeklong trip that she began her journal in hopes to share it with her impending child. A few days before her departure, on board a faster vessel, a messenger was dispatched by Ervin with strict orders to take a sealed letter directly to Horace once the ship landed in Northern Scotland. In the letter was information about her arrival and payment for her elimination. With time to spare, the messenger completed his task and immediately started his return to Bristol. 50 pounds in hand, Horace only had to wait for Elizabeth to arrive and start the plan. Later that night, after he was passed out from a drunken celebration, Colleen discovered the secret letter. She could hardly believe her eyes as she read the despicable plot her worthless husband was tasked with. Her mission slowly became clear as several days went by until Elizabeth eventually arrived.

Unaware his wife knew what was going on, Horace ordered Colleen to meet the ship and bring the teen to their cottage. She suggested that she stay overnight with the young girl and get needed supplies before returning. Horace agreed knowing he had an opportunity to have some open play time with one of the neighboring lassies. The 3-hour journey by cart gave her ample time to get acquainted with Elizabeth and size up what to do next. When the two women met it seemed like an immediate bond of friendship. For Colleen it was partly from pity and sympathy. For Elizabeth it was partial relief from the voyage and a strange peace of mind for her that she had not felt in a long time.

Later that evening, after a hearty meal at the port inn, Colleen unveiled the plot against the teen. When the shock wore off the two women decided to hatch a plot of their own. While the town slept, they quietly snuck out and headed for the cottage. Silent as the night, they arrived and as Colleen had calculated, her cheating husband was passed out in their bed with the wench he frequently played with. Both totally intoxicated and naked, they laid there unaware of anything going on. In a final fit of rage Colleen picked up her wooden kitchen mallet she'd used to pound out meat and proceeded to swing it one last time. The dull thud found its mark to the back of Horace's head. Rapidly she turned it on the slut's skull as both lay there motionless. Elizabeth was surprisingly unshaken as she watched the ordeal unfold. A revengeful smile came over Colleen's face as her eyes spoke of final relief from her long years of torment & despair.

The women quickly sifted thru the strewn clothes for any money and valuables. They gathered up whatever supplies they would need for their pending escape trip and packed it into the horse drawn cart. Only one more thing left to do. They grabbed up all the black power they could find, spread it generously over the bedded bodies and touched it off. Immediately, flames burst into a roar as the two women beat a hasty exit. Before they were safely in the cart the entire cottage was ablaze with a fury of crackling heat. A mile down the dusty road, the light of the remote cottage was still bright & strong. They were free now, and no one the wiser. The towns people would assume the charred remains were Horace & Colleen. As for the wench, she was well known to repeatedly wander off for days & weeks at a time, usually drunk too. As for Ervin, word would get back to him eventually that the two bodies were Elizabeth & Colleen. He figured Horace had disappeared and would never be seen again. They headed southwest, their destination: Glasgow to hopefully board a ship bound west and out of Scotland forever.

Noah began to open up more & more to Eli about the tales Colleen had shared with the burly Dutchman over the years. He felt it was high time the young lad knew the whole truth. He knew now that even though Eli was barely 11 years old, he could handle the facts about his birth mother as well as the only mother he knew. And maybe even some insight to the lad's astonishing ability to grasp things quickly and easily.

The road was long and tiring, but it gave the two intrepid lassies the time to become closer than they ever anticipated. Among the items they gathered up before they torched the cottage was a unique looking bone handled knife. Elizabeth recognized it immediately. On the butt of the handle was carved the initials: NG, her father's blade he had made. The pieces of the puzzle about her family's death started to fall into place. Colleen explained that Horace would occasionally be gone for weeks at a time only to return with coin in his pocket & bobbles unknown. The teen wondered if it went deeper, say, back to Lord Ervin. Could he be behind the so called "Bandit Raiders"?

When they arrived in Glasgow it was late-March 1741. The town was bustling with business & trade mostly from the start of the spring shipping trade. But it was a frantic time for local farmers starting their spring crops. The two women felt uncomfortable about lingering in the port long and knew they had to get to Ireland as soon as possible. Belfast was a short sea trip for any outgoing vessel. They knew the money they had was to last them till they were safely out of Scotland and farther away. It was a few days in port when they managed to hitch a ride on a small cargo ship bound for Ireland. Colleen sold the horse & cart to a local farmer for almost enough to cover the expenses for the two lassies trip to Ireland. On the ship's manifest they were listed as the McGriff sisters.

During the short voyage, they overheard some of the crew speak of the bounty in the "New World" and a growing seaport called Charleston in the Carolinas. This was just what they needed to gain a fresh start on life. And with Elizabeth almost 5 months along, they knew time was of the essence to get there before she gave birth. Even in Ireland, they felt it still too risky to stay. Lord Ervin had ships coming in & out of Belfast as well as Londonderry so fear of someone recognizing them was too much to chance. The money was depleting fast as they sought passage to the Americas. Belfast had no ships scheduled for route to the New World, but rumor had it that they might book passage there from Londonderry to the northwest of Belfast.

Working odd jobs in Belfast as well as other small villages on their way northwest, the two adventures made it to Londonderry in mid-April. The good news was the rumors were true, the bad news was they missed a large cargo ship bound for Boston by mere days upon their arrival. Now it was a waiting game in hopes they could book passage before too long. The choice had to be made and soon, 1: stay and have the baby in Londonderry or 2: hope to escape to the Americas before it was too late. As the days & weeks passed waiting for that "freedom ship" to dock, they found work to help them survive. A local farmer a few miles outside the seaport hired the self-proclaimed sisters on to cook and clean for the field hands.

On a rainy day in mid-June, Colleen was headed for the port town to pick up supplies for the farm. At the wharf she saw a frightful sight, one of the ships owned by Lord Ervin was in port. On board was a sailor she recognized from Horace's crew who was part of the bandit raiders. She managed to get what she needed and left quickly before being seen. There was a smaller cargo ship anchored in the harbor that was bound for Charleston the next morning. She learned this from a young 18-year-old sailor, *Everwyn Morwer who was the navigator on the small flute. Everwyn was Welsh decent and had been putting out to sea since he was 12. As they chatted, Colleen got the impression he wasn't too fond of the Royal Shipping lines. She explained briefly the McGriff sister's situation and pleaded for his assistance. He thought it over a moment and agreed to sneak them aboard, considering that the flute's Captain was also his uncle.

Racing back to the farm, she informed Elizabeth of everything and the two decided it was time to leave on that ship anyway possible. Everwyn assured her that they could make the Carolina port within a months' time. The flute was already carrying half a dozen passengers including a young doctor & his wife who were planning to setup practice in the expanding Charleston port. Around midnight, under the cloak of darkness, the two women boarded the ship, and their final leg of a long journey began. Even though they were aware of the risk that Elizabeth would give birth at sea, they knew it was better than being discovered.

Overcast & misty, the ship sail on the tide at daybreak on June 20th, 1741, with a heading west southwest. The seas were calm with the wind's favorable as they rounded the northern tip of Ireland. But two days into the North Atlantic, the conditions turned on the small vessel. Choppy waters, teamed with cross winds, made their speed slow by half. As the young navigator charted their course to a more south-southwest direction, the ship luckily caught a more manageable stream. This allowed the passengers aboard to finally stretch the sea legs on deck and get a breath of fresh sea air.

One morning, Colleen & Elizabeth noticed a young lad peering intently at the view off the port side. In hand was a sketch pad and charcoal stick. As they looked over his shoulder, they watched the creation unfold of the distant Irish coastline. Introducing themselves to a fledgling cartographer, Darin Cavety, a fair-haired artist from England. He too was bound for work in Charleston with the hopes of opening a map making shop there. As an orphan of 6, he was sold to a butcher to labor in his shop. Next door to the meat house was a unique antique shop that the boy would frequent regularly. He was fascinated mostly with large globes & framed paintings of world maps. The Antique dealer was a kindhearted old gent who took a liking to the curious lad. With the passing years, the boy showed serious promise as a detailed artist. So, when Darin turned 17, he took the old gent's advice and lit out to seek his fortune that brought him to this voyage.

July 15th, 1741 brought up an unexpected storm from the west that raked the flute off its course, thus slowly it to a crawl. Sails from the mizen & main masts were shredded open and one of the hulls bracers cracked. Luckily no one was lost but several of the crew were dealing with minor injuries. The doctor & nurse wife was a blessing to be aboard and tended to them with expert hast. As best as he could calculate it, Everwyn figured their navigation course was thrown off by some 50 nautical miles or more. This delayed their expected arrival in Charleston by no less than 4 days. When the storm passed the crew went to work in a flash to make repairs.

The voyage was starting to take its toll on Elizabeth. Even though she showed no signs yet of giving birth, her health was falling off day by day. More than just the usual sea & morning sickness she was feeling the weakness slowly take over her body. Even with the doctor checking on her periodically, Colleen could see that her dear friend's condition deteriorating as the long days at sea became almost endless & arduous. The food & water were ordered rationed from the captain when it was discovered that the storm had spoiled or lost half. July 20th, with the ship repaired to capacity, the captain announced they should make Charleston within 2 weeks or less with hopes of favorable winds & weather.

Day break of August 2nd shone brightly as the warm sun glistened off the calm blue waters. The billowing sails fluttered with the eastern breezes filling the white canvas like large pillows on high. All seem well as the ship cut briskly through the ocean waves. But below decks Elizabeth suffered a rough night with repeated pains. She knew it was time, as did Colleen and the doctor. The captain had her moved to his cabin when her water broke knowing his ship was about to add another passenger to the list. Several hours past as muffled cries of pain echoed throughout the cabin. Thankfully the seas were calm helping to ease the pitch & roll of the ship.

Elizabeth was fighting for her life to pull through this and birth a health child. At 11 am a high-pitched cry pierced throughout the ship, a fine baby boy. There was a short silence from the new mother then suddenly she screamed again. The doctor worked diligently as he eased out a second child, another boy. But this one was silent... dead silent. A stillborn baby sat motionless in the blood covered hands of the doctor. All the tear-filled eyes in the cabin turned slowly toward the mother, sweat covered, flushed & bewildered. The doctor quickly wrapped up the stillborn infant, handing it to Colleen and whispered to her, "take the child out of here, let's concentrate on those alive right now"! She nodded and left quickly. The nurse-wife had cleaned up the still whimpering baby boy, handing him to his mother knowing this would ease & comfort her. A bright smile blossomed from Elizabeth's face as she gazed into her child's glistening blue eyes.

Her voice weak as she spoke out, "Is he ok doctor?" Smiling happily, he replied, "Yes, he is just fine a strong health boy. All he needs now is a name"! She looked deeply at her newborn son, paused, then replied, "Eli.... Yes, I like that.... Eli McGriff". Word spread quickly throughout the ship of the good & bad news. The captain, patted the back of the doctor, giving him a hearty well done as he exited his cabin to get back to his task at hand. Returning to his position on his quarterdeck, the aged captain peered out to sea. His mind began to recall of an old wife's tale he had heard repeatedly. It was about how the survivor of stillborn twins being blessed with all the knowledge & wisdom from the dead one. Then he whispered, "That boy will be something special, I'd bet my life on it"!

Colleen emptied out a chest in the storage compartment and gently place the tightly wrapped up infant inside and closed it. She took just a moment to gather her wits before heading back to herself proclaimed sister & new nephew. She had in the back of her mind that this whole ordeal may have taken a dreadful toll on Elizabeth, so she had to prepared for the worst. Returning to the captain's cabin, she assured the doctor & his wife that she had things well in hand for now, as the fatigued couple slowly left. With mother & child now well asleep, Colleen sat down next to them to relax some too.

A few hours of silences passed when Colleen was awakened from a nap by the soft touch of Elizabeth's hand on hers. A majestic glow cascaded from the new mother's face as the two exchanged smiles. She motioned for her to take the sleeping Eli, as the gentle exchange was made. Elizabeth began to whisper weakly, "I need one last favor of you my dear sister". Colleen nodded willingly, "Name it dear one". Elizabeth paused for a second to catch her breath and spoke, "Promise me you will take good care of Eli when I'm gone". Beads of tears swelled up and poured from their eyes, they both knew the inevitable was now at hand. But before she could reply, the soft hand of her dear sister fell down in eternal rest. Her tear-soaked eyes closed for the last time. Colleen looked down on the deep sleep baby and softy said, "I swear on all that is holy, I will raise you to the best of my ability, my son, Eli McGriff". Later that night, under the serenity of a stary sky, the crew and passengers gathered on deck. Wrapped together in traditional mariner shroud, they were buried as sea with Elizabeth holding her son in her arms.

The following evening, a cry bellowed out from the lookout, Land Ho! Charleston off the starboard beam"! Within an hour the Welsh flute docked under very few towns' people eyes. There on the dock was the harbor master whose task was to record all arrivals & departures including passengers. Knowing this would happen, young Everwyn Morwer had forged a set of papers earlier that morning for Mrs.

Colleen McGriff & son Eli McGriff. He finished off the farce with a witnessed & signed statement by the port director in Londonderry. A deep sigh of relief came over Collen when the harbor master stamped her papers and said, "Welcome Mrs. McGriff to Charleston". She turned back at the ship, most of the crew busy offloading the cargo. She smiled gratefully and softly said, "Thank You... Thank You All". They all knew there would be an unspoken vow of silence as they all continued on with their lives.

It took no time to get settled into her new home & surroundings. Charleston was just hitting its peak in growth. Businesses popping up left & right almost daily. Colleen got work as a cook in one of the thriving taverns just off the wharf. That was where she eventually met Noah as the two became friends. He traveled back & forth from the port as a first mate on a Dutch Cargo ship. Eventually he had his fill of it after 10 plus years at sea so a couple of years later he decided to settle in Charleston. Purchasing a small fishing boat, Noah began to make an easier life for himself there. Eventually, he opened a small fish market just off the docks where Colleen was hired to take over and assist him.

As Eli grew in size, so did his mind, grasping the basics with ease & speed. Before he was 5, he was reading & writing. The Dutchman began to take a shine to the smart little lad. As for Colleen, she kept her word and more. She raised Eli as if she gave birth to him including adding to the journal Elizabeth had started. The day came when the lad asked about his father. She simply told him he was a merchant sailor who died at sea. She knew the day would come when he would have to know the truth, but for now it was her first priority to help him grow. By age 7 he was crewing with Noah on his fishing boat, learning more every day the proper ways of a mariner.

More importantly, the youngster was learning how to enjoy life in the ever-growing port town. He easily made friends of all nationality too. Charleston was a checkerboard of French, Spanish, German & Dutch. Through shear repetition, Eli began to actually pick up the various languages spoken and by age 10 could easily understand & ever speak some of it. Noah saw this, so when they were together on the boat, they would speak Dutch only. He was growing physically too, getting tall & stronger than others his age. During this period in time, it was uncommon for most children to be "home schooled" rather than sent to local schools in the larger towns & villages. Eli was that exception.

It was around Mid-May 1752 when an English ship arrived in Charleston, a Royal Shipping Line Company vessel. On board was a deckhand named Joseph Fahen who was a former partner with Horace McLeary as one of the members of the bandit raiders. As he helped to off load the ship's cargo, he caught sight of a buxom redhead that looked strangely familiar...Colleen. But he had heard they both died in the cottage fire 11 years ago. Keeping out of sight of redhead fish vendor, he decided to look into this more. Colleen was unaware she was being watch as she continued on with her usual business. As for Eli, he was with Noah down the coastline on their usual 2-day fishing run. Later that evening, Fahen went ashore with the rest of the crew. Overhearing the name Colleen from a local man in the wharf tavern he knew he had pegged her right; it was the same Colleen. The shady sailor saw a chance to make a sizable profit from this information if it got back to the right person, now Viscount Ervin. Years before he was finally recognized by the royal family and bestowed his new title. A day later the ship sailed with Fahen aboard, bound for Boston then back to Bristol, just as Noah & Eli were sailing back into port.

It was early July when Fahen's ship docked in Bristol. He wasted no time seeking out a private audience with the Viscount. After telling him the startling news about Colleen, Ervin's face turned a ghostly white. He composed himself, took a deep breath as he turned to the spying seaman and said, "I want you to dispose of her Immediately"! He unlocked his large desk draw and tossed a sizeable pouch of gold coins at Fahen. "A fortnight from now your ship departs for Charleston, BE ON IT", Ervin Commanded. The informer just smirked, then nodded his head & left. The Viscount sat there pondering what really had happened 11 years ago. He figured now that the 2 unidentifiable bodies in the Scottish cottage had to be Horace & Elizabeth. Somehow, Colleen escaped and was the only one to know the despicable truth. With her eliminated the books can forever be closed.

Late night on September 13th, 1752, Fahen's vessel docked in Charleston just ahead of a storm front coming in from due east. Rain was pelting down heavily as occasional gusts of eastly winds & thunder would kick up. The captain ordered the crew to batten down all hatches and remain below till daybreak. When all of his bunkmates were fast asleep, Fahen saw his opportunity to dispose of his target without anyone seeing him. Sneaking off silently he made his way to her two-store house he had seen her go into months before. Opening a window, he silently crept inside. All was peaceful inside as he presumed, she was alone and asleep. There she laid in bed as he eased in to attack her. Quickly gripping her throat with both hands, he began to choke the unsuspecting woman. But the skinny assailant didn't anticipate her strength as she fought his assaults. The struggle went on for several seconds till they both kicked over the bedside table. Her voice muffled unable to scream for help. Fahen could feel she was fading fast as he lunged in harder for the final kill.

Then all at once there was a resounding thud as Fahen collapsed on top of the gasping woman. Her eyes slowly began to refocus to see Eli standing over them still gripping a large iron skillet. A blank look engulfed the boy's face for a moment, then uttered, "Are you alright Momma"? She regained some of her strength enough to push the still body off her onto the floor. "Yes... yes, I think so son", she whispered out. She sat up checking to see the condition of Fahen, his skull was cracked open, he was dead. Slowly, a pool of dark crimson blood began to encircle his head. With passioned relief she took the skillet from his hands and hugged the boy hero, uttered in his ear, "Oh My God Thank you Son ... Thank you"! She gripped his shoulders firmly and ordered him to fetch Noah who lived only a few houses away. The boy lit out with all the speed he could muster. She checked one last time to assure herself the bastard was dead. Yep. As a door nail.

Within a matter of moments Noah & Eli burst in from the torrential down pour that was soaking the streets. Noah embraced her and told her to rest he will take care of this now. He told Eli to look after his mother while he took care of the dead bastard. Grabbing up the blood-stained sheet off her bed he expertly wrapped his head, thus slowing the puddle of blood still oozing out. He then wrapped the body in a blanket and heaved it over his strong wide shoulders. "I'll be back in a few minutes to clean up the rest of this mess, meantime, you rest", as he left out. Stepping lively through the darkness & heavy rain, Noah took the bundle back to his house undetected. He knew what this type of storm was about to bring to Charleston, it was a hurricane. There is an air about them, you can smell it as it swelled up of the ocean, and Noah had smelled this many times before. After safely stowing away the body in his woodshed, he returned to the McGriff home, soaked to the bone from the ever-increasing rain.

Eli had managed to make his mother as comfortable as possible and was cleaning up the pool of blood left on the floor. Within a few minutes, Noah and the unphased boy had it all gone while letting the down pour outside the door rinse the blood away from the clothes used. As her voice gradually came back, she explained who he was. She recognized Fahen immediately, knowing he had probably come from the Royal owned ship that docked. Noah ordered her to rest for now and told them both to start preparing for a blow from the oncoming hurricane. "I'll get rid of that asshole tomorrow, don't you worry, for now we will ride tonight out here together", he calmly said. He tucked in Colleen snuggly then told Eli to try and get some sleep as Noah walked over to stoke up the fireplace and dry off.

A few minutes after Eli retired to his upstairs bedroom, Noah came in to check on him. He softly spoke," Your mother finally fell off to sleep, I think she'll be ok with rest". The boy nodded not saying a word, just a blank distant look in his eyes. Noah sat down on the bed and said in a comforting tone, "I'm not gonna ask if you're ok. I see already you are.... what you did tonight took a lot of guts & I'm very proud of you". The boy nodded again as his eyes got heavy. Noah stood up and started walking out when he heard the boy say with firm conviction, "I'm Glad I killed him, I'm Glad"! Noah stopped, then turned and said, "Me too". Those two simple words was assurance enough in Eli's mind to allow his conscience to rest for now.

When day broke the wind was howling, rain pelting harder with every minute that past. Off in the distance, Noah could hear the rolling of thunder approaching closer. He got up from his chair positioned at the foot of Colleen's bed as he watched over her throughout the night. The fireplace was down to small piles of burning embers when he threw a few more logs on. About the same time Eli came downstairs from his room, rubbing his eyes to waken more and ask, "How's momma doing"? Noah glanced over at her and said quietly, "She's still resting, thank God, that ordeal took a lot out of her". Smiling briefly the boy replied, "Took it out of me too". Noah told the boy to make some coffee as he put his heavy coat on to brave the weather, "I'm gonna run back to my place & check on things. I'll grab up some supplies we are gonna need & be right back", he stated as he walked out into the growing storm.

It was about 8 am but the sun was totally blocked out by heavy rain clouds, the gray-green ones that are the obvious signs of a hurricane. Fighting off the occasional bursts of wind, he decided to look over the situation at the docks which were only a few hundred yards from his house. The harbor waters were already churning up white cap chops as several small boats that were tied up along the wharf were bobbing around like tops. He rechecked his own fishing boat to reassure he had lashed her down tight. He strained his rain-soaked eyes to see the large Royal cargo ship docked at the center of the wharf was swaying fore & aft with every wave slapping her hull. No crew was on deck offloading their cargo yet due to the weather. The only other ship was the HMS Hornet, a fourteen-gun sloop of war securely anchored at the mouth of the harbor entrance.

Only a handful of town's people were outside, most racing about to secure their shops & stores. Noah returned to his house, first thing he checked on was the wrapped-up body in his woodshed outback of the house. All seemed the same as he left it several hours earlier. He grabbed up a change of dry clothes, and all the food and provisions he had and headed back to Colleen & Eli. She was up and about making breakfast for everyone when Noah returned. Other than some obvious burse marks around her neck she seemed fine but still a bit weak. As they sat down to eat, she proceeded to tell them who it was and why. They listened to her tale intently as it seemed to make perfect sense. Noah slowly reached into his jacket pocket and produced a leather coin pouch he had found on Fahen while he was wrapping him up. Inside was the remains of the payment he got from the Viscount. There was roughly about 30 gold crown coins left and on the pouch was the Royal Shipping Line crest embossed clearly.

Noah knew sailors weren't paid anywhere near that amount and never in gold crowns. A usual crewman was paid in shillings which came to roughly about a pound or two. As for the coin pouch that was not a normal thing you would find on a common sailor, except maybe a captain. Colleen knew it had to be Ervin who gave him the leather money pouch. For several years, everyone knew of the rise in royal family of the Viscount, even those in the colony towns along the east coast. Noah placed the pouch on the table, "this is yours now, you & Eli both", he proclaimed. Not a word was uttered, as the three sat there slowly finishing their breakfast. Only the rising sounds of heavy wind & rain broke the quiet with the occasional creaking of the wood framed house. The storm was approaching fast on Charleston and all they could do was hunker down and pray.

Strong winds began the evening of September 14th, becoming more violent as the storm blew closer. Rain sliced down steadily through the following early morning, as a terrifying night gave way to a horrifying day. The storm surge poured in around 9 am, overflowing seawalls and adjacent creek beds. Before 11 am nearly all the vessels in Charleston harbor were on shore, some driven into the marsh, some riding the flood that crashed into wharfs & buildings. The three could hear sounds of roofs being ripped off neighboring houses. The storm surge had sea water pouring in through the front door as they moved upstairs around noon on the 15th. Noah knew the eye of the hurricane was close as the winds & rain slowed to an almost eerie silence. Minutes later the winds shifted from the backside of the eye and the fury resumed.

Just then, a ground shaking explosion rocked the town, echoing for miles around. The Royal ship had broken from its mooring with the surge carrying it into several buildings on the wharf. The powder magazine touched off and the hull ignited throwing wood & cargo fragments everywhere. Water now had risen more than ten feet above the normal high-water mark, the sea covering the entire peninsula. Thankfully, the house the three were in was surrounded by several others on every side. Thus, forming a slight barrier for them. But when a second explosion hit, tragedy struck them.

A large section of the roof from another house came hurtling into the second-floor window and caving in part of the wall. Noah raced to clear the debris that cascaded over Eli who was hit with minor cuts and bruises. Then they turned to see a horrifying sight, Colleen sat wedged against the back wall with a section of the roof beam pressed hard at her chest. The two worked feverously to get it off her and gently move her to a safer spot. Clearly in agonizing pain, a trickly of blood began to form from the corner of her mouth. Once moved into a better spot in the devastated room, Noah sealed up the gaping hole in the wall as best he could.

Minutes later, they could hear the sounds of the winds begin to die down as the rain slowed to an easier downpour. Thankfully the winds shifted, the tide ebbed, and the water flowed out as quickly as it had come in. The downstairs was free of seawater now they could gingerly carry Colleen down to a dry safe spot. While Noah tended to her best he could, Eli relite the fireplace. By 3 pm the wind had died down proving the storm had finally passed. Colleen was in severe pain as she pointed to large wooden cabinet in the kitchen area and telling Noah to pull open the bottom doors. She mustered up every bit of strength and said, "Chest inside, get it out... not much time left... he needs you now... "Her eyes fell shut, her body limp, the pain was gone forever. The two sat aside her as tears poured out while embracing one another. It was the first time Noah had seen the boy openly weep since he was a toddler, little did he know it would be the last time too.

After they both tended to properly wrapping her up to prepare for her burial, they decided to head over to see what had happened to Noah's house. Very few people were outside yet as they slowly trudged through the debris & devastation that was Charleston. The Hurricane reduced the town to a very melancholy situation. Although there were no accurate figures as of yet of the deaths or injuries, it was presumed many drowned; others killed or dangerously injured when their house fell apart. Later it was estimated 500 buildings were destroyed completely. Broken chimneys, lost roofs, shattered windows, and dislodged foundations. The wharf & piers were smashed, every building upon them beaten down or carried away. They stood motionless in front of what use to be Noah's home, now a mass pile of rubble including the backside woodshed. The only thing remained was shreds of the blanket Fahen was in. As they learned later his body was found washed up in the marsh on the back part of town.

The two companions eventually found their fishing boat almost a thousand yards from the docks in a creek gully. The Mast had snapped but miraculously the hull was in tack with only minor damage they could repair eventually. There were several other small crafts scattered around that weren't as lucky. With the exception of very few, the bulk of the vessels of Charleston were destroyed. The HMS Hornet somehow managed to ride out the storm with minimal damage. Before she sailed back to England, she carried with her the news of the destruction as well as the list of 95 names who perished in it. On that list was all the members of the Royal Ship that blew up as well as the town folk of Charleston, including Colleen McGriff. She was buried along a small rolling hill just west of town that overlooked the harbor, a place they knew she would want to be.

As grief stricken as the towns people were, it was priority one to get their lives back in order with the utmost of haste. This included the main export farms of corn, indigo and rice that were wiped out from the hurricane. Within a few days, the two survivors began repairs on the McGriff house. Using a lot of the materials from Noah's house that was totally flattened to the ground, they were able to get the house back in order, including several stronger improvements. They managed to salvage their fishing boat and carted it back to the dock area. Oh yes, one more thing, they got around to opening the bottom doors of the large wooden cabinet in the kitchen area. They discovered a watertight iron box and inside is where the tale began.

CHAPTER 2

The Gathering

For almost 2 weeks, everyone worked feverously to get Charleston back in order, including the soul protection of the British fort at the mouth of the harbor. Most of the city's governing building were damaged or destroyed, added to the list was the town hall that housed all the of shipping & personal records. The misfortunes continued to ravage the Carolina port when a second storm rushed through on the afternoon of September 30th. Luckily, this one was not as overpowering and pushed past within a matter of a few hours. The main thrust of the hurricane did extensive damage further south along the Georgia coastline. The bustling port of Savannah was ripped apart leaving them in the same peril as their northern neighbor. Cartographer, Darin Cavety had married 7 years before to a plantation owner's daughter, Constance who gave birth to their son Trevor. Mother & child were visiting the Savannah plantation when the storm hit as they perished during the violent siege. Word got back to Darin within days at his Map making shop in Charleston.

Over the years, Darin had become a respected member of the community, which included accepting the position of assistant to the harbor master. He and Noah grew to be good friends during this time. When the tragic news reached the husky Dutchman, he & Eli immediately went to console the devastated man. Noah had another reason as well, with all the town's personal records destroyed it was an opportunity to change Eli's name to Studman. Noah felt if the paperwork officially showed Eli was his legal born son, it would eliminate any doubts from the possible probing viscount back in Bristol. Besides, most of the Charleston community naturally assumed Noah was the father of the boy already. Darin agreed and within days it was made official as he added it to the town files as Elijah Studman.

As the weeks turned to months, everything was slowly revolving back to normal in Charleston. This was a period in life when people had very little time to lament or grieve on the dead. They forged forward to survive & grow in this new land they called home. Those who immigrated knew of a life of conflict, war & terrane. Most left for the New World to escape it all, some were forced to leave, and others enslaved. But no matter what the reason, this was home now, and they refused to give up the fight for a better life. Maybe that was one of the main reasons they were somewhat, cold hearted toward death of a loved one. Life must go on no matter what the cost. It also made for special times becoming a truly joyful moment, like Christmas.

Noah & Eli were quickly back to their productive work as fishermen after rebuilding and improving their boat as well as reconstructing the fish shop on the wharf. They hired a local 16-year-old orphan girl named Ruth Jacobs to help run the shop while they were at sea. She had lost her parents in the storm and was basically all alone. Her family had worked at one of the dock taverns but when it was destroyed, the young cook & waitress had to find another way to survive. Ruth possessed a very common look about herself, both in face and body. She knew her appearance wouldn't get her far so she had to enhance her skills to make it in life. Thankfully, her family home, that was close to the fisherman's cottage, took little damage from the storm so she was able to have a roof over her head.

A few days before Christmas, the town gathered together for a traditional holiday feast in the square. Everyone donating what they could to the massive party, including the 2 fishermen who kicked in over

00 pounds of fresh fish. On Christmas morning, there were two unique gifts under the Studman tree. Eli had worked secretly for weeks on fine leather 3-point hat for his new father, which included an artistic emblem centered by the initials, NS. Eli was thrilled when he opened his gift, revealing a sturdy handmade leather scabbard incasing his grandfather's bone handled 9-inch bladed knife. Noah glazed into Eli's eyes and said, "It's time you take up the knife your mothers wanted you to have". It had been cleaned and sharped to a razor edge, for the ever-growing lad.

Over time, Noah watched his son grow inside & out. Eli spoke very little to most people, he would instinctively listen, watch & learn. Noah called it "sponging", soaking up everything he could gather and mastered it quickly. Eli would re-read the journal late at night to the point of memorizing every line, visualizing every detail of his family past. By the time he turned 14 he was better than any sailor twice his age. He could speak several languages, as well as read & write them. Mathematics, Navigation, Logistics & Strategy came easy to the handsome 6-foot-tall young man. Noah knew it was time he learned about his physical skills and how to defend himself. With pistol & long rifle, they would hone his accuracy on both land & sea, something Noah was prolific at.

By now the Studmans had upgraded their vessel to a 40-foot cutter they bought from a Savannah fisherman who was through with the sea. He bought a small farm several miles inland and decided to work it with his growing family. The cutter was originally built in 1742 for small cargo hauling with a capacity of about 35 tons. The sails were tri-rigged thus making it easy to man with 2 to 4 crewmen which was perfect for the father & son. Making several improvements, they were not only hauling fish, but they also started carrying cargo back & forth from some of the closer ports to Charleston. Mostly personal items for the local shop owners & port merchants who needed it delivery in a matter of a day or two, not weeks.

While in port overnight at Savannah, they were dining at a favorite tavern that was renowned for their excellent food. One of the cooks was a 24-year-old oriental man only known as *Tohru. He had migrated there a few months earlier from destinations unknown, as he just strangely showed up in port one day. He spoke broken English but was fluent in his native language of Japanese, something no one understood on town. Tohru was mostly outcast by everyone and looked down on, with his only attribute being a superb chef. Paid very little and forced to live in a dilapidated old shack, it was clear he hated his life there. Basically, the oriental man was a joke to the townies who would have their fun ridiculing him at every chance. He hated it but he also knew if he lashed back, it would be the end of whatever he had there, even though it was little or nothing.

Later that night, Noah & Eli were asleep aboard their docked cutter when they awoke to a ruckus on the wharf. A half dozen drunk sailors were having their fun with Tohru who was heading back to his shack nearby. They decided it was enough, seeing the unarmed man out numbered 6 to 1. Noah bellowed out, "Ok that's enough! Leave him be"! The ringleader turned and said, "Fuck off Ya old Bastard or I'll cut Ya into fish bait and force feed Ya to this Chink"! Two of the drunk seamen turned to run at Noah & Eli when Tohru tripped them both up in a split second. Before they went face first into the stone wharf, he simultaneously cracked both in the back of the neck. They plummeted unconscious face own. A third sailor saw this and pulled a knife out to cut the fast little man, but before he could wheel it, Tohru disarmed him with a flashing kick while a pinpoint fist punch found its mark at the man's throat. He dropped to his knees immediately gasping for air. Noah & Eli launched into action as the 3 remaining bullies fell from their powerful blows in a matter of seconds. The wharf went silent, 6 sailors down for the count as the 3 men stood over them, daring any and all to try it again. As they walked off Noah leaned down at the bleeding unconscious ringleader, gripped his greasy long hair and whispered, "Next time I'll cut off your balls and feed them to your faggot mates"!

Noah had noticed several small cuts & bruises the oriental had taken from the bully abuse, "Come with us and let's get you cleaned up", Noah politely ordered. Tohru smiled slightly, then bowed his head as they walked back to the cutter. Once they bandaged up the wounds, the grateful little man finally spoke "Tank You... You first to help me... I always member dis". The 3 sat there getting better acquainted through most of the night. Finally, Eli said, "Tohru, you stay onboard with us tonight, we ain't sailing out till the morning tide". He smiled, bowed his weary head as they all fell off to sleep. Both Noah & Eli had the same thoughts in mind as they shared them the next morning. They explained best they could to Tohru that he should sail with them back to Charleston as part of their crew. Noah went on to say, "We got plenty of room at our house there, besides we need another on board to help us, not to mention we are both lousy cooks"! As the 3 laughed walking together to his shack to gather whatever gear he had.

Tohru continued to amaze the Studmans with his knack for seamanship. As they learned over time, he had sailed from his home in Okinawa at age 13 on an East Indies Freighter. Making the ports of Guam, Singapore, Melbourne, Fiji, & then Panama. That was where he caught a cargo ship headed to Port Roya signed on as ship's cook. For several years he bounced around the Caribbean from one ship to another till he landed in Savannah. He & Eli found they both had a few things in common, they both possessed the unique ability to learn language quickly. Before long the two unusual comrades were speaking each other's native tongue. The other was both of their grandfathers were handy at blacksmithing. The oriental father specialized in the ancient art of Samurai sword creation, as Tohru unveiled the beauty he had with him, carefully wrapped in a black silk satchel. Noah & Eli looked in awe at the gleaming sword as it was unsheathed from its onyx casing. The 3 made a pack, they will teach him how to shoot and he will show them the art of Samurai sword fighting. It was right then they knew, now we are 3.

During the next few months, the 3 were able to do some expansion improvements on their house including adding a new back room for Tohru. The kitchen area was rebuilt to bring in a wood burning stove. They turned the woodshed out back into a small makeshift blacksmith shop. Improvements were also rendered to their cutter they named Tripoli, since they were using her mainly for short cargo runs from Brunswick to the north and down south as far as St. Augustine. Exporting rice, corn, & indigo from Charleston then importing back with cotton, grain, coffee, tobacco, from Brunswick. St. Augustine proved to be a profitable port for to sell their cargo but there was very little the Florida port offered as export with exception of the occasional bundles of bananas.

But fortune shined on the Tripoli crew in early July 1756 when they were off loading their cargo. A Spanish Flute was forced to port in St. Augustine after having suffered hull damage from its voyage out of Jamacia. In their holes was a large shipment of rare lignum vitae, a sturdy iron like wood needed for rigging components, blocks & sheaves. Far too heavy to chance hauling it on the Atlantic crossing to Spain, their Captain decided to sell off all he could. And with only the Tripoli in port at the time, Noah saw an opportunity to make a sizeable profit, especially since they had sold off all their cargo hours before. The two captains came to an accord as the small cutter was loaded to the gills with the unique cargo.

Before the Spanish harbor master caught wind of the secret transaction, they sail out bound for home port Charleston. Like the British controlled ports, Spain had taxation restrictions on all import/export goods that was governed & enforced by the appointed harbor masters. But Spain wasn't quite as greedy as the ever-growing power England had. It was a slow smoldering fuse among the colonies that would eventually ignite into a revolution, but for now the colonists quietly took it. On the short voyage back home, they agreed to store most of the rare cargo, this way they could slowly sell it off privately to other vessels & shipwrights. One in particular they had in mind was a ship building apprentice in Brunswick, Fabrice Naviree. The young Frenchman who they had befriended a few months before.

Fabrice had arrived in the Carolina port a few days after his 21st birthday in early April 1755 from his home in Marseille. There, he had study architecture & horticulture as well as the arts & sciences. With this wild combination of knowledge, he planned to put it to good use toward his passion of shipbuilding. But after 2 years of being ignored for his insane ideas, he headed west to the Americas in hopes of starting a new life there as a shipwright pioneer. Besides, he knew from his studies that most all the truly vital materials could easily be found in areas like Jamaica, & the Bahamas for lignum vitae. The white oak for hull, keel & frame in Virginia, eastern white pine for sturdy masts from Georgia, as well as longleaf pine for beams & decks from the Carolinas.

Putting these materials together he calculated that a ship could be built for speed, strength & durability. The Frenchman spent many a night sketching out in detail the innovative hull structure, mast placements and decking. This included the maximum use of cargo storage & cannon displacement as needed. The drawback... a ship of this quality would take extensive time and money to build. As he shared his ideas with them one evening aboard the Tripoli, Eli's mind raced with excitement at the thought of such a vessel. A perfect ship to initiate a perfect plan that burned within him more & more every passing day. Slowly the pieces of the puzzle were falling into place, but for now... learn.

With the help of Darin, the assistant harbor master, they were able to store most of the rare wood away at their secluded blacksmith shop behind the house without being detected. The British appointed harbor master was fortunately away on crown business when the Tripoli docked. The four men sat down to a hearty meal at the Studman home that evening. This was a chance for Darin to bring the men up to speed on what was happening during their fortnight away. Naturally the main topic was the ever-increasing taxes leveed on almost everything coming in & out of Charleston. Even the small fishing business was being taxed now and by the pound too. Noah had hired two local fishermen to use their small, long boat, thus keeping the fish market going. Most of the profit went to the hired crew and Ruth who still managed the wharf shop for them, with Noah & Eli getting around 10% of the profit.

But the men could see something else was gnawing at Englishman, he really hadn't been the same since he lost his wife & son a few years back. Being single gave him time to ponder at night about what direction his life was headed, especially his depleting loyalty toward his homeland. Forced by England to over tax the cargo ships & local merchants who were barely getting by. He was also missing his first passion of map making. Even though he still had his shop there, he was spending more time as assistant harbor master than he wanted. He craved to be back as sea, even if it was short coastal runs. As a jest Tohru laughingly said, "why don't Ya forge up some orders from da king to map da coastline from here to say... Virginia? You can hitch a ride with us"! Instantly everyone got a good laugh over the idea, but when it died down, a look of amazement covered Darin's face. As he uttered, "Sure... why the hell not! I got everything I need to do it! I'll show the orders to that asshole of a Boss of mine, he has to honor it since it's a royal command". He would simply tell the harbor master a courier arrived by ship while he was away. As luck would have it, a Royal Shipping Lines Carrack had arrived & departed during his absence.

The next morning Darin rushed over to the Studman house with documents in hand. As he read aloud in official mock fashion, "By order of Royal decree, Darin Cavety, Cartographer to the Crown is hereby ordered to map out, in detail, the coastal lines of the Americas from the Port of Charleston, northward to the Virginia Colony. He is to contract the first available vessel to successfully complete this task and be done with the utmost of hast. By Order of King George II". He turned to the awe struck 3 men and jokingly commanded, "I hereby contract the vessel Tripoli to undertake this Royal mission"! As the 4 men broke into laughter. Darin explained that the harbor master should return later that afternoon and we can head out when you all are ready. He included that the Tripoli would be paid the sum of 100 pounds plus whatever was needed for provisions for the journey.

Fact: Brunswick was settled back in 1726 but it wasn't till 1754 that it became a British controlled county seat. So, the coastlines north & south were only known by sight from a handful of local mariners at best. And with the start of the 7-year war against the French in May of 1756, then eventually with Spain, most British vessels kept to the open seas and trade routes, not to mention the occasional pirates & privateers. There were long stretches of small spotted islands, rocky shoals, high cliffs, & winding inlets that snaked around for miles between Charleston and Brunswick. And with every storm, mother nature would change her appearance and accessibility.

With ample provisions aboard and cargo secured, the Tripoli set sail on the morning tide of a bright sunny July 15th day. It didn't take long for 3 to see the positive change in their added shipmate. It was just what the doctor ordered; the salty sea air filled his lungs again with vigor as he worked happily along with his close companions, now his shipmates. By late afternoon he was back at what he loved, sketching out the virgin like coastlines as the ship glided along within a few miles of shore the entire way. When night fell, they would anchor in a comfortable shoal till daybreak and continue on their merry way north. The winds & weather were fair as the sleek little vessel skimmed through the calm water, making the port of Brunswick 2 days later.

After unloading all the cargo but the one piece of lignum vitae, they sought out the French shipwright. It didn't take long, as Fabrice was near the docks repairing a small fishing boat. After greetings & introductions for Darin, the 5 men strolled back to the Tripoli where Noah unveiled the rare wood. Fabrice was overjoyed with the sight of the rare wood. Even though Lignum was abundant in dense areas of the mountain regions of Jamacia & the Bahamas, very few trade ships would carry it dues to its cargo weight and the initial costs. To a shipwright, this was more valuable than gold or silver. "How much of this do you have"? Inquired Fabrice. "Right now, about 30 logs stored back safely at our house in Charleston". Quickly calculating in his head, the Frenchman explained he would need at least 40 to 50 more to construct his dream ship, a fully loaded Brig. He already knew where to put his hands on the white pine, Savannah gets it in from farmers there who clear their fields with it regularly and bring it to market to sell off. The longleaf pine can come in from land clearing west of Brunswick & areas northwest of Charleston. As for the last needed ingredient, white oak, Fabrice had heard of new settlements around Williamsburg & Jamestown in Virginia that have a plethora of strong wood. The crew's eyes lit up at the thought of owning a Brig.

Fact: Most Brigs built during this period would average from 75ft - 165ft (23m – 50m) with a cargo capacity up to 480 tons. Used primarily as fast sleek war ships that could carry up to 28 guns depending on the length of the decks. When used mainly for hauling cargo, it served well as a long-range vessel with more than ample cargo space. What Fabrice had imagined was the perfect combination of the two and a lot more. But this build would have to be secretly done, war was starting its rage between Britain, France & Spain, so the taxes on all goods was affecting the colonies severely. There were already the winds of revolution lingering in the air against the British Crown, not to mention the occasional sea & land attacks from privateers who would kill to have the ship Fabrice had in mind.

"What you propose would cost us a small fortune", uttered Noah. Fabrice quickly replied back, "Yes, I know but what if we partnered up"? He went on to say that he was barely scrapping by in Brunswick as an apprentice. Plus, this undertaking will require the needed materials safely put away from prying eyes and a secluded place to build it. He added that with a shortage of proper manpower, the build will take several months or more to complete. Thinking this over for a few minutes, the men agreed to the plan with first priority to find a hideaway to start material storage. Darin broke in jokingly, "who knows, we may find a spot on this charting trip"! As the laughter subsided the men headed off for some dinner as night began to fall. In deep thought, Eli knew now there were 5 for him to learn from as the gathering continued to grow.

At morning tide, with cargo loaded, the Tripoli set sail again heading north through the winding inlet channels that covered the mouth of Brunswick harbor. A patchwork of small sandy islands, together with jagged rock formations dotted the coastline. The background inlets seemed to be a dense forest of sprawling trees weaved by thick vines & foliage. These lowline obstructions acted as a natural buffer from storms in the Atlantic and at the same time recreating its look with every passing hurricane. The narrow passages, combined with the shallow waters made it impossible for large ships to venture into. Their keels would easily get cut open from the unseen rock & coral formations just below the waterline.

Eli was sprawled over the bow sprit, catch nests flanking either side, as he fed back to Noah at the helm the depth conditions ahead of them. Waters were calm crystal blue as he could easily see to the bottom some 20ft down. Tohru was astern preparing meals as Darin sat amidship charting every little detail of the coastline just 100 yards to the portside. Dusk slowly turned to quiet evening starlight as they anchored safely in a peaceful cove for the night. As the 4 men sat eating dinner, they began to share their thoughts that had permeated their brains throughout the day. So much to digest, especially with war raging & revolution on the horizon. "I'm thinking, we can use all that to our advantage... while the Brits are distracted by war", said Darin. He had notices recent changes in several of the English appointed officials & officers in Charleston. Their concerns we pointed more at possible French invasion rather than daily worries from the towns people. The 4 men nodded silently in agreement.

"From what Fabrice was saying, it sounds like da sooner he gets out of Brunswick da better", added Tohru. Even though the Frenchman wasn't a direct threat to the British there, he knew sooner or later it would come to a head. Noah chimed in, "I've seen his plans and talked with him enough to know that he wants his freedom to build his dreams". Silences lingered for a few moments till Noah looked seriously over to Eli, "You ain't said much son... what's on your mind"? Eli paused as he looked into the eyes of each man and spoke, "I have learned a lot from each of you so far. Learning mainly to trust in you all, including Fabrice. I see it as this... we need a spot away from everyone, and we need it as soon as possible. Somewhere close enough for us all to get to quickly too. After that, we gather & build".

On the verge of turning 15 years old, Eli was years ahead of his age, mentally & physically. The men could see the depth and adult conviction Eli already possessed inside. Yet, he continued to stand humble, silently learning everything he could sponge up in his mind. Along their charting trek northward, they would find time for some weapons practice with both pistols & swords. Darin was a bit slow to grasp the instructions from Tohru on blade work, but he seems to handle himself well with pistol & long rifle. Eli was growing in strength & skill to a point where even Tohru was impressed with his samurai technique. His keen eye with firearms was rapidly becoming a match for Noah's long-time marksmanship. The burly Dutchman thought it was time his son was introduced to another phase of manhood.

August 1st, 1756 brought them safely into Port Bath, a bustling colony in the northeast region of the Carolinas. Late that afternoon they completed the cargo transactions, when the 3 men turned to Eli and told him it's time he became a man, as they all slyly smirked. That evening, after they all enjoyed a hearty dinner and several rounds of ale at the port tavern, they strolled to another popular spot. Outside the ornated building burned 2 bright red lanterns at the entrance, illuminating the sign: "The Crimson Garter". Inside, Eli gazed in amazement at the glittering chandlers and plush red velvet furnishings. Then his eyes focused in on the scantily dressed & painted up females that covered the room. A voluptuous raven-haired woman greeted the 4 men," welcome gentlemen to my establishment, I'm Rosie, please make yourselves comfortable".

Noah whispered something to the madam as she devilishly smiled and ordered a round of drinks for the newly arrived customers. Joining them were 3 ladies, handpicked by Rosie. A petite oriental lass sat down on Tohru's lap, wrapping her slender arms around his neck as she sweetly uttered," I'm Soon Me". A Tall blonde beauty cozied in next to Darin, kiss his cheek with her ruby lips and said, "Hi sugar I'm Honey". Leaving the buxom redhead to sprawl over Noah's lap loudly greeting him with, "howdy Big man I'm Cherry"! Eli sad there smiling at the 3 couples but still somewhat bewildered till Rosie snuck up behind the lad and said, "I understand you're 15 today, Babyboy, well Rosie has a very special gift for you". Noah popped open his pocket watch, smiled and said, "Yes, in about 30 minutes he will be"!

The Towering hand carved grandfather clock in the room began to musically chime out the stroke of midnight. At the final tone they all sang out" Happy Birthday" to the blushing lad, as Rosie gripped his hand and said, "Come with me Babyboy it's time for your birthday present". As the 2 strolled up the long curving staircase, all eyes on them clapping & cheering. Once alone in her lavish bedroom, the sultry lady told Eli this was going to be much more than simply losing his virginity. "I'm going to teach you the proper way to pleasure & please yourself as well as your lady", she seductively whispered.

Rosie was of Spanish descent, easily in her early 30s, yet she was amazingly youthful both in face & body, as Eli watched her erotically strip. Being a madam, it was rare she would have sex with a customer, but when she discovered from Noah that it was Eli's first time, she couldn't resist teaching this young handsome lad everything she knew. She paused her sensuous disrobing for a moment to start undressing the eager Eli. To her amazement, as his pants fell to the red carpet, she was in awe of a very well equipped erect young man. She escorted the naked lad over to a lavish bathtub as she finished her undressing and the two slowly emerged in the soothing warm water face to face. There he learned the erotic art of French kissing and body caressing. They spent the entire night in blissful pleasure as he was happily instructed in Fellatio & Cunnilingus, and so much more. When day broke, both were totally pent from an unforgettable night of pure ecstasy. As he lay there in the soft heavenly bed, he smiled & whispered, "Happy Birthday to ME"!

They all met up downstairs an hour after sunrise and were treated to a special breakfast prepared by Tohru & the Brothel's cook. Rosie joined the 4 men moments after they sat down to fresh brewed coffee. The conversation eventually came around to her discovering the men of the Tripoli as she explained that her younger brother was an experienced sailor who was presently out of work. They listened intently as Rosie when into detail about her unemployed sibling.

Marino Tiburon, age 24, had been at sea since he was 14, mostly on small cargo vessels. The family migrated to the Americas when they both were still children back in 1735. Their parents had passed away over 10 years ago, thus leaving the duo to fend for themselves. Marino was an excellent sailor, expert with a knife & blade, but his main flaw was his fiery Latin temper, especially toward the British. One scrap after another had him blacklisted to serve on any English vessel. As Rosie went on detailing her brother's life, the men felt it was well worth looking into hiring him. Rosie was elated at their interest and immediately sent one of her servants to fetch him.

As they were finishing breakfast, in walked a slim dark-haired man, as Rosie embraced him saying, "Everyone this is Marino"! For over an hour the 5 mariners sat at the table getting acquainted, exchanging information about themselves. When Marino mentioned the one officer he ever got along with, Noah's ears perked up at the familiar name, Everwyn Morwer. This was the same Welsh navigator who assisted Eli's two mothers some 15 years before. Eli picked up on the name as well from memorizing his mother's journal. Father & son looked at one another, speechless in the irony of all this. Then after reminding Darin about the 15-year-old voyage, he too lite up with the coincidence. That was enough for the crew of the Tripoli as they offered the Spaniard a place on board with them, who immediately agreed.

After gathering his gear, the men headed to the docks to finish cargo loading and preparations to set sail. Marino went on to tell his new shipmates what he had heard about Everwyn. When his uncle, the captain of the flute had passed away, he naturally figured he would take over command of it. But the captain had debts owed to a certain viscount named Ervin who in turn commandeered the large vessel. Everwyn tried all he could to get it back, including taking it to British high court, but the royal family naturally sided completely with Ervin. The expert navigator was left penniless and out of a job. "Last I heard, he was down in the St. Augustine picking up whatever jobs he could, in between soaking his head in a rum bottle", Marino added.

While, in Port Bath, Tohru did some snooping around and found out some interesting information about a certain desired material, white oak. Seems, new settlements northwest of the city was sporadically hauling in the hard wood to sell. Noah went over to the port trade office and purchased a small amount of it along with their usual export goods. To his amazement, the price of the durable wood was cheaper than he anticipated. With the charting mission completed, they set sail back to Brunswick to let Fabrice know what was happening and meet the newest member of the crew. Picking up a good southerly wind, they arrived in Brunswick in excellent time. The short voyage brought the men closer together with their new crewman. They were confident now he was a welcome addition, plus Eli now had a new language to learn, Spanish.

It seemed Fabrice had some startling news for them as well when they all gathered together that evening on board the Tripoli. A week before he & his port friend Wolf took off one morning to test out the German blacksmith's newly repaired pinnace. Wolfgang Schutze, a 29-year-old immigrant from Austria came to seek his fortune in the New World when he was 17. He was the descendant from a prominent blacksmith family who worked in perfecting hardened metals into combined materials, steel, iron cast, brass & bronze. Wolf, as he was known in Brunswick, took what he learned from his ancestors & accelerated it to creating some of the finest weapons ever seen of its time. But Wolf, like his French counterpart, had kept his best work hidden from prying British eyes. Cannons of unbelievable power, accuracy & durability, including innovative shot process. His concept was to combine powder & projectile in one sealed canvas charge, thus cutting reload time down to almost nothing. He was also working on a new flint lock device to eliminate the unreliable fuse firing system.

After only a few hours south of the mouth of the Brunswick harbor, the low draft 35ft vessel discovered a hidden inlet. Feeling adventurous they slowly made their way in through a narrow passage till they came to what seemed its end. But as they turned the bow westward, they could see an opening through overgrown vines from large trees that flanked the shallow throughway. A few yards of slowly clearing by hand unveiled an awe-inspiring sight. The inlet spread open to an almost 50-yard-wide channel that reached inland for about a quarter mile in length. The heavy foliage flanking them ashore was a foreground for towering, jagged rock formations. Fabrice would take sounding every few yards, noticing the depth in the channel was less than 20 feet at best, and this was during a high tide. Thus, making it impossible for a large deep draft ship to enter without running a ground.

Ahead they slowly approached a small sandbar that extended across most of the channel. To the port side was a large overhanging rock pillar that once was part of an arch to the shoreline. To the starboard side the sandbar gave way to a very small watery breech just wide enough for the men to slowly work their way through. Using oars, they pushed the small craft past to a wider & deeper opening on the obstruction's backside. Some 500 yards ahead they started seeing the making of a deep lagoon, surrounded on 3 sides by massive stone walls that mother nature had majestically made. To their astonishment sat a large flat beach area to the port side of them about 100x100 yards in size. Overgrown with plants, & trees that seemed to be there for centuries without man ever disturbing them. The sandy land ended with massive stone backing that towered over 50 feet high.

After hearing this astonishing tale, they wasted no time as both ships made for the hideaway. Once landed they carefully began exploring every inch of the area. In the far southern part of the flatland was a small waterfall that pooled & eventually ran down into the lagoon. To the side of the freshwater cascade was a wide shallow cave inlet with a few smaller ones cut into the heavy rock walls. On closer inspection the French ship builder was elated to discover the massive trees were family to the longleaf pine needed for his dream build. Tohru noticed a black substance inside one of the smaller caves as he called to Wolf to see it. The German's mouth hung open for a moment, then he bellowed, "Holy Shit!... Carbon"! He knew it was the main ingredient to turn iron to steel. He also knew where there was carbon there was iron ore too.

They had food there too, fish, blue crab & sea turtle were plentiful in the lagoon. Tohru had not cooked turtle in years, so he was in heaven preparing a feast for the men that evening. Figuring they would wait till morning high tide to head back to Port. It also gave them a better chance to get to know Wolf. Obviously not the sailor the others were, they wondered how he came about the sturdy pinnace.

Laughing out loud he spun the tale of a poker game he got into several months back with a former customer. He had made the man a matching pair of dueling pistol that were a work of art. The old man figured he would rope Wolf into a game of chance to get his money back, but it backfired. Little did he know that the sly German was an excellent card player. Short story of it all, the old man was out cheated by Wolf after he put up his last possession the pinnacle. When the man refused to pay off the bet, Wolf put a pistol to his head and said, "Your ship or your brains... what will it be"? They all knew right then & there, they were 7 now and time for Eli to learn German!

The following morning the 2 ships docked back in Brunswick as they set in motion their plans. Everything went back to normal so there was no chance of any outsiders homing in on their business. Marino agreed to stay on with Fabrice & Wolf as an extra hand to help out both in port and at the cove since he had some experience with an axe and construction. The rest did their normal cargo exchange in port and headed back to Charleston to drop off Darin. Once there, it was a day or two of business as usual then headed south to Savannah on their normal trade route. They give instructions for Darin to load up the remaining lignum at the Studman house when Wolf, Fabrice & Marino arrived a few days later. They would start storing the needed supplies in the caves a little at a time to avoid any suspicion.

The Tripoli docked in Savannah with ease. At the docks was one of the Royal Shipping Line vessels that had arrived the day before from St. Augustine. That night in the wharf tavern, Noah chimed up a conversation with one of the inebriated crewmen. Eventually the chat got around to a certain navigator. The half-drunk sailor spouted," Yeah, I know that old rummy, he's still probably face down in the gutter somewhere there"! Noah raced back to the Tripoli, and she sailed off immediately southward. He & Eli both felt a strong sense of duty to help the one man who made it possible for Eli to be where he was. Not to mention the fact that Everwyn would jump at the chance for some personal revenge on a certain backstabbing viscount.

It was a matter of a few high winded days at sea when they arrived in St. Augustine. The docks were strangely empty with the Tripoli the only ship in port. After taking care of the cargo sales the 3 went in search of their friend as heavy rain began to cascade down on the Florida port. Word went out fast of a pending storm headed their way, typical for this time of year along the southeastern seaboard. One tavern after another they would dash in, inquiring about Everwyn with no luck. Hopes were fading fast for the searchers when noticed a few old bums gathered around a small fire in an alley. Noah walked up and said, "Any of you know a man named Everwyn Morwer"? Silently one dirt covered man spoke, "Who wants to know"? Noah looked beyond the long greasy hair & straggly beard, peering deep into his blood shot eyes. "Everwyn it's You! I'm Noah Studman from Charleston, my wife was Collen McGriff"! Eli added in, and I'm Eli McGriff"!

Everwyn stood there desperately trying to remember where he had heard those names before. Then it came to him, recalling the voyage 15 years hence. "Yeah, I remember now... damn boy you grew up a lot"! As his laughter reverted to severe coughing and spitting up what little he had in his stomach. "You're coming with us, it's time we helped You out for a change", Eli said with determination. Still coughing, the men helped him back to the nearest Inn for some needed nourishment. While the rains continued to pour down outside, inside, they managed to get him cleaned up and get some decent clothes on him. They explained briefly what had transpired since their late meeting 15 years ago, as Everwyn told the story of how he came to be in such a poor state. "Well, that's old history my friend, you're coming with us now...We are in need of a good Navigator"! Noah uttered. "The only thing I have left to offer is just that too, and nothing more". He replied. Eli softly said, "There IS something else you have that we want... your friendship"! Smiling wide the men clasped hands in a lifelong accord. Now we are 8, Eli thought proudly.

They spent a few days helping Everwyn to get back to health enough while the storm passed them over. It also gave them time to bring the newest member of the crew up to speed on all their plans which included the material gathering for the potential brig. Everwyn thought for a minute and remembered a large shipment of lignum that came in several months ago from the Bahamas. The shipment was far too large for one ship to carry it across the Atlantic to Bristol all at once, so it was stored in a Royal Shipping warehouse. The original shipment was for over 1500 tons of the rare heavy wood, contracted by the Crown. Everwyn estimated that a little more than half was still stored away. With the Tripoli empty they knew they could safely haul about 25 tons, roughly 100 pieces. The next Royal cargo ship wasn't due to arrive for another 3 weeks, minimum.

The Warehouse was at the far end of the wharf, patrolled at night only by one or two city guards from the small fort. The city at the time was still under Spanish rule even though war had broken out once again between Spain & England. To secure the warehouse from Spanish raiding, Viscount Ervin had forged letters of marque showing that the warehouse was storage for Spanish privateers. So, when a Royal Shipping vessel pulled into port, she would fly Spanish colors disguised as privateers to keep from being commandeered.

In the early hours of darkness, under the cover of light rain, the Tripoli snuck around to the warehouse dock. Tohru moved through the shadows of the wharf till he came up behind the first guard who was half asleep in the guard shack. Quietly clubbing him with a ship's wooden belaying pin. He waited in the darkness as the second guard was finishing his patrol and clubbed him as well. Placing the two unconscious Spaniards side by side in the shack. He produced a bottle of rum, pouring it generously over the guard's faces and leaving the empty bottle next to them. Picking the lock, the 4-stealth thieves loaded the Tripoli till she could take no more. They relocked to doors and sailed off north bound for Charleston.

When the guard changed later that morning at sunrise, the Spanish Captain assumed his two men had themselves a drunken spree. He opened the locked warehouse and saw nothing had been missing since the Crew only took around 100 pieces of the more than 3,000 pieces remaining. The lignum was neatly stacked in 6-foot-high squares, so before they left, they restacked them so what was missing couldn't be seen from the naked eye. But a note was buried inside one of the stacks that read, "Property of Royal Shipping Lines", signed Viscount Ervin. In hopes that would piss off not only the Spanish but the British posers, or as Tohru would say jokingly, "Light Da Fuse and Run"!

The voyage back to Charleston gave Everwyn his sea legs back, teamed with a newfound confidence in himself. Fueled with the fires of revenge, he & Eli quickly became a close nit duo with every passing day. At night, he would teach the curious lad how to navigate from the stars, and during the day show him how to do dead reckoning since they didn't have a sexton onboard. Everwyn was looking forward to seeing Darin again after so many years had passed. Anxious as well to meet the rest of the assembled crew, especially Marino and to thank him personally.

The night before they arrived back, Eli was at the helm while his shipmates were catching some needed sleep. Calm & quite his thoughts began calculating what he had amassed: A strong skillful Dutchman, A multitalented lethal Japanese, A sly knowledgeable artistic Englishman, A master craftsman Frenchman, A visionary German blacksmith, A fearless fiery Spaniard, & A educated experienced Welshman. Seven men to learn from, grow with and eventually use to extract his revenge on the bastard he regretfully called his birth father. He knew the gathering was now complete, it was time to slowly formulate it all together. Meanwhile, he would do all he could to quietly whittle apart the Royal Shipping Lines with a little help from his friends. With a devilish smirk he proclaimed to the night winds, "Take care Lord Ervin, Eli is Coming"!

There was a joyous reunion on the docks that evening when the Tripoli pulled into port. Darin & Everwyn embarrassed with brotherly glee after so many years apart. Noah told Darin of the unexpected cargo as they rushed half of it into covered carts to store it at the Studman home. "We will take the other half of it to the cove on the morning tide, Wolf can come get the rest when we see him", Noah exclaimed. Eli told them that he would stay aboard to insure no one would snoop around the ship till they returned. "I make you some food to feed that ugly face you got"! Laughed Tohru. Darin sized up Everwyn and told him he had some better clothes that would just about fit him, "I'm thrilled to see Ya mate but Ya look like death warmed over"! Joked Darin. "Yeah, while you're at it take a fuckn' bath too Ya smell like whale shit"! Noah roared other with a smile. "OK...OK... I get the point you bastards"! Everwyn smirked.

About an hour later they all returned to Eli at the dock, with a positively notable change in Everwyn's appearance and smell. Darin had waited till all could hear about the latest news around town. It seemed the aging harbor master had taken ill with the gout and was unable to do his job properly. A formal message went out on a London bound ship 4 days before with the information and a request that Darin take over as Crown appointed harbor master. This was perfect, they could have Darin on the inside as their eyes & ears to the ongoings of England and especially the Royal Shipping Lines. Along with the message he also sent off the newly completed charts of the coastline with one minor exception, a certain cove inlet. He marked it on the map as just another impassable area covered with rocky shoals. He added that war had broken out with England & Spain. The men all laughed as they told Darin they knew already from the reports in St. Augustine. "Ok, what's the joke"? Darin asked. They told him about the note they left in the warehouse and Darin damn near fell off the boat laughing. Everwyn chimed in, "I'd love to be a fly on the wall when that Son of a Bitch hears about his precious warehouse"! As they all nodded. As you could read their minds thinking the same thing, "This is just the beginning"!

The timing couldn't have been any better when the Tripoli slid into the cove a few days later. Working up a sweat on the beach was Fabrice, Wolf & Marino. They got a double surprise as they saw Everwyn hauling off the first of the lignum vitae. In no time at all, the seven shipmates had it safely stored away with the rest in one of the larger caves. The 3 men had been very productive, in just a few weeks, they managed to cut down most of the trees on the front side near the lagoon. Little by little, the pinnace brought in tools & supplies to their little hideaway. It was agreed that Everwyn would stay on with the Brunswick crew, this way the original Tripoli crew could carry on with business as usual. They decided to continue on like nothing had changed from their daily lives. It was imperative every man maintain their normal routine to avoid any suspicion from outsiders. "We have all the right people, in all the right places, it's only a matter of time now"! Exclaimed Eli.

CHAPTER 3

The Awakening

The fall of 1756 was a particularly abundant harvest for several of the colonies, from Virginia down to southern Georgia. Mother nature was kind enough to minimize the Atlantic storms that season to only a few minor ones, thus a heavy influx of new settlers was arriving steadily from Europe. With war engulfing most of the major countries, people were fleeing in droves to the new world. Record numbers claimed in areas like, Boston, New York, Richmond & those pushing westward into the Ohio valley. England was waging war with France & Spain as Prussia threw its hat in against the Crown. Europe was in turmoil leaving the American colonies somewhat peaceful from the conflict, for the time being. But England still sought out the new world as a vital source of income through export & taxation.

By now, Everwyn & Marino had teamed up to use Wolf's pinnace for short fishing and light cargo runs when the 4 Brunswick based partners weren't working at the cove hideaway. Fabrice had overhauled the small vessel to expand its cargo carrying capabilities by about 40% so supply trips to the cove were considerably more productive. To save on daily expenses the 4 bachelors eventually moved into Wolf's house he owned outright which was large enough for them.

In Charleston, all was going well, including the sideline fishing business. Ruth and the 2 hired fisherman were bringing in their catch to market almost daily now. Great news arrived in late-October as Darin was officially appointed Harbor Master by the Crown. As for the old gout ridden one, he left for England to live out his remaining years at his home in London. Darin hired a young assistant a few weeks later, a local lad named Jacob West who was a native of Charleston since his birth there in 1738. Darin trusted him as his assistant but nothing beyond that. Jacob & Ruth had gotten romantically involved a year before & eventually married. He would lend a hand from time-to-time helping Ruth at the fish market and even make a fishing run occasionally, so Darin was comfortable trusting his new assistant more and more each passing day.

A funny thing happened on the way to the warehouse! Back in St. Augustine in early October, disguised as a Spanish Privateer, a Royal Shipping Line Carrack docked to pick up another load of lignum vitae from the port warehouse. Under the eyes of the Spanish Harbor Master & the Captain of the guard, a strange note was discovered amid the stacks of the valuable wood. Within moments the heavily arms Spanish garrison had surrounded the warehouse and British owned Carrack. The captain & crew were imprisoned as spies, the warehouse, contents & ship was commandeered when letters were discovered onboard matching the name Viscount Ervin. Just a little payback to get the ball rolling.

The winter of 1756 was relatively mild in the Carolina ports giving the 8 men a chance to build up the cove little by little. The largest cave next to the waterfall became a perfect spot to house them rather than waste time and materials building any. The 40-foot-high celling was solid rock with one exception, a small hole against the back wall would appear during the daylight hours. While both crews were there, they decided to investigate it. Fashioning a makeshift ladder, they managed to set it up against the wall to the unknown surface above. Tohru being the smallest, volunteered to go up, and in no time, he plugged through opening. Chiseling the space wider, the rest climbed up to discover a truly wonderous sight to behold. It was a sprawling open area covered in thick foliage and massive, towering white pine rees. Even more, there was game everywhere, deer, rabbit, wild boar, & wild turkey. In marsh areas close by, Wolf was elated to see large deposits of bog ore (limonite) that was used for making charcoal. The hardened coal was the hottest substance used for forging metal. It seemed the more they explored the hideaway the more mother nature smiled on them. Off in the distance, a mile or so away was yet another barrier of rising stone walls.

As Fabrice rubbed his hand on one of sprawling white pine trees, he could in vision it as a strong main mast. He spoke out to the others, "All we need now is white oak for the hull, keel & frame and I can get started"! There was more than enough lignum stored away, the longleaf pine they had been cutting down from the beach area was more than ample to fashion into beam & deck. Noah & Eli agreed it was time to start making cargo runs back at Port Bath to gather up the white pine a bit at a time. Eli thought it would be a great chance to get some more lessons from the voluptuous Rosie.

The God given gift in his pants had become quite the treat for a few young ladies since his 15th birthday indoctrination. The young lad had gathered up some erotic adventures over the last few months, coining the phrase," A girl in every port"! Added with the unique teaching from Rosie, Eli was beginning to live up to his name, Studman. And as he grew older, his youthful look evolved into a dashing sight the ladies would melt over. Long head of cascading chestnut hair framed a chiseled clean-shaven face with sturdy high cheekbones that enhanced his piercing hazel eyes. A 6-foot frame flanked by wide shoulders and muscular arms the girls craved to feel around them. Mature enough to know this was purely an occasional sideline pleasure, his mission was firmly locked in his head, revenge.

Tohru had fashioned a few bows & arrows for the men to hunt with at the cove. It would be much easier to take down a fleet footed deer or a swift charging boar. They added salt to the list of returning cargo to help preserve the meat in a brining process. With the men gathered in their comfortable cave dwelling, Eli felt it was time he spoke up of his plans. "For all of us this is a great chance to make some really good money & make a better life. For some of you it's a quest to fulfill dreams long desired. But for a couple of us it's a matter of overdue payback"! He went into detail about what had happened over 15 years ago to his family back in Wales. "I'm proud to call myself a Studman, but I'm the last of the Griffin name. If it takes forever, I WILL avenge it". Those who didn't know sat silent, thinking what they would do if they were in Eli's shoes. Those who knew the tale had already resolved to see it through, no matter what. They all took soleus that even though they were without family for the most part, they now had an unbreakable bond, a brotherhood.

Back in Bristol, in mid-November, the news arrived of the Spanish confiscation incident in St. Augustine. It rocked the British Trade Union that immediately had them up in arms, but it was the Royal Shipping Line that took the brunt of the loss. Losing the remains of the warehouse goods as well as the 1200-ton Carrack cargo ship costing Viscount Ervin over 35,000 pounds. What was worse, the loss of respect from the royal family, including the king. He commanded that Ervin make good the loss personally or he would be removed of his post & title. Reluctantly, he was forced to agree to the terms and was given one year to pay it back, with interest. He instructed his eldest son Ervin II to get to work on it immediately. The 31-year-old had been the company's accountant for 12 years as well as taking care of the family financial books. His father had an arranged marriage in 1744 for him to a young lady in waiting to the court named Lanora Winston. She was the sole daughter to Baron Winston and blood kin to the Queen. She gave birth a year later to a daughter they called Elinore who was pampered & primed for a royal life. As she grew and blossomed into a ravaging beauty, almost the spitting image of her devastatingly attractive mother. But her birth took a toll, as doctors informed Lanora, she wasn't able to give birth again less taking the chance of miscarriage or even death.

Sitting at the plush Ervin estate, father & son came up with a plan to raise the money quickly without effecting the company, auction off small worthless pieces of land they held the rights to in the new world. Land that the crown didn't control so Ervin claimed it a decade before and did nothing with except levee taxes on. Or so the books showed, in actually, the Ervin family was skimming off the profits into their pockets. This was mostly swampy marsh land, uninhabitable to even the newest of colonial settlers coming into the Carolinas. Using the latest charts provided by Darin, the conniving duo chose several parcels of land to quietly auction off in Charleston. Notices arrived & posted in the port a week before Christmas stating. "Here Ye Here Ye, by order of Crown, a one-day auction will be held on December 24th, 1756, for designated sections of land here & around the Port of Charleston"! Signed Viscount Ervin, envoy to the King. 141 forged land deeds were aboard the Royal vessel as it sat in port awaiting Christmas eve. Darin, as Crown appointed harbor master was privy to the locations of the areas to be sold at both ports. Astonishingly enough, one of the deeds had zeroed in on the uninhabited cove of theirs. Luckily, the Tripoli crew was in port when the news arrived.

The 4 men sat that evening at the Studman house to decide what to do. The money they had on hand was less than 100 pounds, but the Brunswick crew may have some to contribute as well. They dispatched a courier to ride with hast to Brunswick with a sealed letter, instructing the 4 mates there to come to Charleston immediately with as much money as they could spare. Darin said, "I spoke with the auctioneer, he was figuring to raise around 100 to 150 pounds per deed, but we might get lucky since the hideaway area is so isolated and impassable". Darin had a chance to read one of the fine print deeds, stating, "Documented owners would be subject to annual taxation per acreage. Failure to comply would result in forfeiture of said land". The deed number of the cove and surrounding 100 square acres was lot #133. "What if the buyer was...John Smith"? Asked Eli. The 3 stared at him with blank faces till they understood his meaning. They would have Darin forge up some papers for Everwyn since he was English descent in appearance and not known at all in Charleston. Dressed up as a farmer they would get him to bid on lot #133 and no one would be the wiser.

Two days later the pinnace arrived with all on board including aka, John Smith as the 8 gathered up to explain the plan. Combining their funds, they now had almost 150 pounds. Wolf suggested a possible way to make some more quickly. Knowing there was a lot of money pouring into Charleston, there would have to be a card game or two popping up. He too was a new face in town, with locals assuming he was there for the auction along with hundreds more. Besides, who would ever guess a tattered looking blacksmith would be a card shark. The sly German's premonition was right on the mark as the jingling of coin carrying newcomers filled every Inn & tavern the night before the auction. Several games of chance literally appeared out of nowhere in the busy public establishments, as Wolf took his time to pick just the right pigeons to pluck. He sat down at a scoped-out table of men playing poker. He planted down a half empty bottle of watered-down rum for all to see as he slurred out, "Mind if I join in"? The 4 others could see he had been working his bottle to the point of inebriation. They had a new drunk to take advantage of. "Sure Friend, your money is welcome here", smirked the fine suited man across from him. The game was draw poker, Wolf's specialty as the game resumed. A few hours past with Wolf going up & down intentionally. What the 4 men didn't know was Wolf had palmed 2 kings and waited for the right moment to slam the door on them.

The hand came around several minutes later as he was dealt the 2 remaining kings in the deck and waited his turn. Gulping down the last drop of diluted rum he uttered," I'll take 3 cards"! As he got them, he intentionally knocked over the empty bottle making it crash to the floor. In that split second while the table was focused on the shattered mesh, he made the swap, belched loud & said, "Opps sorry about that, my mistake"! Acting blurry eyed and out of sorts he waited for the rest to play. The bet increased with the first man, as the second one folded. The third man called it as the suited shark saw his opportunity to blow out the drunken German. "I'll see that and raise Ya 50"! The next man thought for a moment and then folded, bringing the bet to Wolf. A pause to survey the situation the German made his move, "I see Ya & raise Ya 50 more"! The next man immediately folded in disgust leaving Wolf to battle it out with the obvious table winner. He had just enough to bump the bet up to 60 more, clearing what money he had left in front of him. Wolf looked deep into his opponents' eyes and said, I call Ya, what Ya got"?

Wolf had been watching the card shark all evening knowing he was dealing from the bottom of the stacked deck. On this particular hand he caught a glimpse of a red queen at the bottom, knowing what the setup would be. The Shark laid down his 5 cards, 3 of clubs and 4 queens. Smiling through his decaying teeth he spoke, "Beat that friend"! His jaw dropped to the floor when Wolf unveiled an ace of spades joined by 4 handsome Kings. "Thanks Friend... I just did"! Beamed Wolf. As he racked the pot into his hat he stood up and put it on his head. Without them seeing the 3-lingering cards he had palmed were now safely underneath too. "Happy Christmas Gentlemen"! He said as he walked out with more than 200 pounds, leaving 4 men dumbfounded & speechless.

Scattered throughout the crowded tavern was Wolf's 7 brothers, as they all watched from a distance the master at work. One by one they slowly eased their way out. Tohru was nearest to the door went he saw the outraged loser make a beeline for the exit to track down the Drunken German. A few steps before overtaking Wolf, the card shark pulled out a knife. Suddenly he was thrust into a dark gap between two building and a razor shape blade at his throat. "I say only once... drop Da knife"! Tohru immediately heard the clank of it hit the cobblestone street. "Now you get lost... I see you again I gut you like a fish"! Tohru had never seen a man piss himself while running off like a scared jack rabbit.

Minutes later, the 8 were reunited back at their safe haven of the Studman home, all still laughing about the urine-soaked asshole who was on his horse at full gallop miles away by now. Tohru flung the captured pearl handled dagger into the table as vibrated back & forth. "A souvenir for Ya Marino, Happy Christmas"! He laughed out. Wolf gently took his hat off and dumped it around the deep stuck dagger, "And a very Happy Christmas my brothers! Dinner is on me"! Stoking up the fireplace they enjoyed the warmth of fellowship & the pending Holiday. "A toast... to the Cove & her soon to be owners"! As Noah raised his ale mug. Everwyn added in. "To Griffin Cove", as they all firmly nodded to the perfect name. Eli's eyes glistened with deep pride at his shipmates... his brothers... his family now.

Christmas eve in Charleston was teaming lively with festive town folk and the ever-arriving outsiders for the pending auction that morning. The 8 men knew it would be a few hours before the Royal Shipping Line appointed auctioneer would get around to lot #133. Darin was the first to arrive minutes before the sale started since he had to be present for it all for official recording. Gradually, the rest came sauntering into the crowded town square. There was an enlarged map setup next to the auction stand showing the various partials of land to be sold off, with each marked out as they went. The sections ranged from just south of Charleston to a few miles north of Brunswick with #133 being one of the last to go. A pattern of sales was starting to form at the various costs going from as low as 75 to as high as 500. As the day lingered on fewer bidders were amassed and by late afternoon both the people as well as the prices were dropping off.

Lots 132 & 134 were at least 10 miles away & inland from the desired Griffin Cove. All but Everwyn (farmer John Smith) was near the stand when lot #133 came up. The others were milling about the square, but their ears were trained on the sale. Finally, the obviously fatigued auctioneer wearily spoke, "Lot 133 is now up for sale, I will start the bidding at 100 pounds"! Several seconds passed with no takers. "Anyone bid 75 pounds"? Still nothing uttered from the sparce crowd. "How about 50 pounds for this great section of land"? A moment later, the tattered clothed farmer shouted out, "I'll go 10 pounds"! A low murmur of laughter came up from the scattered few there. The auctioneer replied back, "How about 20 pounds, do I hear 20 pounds from anyone"? Silence filled the air, "15 pounds do I hear 15 pounds"? The auctioneer knew he had to sell them all off no matter what the price, and with only a few left he finally gave in. "10 pounds going once... going twice... SOLD for 10 pounds! Come up and make your mark sir". Darin turned to the farmer and said, "Name please"? Everwyn replied, "John Smith". He scrawled out a poor attempt at signing an "S" and paid the 10 pounds for the deed to lot #133. Beaming smiles from various areas of the town square could be seen on the faces of the new owners of Griffin Cove. An unsuspecting Christmas gift from the Royal Shipping Lines and Father Christmas, Viscount Ervin.

Back at the Studman house the men celebrated their 10-pound victory with a splendid meal, and a surprise gift for Everwyn. Noah spoke up for the rest, "No true navigator is complete without the proper tools"! As he was given a high-quality sexton from his grateful brothers. Among the other gifts exchanged that night was a carved wooden model of the brig to be built by Fabrice. Wolf had forged up a set of matching double barrel pistols, one for every brother with individually carved handles. Marino surprised everyone with hidden talent he had for tailoring, making the crew a set of heavy leather gloves, perfect for work on land and at sea. Darin had been working secretly at something that touched them all, as he revealed a large parchment of artistic splendor, an upright golden winged Griffin with its talons up & long tail poised to attack. The most heartfelt gift came from Noah & Eli. As the 2 announced that from now on they all shared equally in the profits that was brought in. "Aside from the materials & provisions needed for our Brig & Griffin Cove, we split everything 8 ways", announced Eli. For the first time they all saw their future captain before them, the young lad who was becoming much more than a man, he was growing into their leader.

They all headed back to their normal routine a few days after Christmas, with the Tripoli making its run northward to Brunswick. Per Fabrice instructions, they laid over 2 extra days while the skilled shipwright completed some needed repairs on the vessel. At the same time increasing her cargo capacity by 25% to accommodate the needed white oak they were to pick up in Port Bath. Meanwhile, the pinnace, now named "Rover" was at Griffin Cove dropping off supplies of salt and storage barrels to secure the upcoming hunted meat. They fashion a more durable permanent ladder to the area above as well as widening the opening to allow the cut wood to be roped down. They also built a flexible cap cover over the ceiling hole to prevent rain or stray wildlife from falling down into the cave.

Winter of 1757 was upon the colonies as snow covered most of the lands north & west of the Carolinas. The frozen country sides made it difficult for farmers, merchants, miners & loggers to bring their wares to market in the various ports. The 8 men knew this would eventually happen, so they used the time to work more at the cove, building, harvesting & hunting. During the cold months of January through late March the slide platform was built to house the pending hull creation close to the lagoon. In one of the smaller caves, Wolf & Tohru constructed a forge and smelter, more than sufficient for their metal working needs. They had stocked up an ample supply of charcoal they had made to fire up the furnace to maximum capability. Setting up a winch pully, the much-needed timber from higher up was brought down to the ground level and stored. In no time at all, the provision barrels were topped off with dried salted fish, deer, boar, rabbit & turkey meat. In another short cave, Tohru fashioned a small smoke house to add a bit of flavor to the hunted meat. Barrels of ale, from Brunswick were placed in the cold fresh pool at the base of the waterfall. The gathering of carbon, plus iron ore & bog ore was slow but productive as spring crept back into the ever-growing Griffin Cove.

As the weather turned warmer, so did the waters of the cove, giving the men time to start the gradual task of dredging the sand bar that served as a barrier to the inlet. Working mostly at low tide the sand, scattered coral, & rocks were hauled out allowing a wide deep draft while it still prevented any large vessel intruders from entering into the cove. The sand bar itself was left undisturbed as it served as a natural blockade with a few rock formations and heavy foliage at its core. Several months before they had built a floating blind made of tall water reeds & plants that served as an addition to the natural one to help disguise the canal entrance from the Atlantic. Lashed to the banks with underwater lines, the buffer was totally undetectable to the naked eye.

The men were now back in full swing with their usual jobs when the Tripoli docked in Port Bath in early April. Seeking the much-needed white oak. But the wood was nowhere to be found for sale in the port trade office due to the heavy winter there that was just now letting up its chilling grip. Most everything else was scarce from being consumed by the locals over the long cold months. Noah, Eli & Tohru checked around town to try and catch some gossip about any needed supplies, but everyone said the same thing, nothing to be had for at least a month or more. Rosie was coming out of one of the shops when they caught sight of the dark-haired beauty. "Oh my God, I thought you 3 had fallen of the face of the earth, it's been far too long, so great to see Ya'll again"! She beamed with excitement. After exchanging hugs, the men invited her to a late breakfast with her accepting happily. The conversation started with them thanking her for Marino, who was a valuable part of their crew now with him working out of Brunswick. A brief update of how things had gone for everyone over the past months, as the chat turned to the supply problems. Noah said, "Rosie, the main thing we were hoping to load up was white oak but there's none around". She pondered for a moment then remembered something she overhead a few days ago.

About 20 miles northeast of town was a German farmer who migrated his family to America back in October. He spoke very little English and from what she had heard he came into town about 10 days ago with a broken arm and no money for supplies. She saw this and was kind enough to give him some coin for food for his staving family. The land he bought had not been cleared to plant his crops, it was cluttered with, what he kept calling "Weibe Baume". She wasn't sure what he meant. "Weibe Baume? That's white trees"! Eli translated to her. By now the young man had gathered up enough of the language from Wolf to understand & speak it well. While chopping down one of the larger ones a stray branch had glanced off and snapped his forearm. With the assistance of Rosie & her carriage, they scraped up all the supplies they could find and headed to the farm. A couple of hours later they arrived at the dilapidated place. Eli immediately spoke to the injured German & his wife in their native tongue.

He explained they were there to help them all they could as the much-needed provisions were unloaded into the house. Cascading on 3 sides of the small farmhouse were towering thick Weibe Baume numbering several dozen or more. It was what they had suspected, sprawling groves of white oak. It seemed the German bought the farm sight unseen back in Germany and was told it was primed and ready for farming. His wife and 4 adolescent children were left to fend for themselves since none could speak English.

After the supplies were unloaded, the Husky German wife went to work preparing them a long overdue meal. Tohru examined the broken arm which appeared to have no serious chance of compound fracturing or gang green showing. He reset it with some wood cut splints and rebandaged it. All the while Eli explaining to the thankful man what his oriental friend was doing. A few minutes later, Noah turned to Rosie and instructed her to take the carriage back to town and get a message to the crew in Brunswick to get to Port Bath as soon as possible and bring their axes. Rosie added she would get the word out in town of anyone who wanted a few days' work clearing land."10 shillings a day should get us at least a half dozen willing lumberjacks"! She laughingly added. The Tripoli crew stayed to help fix things up as best as possible for the needy family. Eli translated to them what was going on, when the farmer asked in German, "How can we ever repay you for all this"? Eli told him simply that they wanted the rights to buy all his white oak. For a moment the man was puzzled, then he replied in broken English, "they yours... all of them...no money I want"! Eli smiled back at the teary-eyed farmer, firmly shook his good hand and said," Danke Mein Freund"!

Rosie came back about 4 hours later followed by the town doctor on horseback. She had grabbed up some clothes & blankets for the tattered family as the afternoon was waning down. It seemed Tohru's diagnosis was spot on, the doctor confirmed it was a clean break of the forearm & was healing well. He should have full use of it within a few weeks or so. Before twilight fell the crew headed out as Eli explained they would be back bright and early to start clearing the Weibe Baume, hopefully with help too. Following the distant lights of the port, they arrived back in town as Rosie's guest at the Crimson Garter. The girls were thrilled to see the Tripoli crew back, especially "Mr. Eli Stud" as they jokingly called him. "Cool your pantaloons ladies, This Stud is mine tonight" she boastfully laughed as they headed upstairs for another lesson in advanced erotica!

Manned with sharpened axes, 4 hired men joined the crew at daybreak as they made their way back to the farm. One by one the tall timbers fell crashing to the ground, while remaining stumps were neatly uprooted. With his good hand the farmer would chop off the smaller limbs turning the white beauties into clean logs. Around noonish Rosie & some of her girls boarded carriages to bring them lunch and a well-deserved midday break. By the time the Rover crew arrived in Port Bath 4 days later, over half of the west side grove was cut, cleared & ready for plowing. It was a fond reunion for Rosie & her little brother Marino who brought her a unique shoulder cape he had fashion from a large black panther they trapped a few months back at the cove. Wolf was delighted to finally have a fellow countryman to chat with as he learned more about the Wilhelm family. Setting up some makeshift tents next to the farmhouse, the brothers camped there in order to get a fresh start every morning. The 4 hired men eventually had their fill of hard laboring, and with shillings in hand they went their separate ways.

Hans Wilhelm was head of the family from a poor village near Hamburg. His wife, Ursula decided to leave with him and their 4 children for the new world in hopes of a better life. When the offer came about the farm, they jumped at the opportunity. Hans was very familiar with growing wheat, corn &

beans, but he had brought some very unique seeds with him from Germany, long leaf hemp. Fact: This was a legal commodity to grow at the time with several farms around Virginia amassing it already. Along with tobacco, these crops would easily yield a farmer a sizable profit at harvest time. Han's idea was to plant wheat & corn on the sunny western slope, then set aside the southern acres that were closer to the brooks & streams for hemp and eventually tobacco. The rare European long leaf strain required more oxygen & water than the hemp growing already in the colonies, thus producing a thicker, stronger plant used to make clothes, rope & sails.

About a half mile southeast of the farm was the mouth of an inlet river that eventually flowed back to the port. The 7 men moved the 2 vessels to a safe clearing making the loading much easier than wagon hauling them the 20 miles back to the town. Fabrice & Everwyn had rail split the white oak logs into length wise quarters as this was eventually needed to start the hull building back at the cove. Within a week the Tripoli was fully loaded & headed back to the cove for the first of several deliveries. Rover crew stayed on to continue cutting & clearing the remainder of Han's west pasture. By the end of April, fully recovered, Hans had the pasture planted with corn & wheat, as the southern area was now clear of all the sprawling trees. Over 200 tall white oak logs were amassed, more than enough for the brig's hull, keel & frame. When the last of the cargo was loaded on both vessels, Wolf handed Hans a leather pouch with 75 pounds inside. Speaking in German he told the grateful farmer, "This is only a down payment for the timber, when your harvest comes in let us know, we will be back for some of it, especially the hemp & tobacco". Han's replied," I can't take your money my friend, you all have saved my family's life and I'm forever indebted to you all". As he tried his best to return the pouch, the 7 men insisted he take it, at least as a start to a long & prosperous agreement together for more goods. Teary eyed, Hans & Ursula embraced them all as they sailed out.

With the materials safely stored at the cove they all went back to their normal routine in Brunswick & Charleston. Darin had been periodically briefed via messenger letters when he greeted the Tripoli as she docked. His broad smile was more than just an overdue welcome, he had news they would want to hear immediately. A sealed letter had arrived from the king 10 days before authorizing a second charting expedition. This time he wanted a detailed mapping of the coastline & inlets from Charleston down to south of St. Augustine. The instruction went on to state he was to hire a local civilian vessel with no affiliation to the crown or any other European country. "During the course of the entire expedition you are to remain completely inconspicuous as possible". The letter came with a small, sealed lock box the British ship's captain was instructed to give to Darin personally. Inside was 500 pounds plus an official Crown Scroll granting him knighthood, he was now Sir Darin Cavety. "I'll admit it, when I first saw this, I was somewhat impressed, but then I started reading between the lines more. The money & knighthood is a way to insure I keep my mouth shut while I help the fuckn Limy Navy invade here & probably Florida too"! The men could see Darin's eyes fire up with the deep passion for some royal payback. "So how about I hired the Tripoli again for a little joy ride down the coastline for a few days"? Darin Smiled slyly at the crew. Noah smirked saying, "Ya know, we just so happen to be making a cargo run to Savannah tomorrow if Ya Wanta hitch a ride"!

England had been making numerous attempts to take control of northeast Florida dating back over 50 years. Every time, Spain beat them back while growing in strength with powerful forts strategically positioned inland and on the coastline. It was obvious King George II was preparing for yet another siege this time from both land & sea. Meanwhile, war intensified in Europe making this Florida attack at least a year or more away, plus the king now had Prussia's growing army to contend with. This latest mission for Darin was a prelude to another bogus auction to raise money, this time directly for the crown.

Morning tide saw the Tripoli sail out of Charleston harbor bound for Savannah to drop off cargo and make a few extra pounds before they landed in St. Augustine. On board, Darin had his previously charted map that was accurate to a tee so all he would do was adjust any minor changes mother nature might have made over the past 2 years. The voyage was routine for the Tripoli since they had made this run countless times. Sliding into St. Augustine for the first time since the warehouse folly, they noticed the ports fortifications had been beefed up substantially to accommodate a larger garrison of troops. A Spanish sloop of war was patrolling the outer harbor & surrounding coastline making it clear they were ready for anything.

The following morning, with a light cargo load, they decided to venture south for a day or so since Darin hadn't had a chance to chart the deeper coastline areas. Several short inlets, patched with sandy islands dotted most of the region before reaching the growing settlement of Haulover, about 25 miles south of St. Augustine. Haulover was sparsely populated by a mixture of Spanish & French immigrants who established a friendly cohesion with some of the native Indians. Once landing a safe anchorage within a few yards of the beach, the Tripoli crew waded ashore to check out what the village had to offer. Bananas was about the only thing in abundance as they purchase a dozen bunches to sell later. One thing clearly missing there was the overshadowing presents of Spanish military. It seemed an occasional patrol would ride in to check on the tiny town but apart from that, Haulover was an open town. During this period, much of the eastern coast below St. Augustine was uninhabited for the most part, with exceptions of places like Haulover. The terrain consisted of marsh & swamp land that even the long existing Indian tribes found difficult to live in. Mother nature had planted fierce wildlife in abundance there to protect it, alligators, panthers, wild boar, deadly snakes and more. Even the seas proved a threat to man, schools of sharks could be seen patrolling about a few miles offshore. Razor sharp formations of coral lined the shallows that would gut a ship's hull in the blink of an eye. Mix that with ever present storms made the region a frightful venture for any sailor.

Fact: On July 31st, 1715, 12 Spanish treasure fleet ships departed from Havana bound for Spain. A few hours later they encountered a deadly hurricane with winds clocked at over 150 miles an hour.11 of the 12 ships were torn apart as they all came crashing into the jagged reefs along the Florida coastline. The ship's cargo was hundreds of tons of gold, silver & jewels valued at the time, well over 20 million pounds. 1,500 crew & passengers perished with only 1 ship surviving to return to Spain with the devastating news to King Philip V. Wreckage & bodies could be found washed ashore from the southernmost straits northward for several miles. Many of the ships came apart within several yards of shore at depths of less than 20 feet. Mast heads could be seen rising up for many years after as an eerie warning to remind mariners of the unforgiving power of Mother nature.

The crew decided to head back to Savannah to sell off the cargo of bananas and pick up some needed supplies to add to the ever-growing materials at the cove. As for the crew in Brunswick, Wolf was finishing up a custom set of pistols for a well to do gentleman who introduced himself as Captain DaRoga. Dressed in fine clothing from head to toe, the man had a seasoned look about him, someone who had traveled extensively for most of his 40 plus years. He was impressed with the fine detail & craftmanship the blacksmith possessed when he arrived in port a week before aboard a sloop in desperate need of repairs. The 110-foot vessel had clearly been on the victorious side of a sea battle recently, Fabrice explained to the Rover crew later that evening at the tavern. The sloop was flying the red & golden Spanish colors after leaving Havana with a heading back to Spain when they encountered a Royal Shipping Line Ketch 15 miles off the coast of Brunswick. The 120-footer was armed with 18 (8-pound) guns and saw a chance to rack the smaller sloop and take it as a prize back to Bristol. But the Ketch Captain didn't count on a much more experienced adversary as the fast maneuverable sloop swung about to its target's stern.

 Laying an accurate broadside of chain shot into the British rigging, as the first pass cut apart its top sails, with lines being cut away and canvas flapping wildly. The sloop made a hard starboard tack to come about for a second volley as the Ketch tried desperately to make a port side attack. But the Spanish vessel was too quick as her 6 starboard side 12 pounders sliced the main mast of the Ketch at its core with it crashing down on the deck trapping several of the crew. 2 precise broadsides and the British ship was nearly dead in the water. Captain DaRoga steered his sloop close in to finish them off with a volley of reloaded grape shot that took out almost a dozen British sailors. Before their grappling hooks were latched into the Ketch, she managed to get a few hits into the sloop's hull.

An experienced fired up crew boarded the tattered ship, outnumbering them by half. Within minutes the ship was taken, as her Captain and almost all her crew lay dead leaving 6 Englishman to make a choice, join the Sloop or die. Only one Welsh sailor opted to live on as he watched the others executed quickly. While the Spanish tended to their wounded, only losing 5 of their crew, Captain DaRoga inspected his captured ship & her cargo. The ships log, stored in the captain's cabin reveled stores of rice, corn & indigo picked up in Charleston. A large purchase of milled white pine planks had come from Savannah. The captain knew his sloop couldn't handle all that cargo. After a quick inspection of the Ketch's hull condition, he decided to take her in tow to the nearest safe haven. The crew cleared the debris from the mast less ship, cutting away any unnecessary remains left to help lighten the load as they patched up the sloops leaking hull and headed west. By nightfall they had come up on a secluded spot about 3 miles northeast of Brunswick harbor called Cabbage Inlet. Protected by rocky shoals on the ocean side they turned into the mouth to bring their towed ship to a safe halt on a sandbar a few yards from shore. Once the Spanish crew secured the beached hull to shore, they loaded all its cargo but the long heavy white pine planks. This gave Captain DaRoga a chance to clear out anything else he might have missed in the British Captain's cabin.

In his closet was a variety of well-made officer uniforms, from the British Royal Navy, to Spanish, French & Dutch, complete with appropriate rank & emblems. It was one of the disguised Royal Shipping Line privateers he had heard about. Sifting through the large desk proved his theory correct, several forged Letters of Marque were in the locked drawer along with a solo key. Looking about the ornate cabin he eventually found the mate to it. A false seat against the stern bulkhead revealed a locked strong box that the key matched to. Inside was gold coins, silver ingots, precious jewels & pearls estimated well over 30,000 pounds in value. It's worth was far more than what was left of the Ketch & cargo, but rather than towing it back out to open waters and sinking her, he continued on as planned and sailed into Brunswick at daybreak. With the crew instructed to keep their mouths shut about the beached ship, DaRoga immediately contracted Fabrice to make whatever repairs necessary to his battered sloop that was now flying Dutch colors of trade. DaRoga had heard good things about the French ships apprentice from other satisfied customers and requested him specifically to complete the task. While the Spanish crew silently relaxed in port, their clever captain slowly got acquainted with Fabrice & Wolf.

One evening at the port tavern, Daroga invited himself to the table of the 4 men, as he was introduced to Everwyn & Marino who arrived that afternoon in the Rover. After a round of pleasant chat and ale, the comfortable Captain complimented them on their well-made cutter looking over at Fabrice knowing that was his handy work. The 5 men slyly smiled, then in a low tone voice Daroga said," It's quite a unique foursome you all have, French, German, Spanish & English". The four looked at each other, smiled replying one by one in acknowledgment of the perceptive Captain. "I'd assume then that you all are pretty much independent minded men with one primary goal... to look out for one another above anything else". A silent pause as they peered at each other again before Everwyn spoke up, "Captain, we see ourselves as unfortunate individuals who fortunately have come together for one common purpose, to survive... with the hopes of thriving". That was enough for Daroga confide in them a lucrative proposition he had in mind.

Peering about the tavern to insure no one else was within ear shot, he briefly explained the reason for the beached Ketch hull a few miles away. Looking at Fabrice, his offer was to have his sloop repaired & refitted for the long voyage back to Spain. Glancing at Wolf he wanted his ships cannons inspected & gone over as well as having a custom set of pistols made for him. Knowing through the idle chit chat that Everwyn was a skilled navigator, Daroga said he wanted his navigation equipment recalibrated, including the poor sexton his own navigator had on board. Finally peering in Marino's direction, he was in some needed carpentry work on the worn-out ship's rudder & housing. He paused a moment to catch his breath then said, "In return the Ketch is all yours including almost 100 planks of milled white pine. The hull is watertight with little or no damage, we just demasted her is all", as he laughed along with the others. Finally, he added that the 18 (8 pound) cannons were worthless to him. Wolf, Everwyn & Marino mentally agreed with the offer as they looked over at their French brother. Fabrice was an apprentice to the Old British shipwright who owned the shipyard. He would expect payment for the repairs to the sloop as Fabrice explained to Captain DaRoga. "You leave him to me; I'll take care of the old bastard... I know a thing or two about him", smirked the Spaniard. The 5 men came to an accord agreeing the Ketch needed to be moved quickly before anyone spotted it. With DaRoga describing its location, the 4 knew exactly where it was and where to hide it too, in the lagoon at Griffin Cove.

The following evening as the sun was setting, the Rover lite out to Cabbage Inlet to retrieve their catch. Using both sail & oars the 4 brothers spent the bulk of the cloud covered night towing the hull slowly into their hideaway. As they approached the dredged sandbar to make the turn for the lagoon, they could see the stern lights of the Tripoli anchored 500 yards ahead. Marino Bellowed out, "Hay you lazy Bastards, Wake Up! Come give us a hand"! Everwyn chimed in," Boy oh Boy have we got a surprise for you"! Minutes later Noah, Eli & Tohru rowed out in the launch to help them tow the final way in till they beached the hull successfully against the far end of the lagoon. While the Rover crew got some needed sleep aboard the Tripoli, Noah sailed the Rover solo back to Brunswick closely followed by Eli & Tohru in the Tripoli. As the sun was just starting to break on the eastern horizon the 2 ships docked in the quiet British port.

The Tripoli 3 stayed on to help complete the bargain as Captain DaRoga & Marino caught up with the latest news from his homeland. As for the payment due to the British shipwright, that was taken care of. Amid the numerous documents he found aboard the Ketch, was a rather interesting one from the Royal Shipping Lines via the Crown. It seemed the old ship builder was remiss in paying taxes on his shipyard dating back 3 years. Wearing the captured British Naval uniform, DaRoga posed as an official for the crown when the old man was ordered aboard the refitted sloop a week later. After presenting him the bill for the work done, DaRoga handed him the overdue tax bill as he spoke, "It seems you owe the Crown over 10 times that amount in back taxes"! Shocked speechless, the old man knew such an offense was punishable by confiscation of property and possible hanging. Pausing a moment, the captain gave him a stern look & made him an offer he couldn't refuse," I'll tell you what I'm willing to do...You tear up that bill & I'll consider speaking to his Majesty about this when I return to England"! The old man breathed a deep sigh of relief, thanked him repeatedly, doing everything but kissing the captain's ass in grateful appreciation of his benevolent gesture. As he was making his way off the sloop the captain said," Oh yes one more thing, that Frenchman does fine work, I expect him to get a raise, he's a craftsman". Stuttering his reply back, "Yes Sir Captain I totally agree... I will see to it immediately". Minutes later Fabrice was told by his employer he was promoted to shipwright with him receiving 15% of all work done at the shipyard. Stunned at the 180-degree swing from his stingy boss he just said thanks and went back to work, snickering at the thought of what the hell DaRoga did to the old bastard.

CHAPTER 4

Misfortune Smiles

On the morning tide, as the Spanish sloops sailed for home, the 7 men headed out in both their ships to get a much better look at the skuttled prize tucked away in Griffin Cove. As they arrived, the mast less hull was much bigger than they had anticipated. The 120-foot ship was originally built in Liverpool in 1740 as a "Bomb Ketch" warship. Given the name due to the reenforced hull flanks that could withstand a typical broadside much better than a cargo designed Ketch. The bow & stern were lightly made to enable the ship to turn better in the wind, as was the rigging, thus making it vulnerable to a stern & mast attack. The first thing they did was take off the ship's name bolted to her stern, "Lady Fortune". As Eli tossed it ashore, he got a rousing round of laughter saying, "Well, now she's renamed, "Miss Fortune"! Over the years, she had been refitted for cargo use with the holes cleared for storage. Fabrice slowly walked through the lower bay inspecting every piece of the watertight hull. Silent as he strolled, you could almost hear the wheels churning in his head. The crew had seen him like this before, it was best to just leave him be in his deep contemplation. He could envision what the area looked like when initially built as he stood in the middle of a forward 12x12 foot frame square still bolted firmly to the keel. The now cargo hatch opening was originally used to house the ship's mortar that was built up to be fired at deck level. He had worked up plans in the past for such a devastating hidden weapon but his had a twist to it, a 360-degree rotating twist.

Meanwhile, Wolf & Tohru were looking over the 18 cannons. Shaking his head time & time again he uttered, "What a frigin waste of iron"! With his oriental counterpart in agreement. The British weren't known for their expertise in foundry production, a prime example was these 8-pound cast iron piece of crap. They were too long & heavy due to the overly thickened muzzle. Wolf knew these could be 10 to 12 pounders if the bore was wider. He added, "They ain't even rifled or stroked". Tohru thought a second then said, "At least we no gotta mine for iron ore anymore". Chuckling, they agreed to use one of them for a mold then melt down the rest. This was a real chance for Wolf & Tohru to create a weapon of unique accuracy & power.

In the bow, was a deck level galley Everwyn was rummaging through finding a cast iron stove along with skillets, pots and enough utensils to serve a full crew. Marino brought up several yards of usable rope & line from the gear locker below. There was an ample amount of spare canvas used for replacing damaged sails. Noah was on the quarterdeck checking out the helm & ship's compass that seemed to be quite serviceable. Below the quarterdeck was Eli in the large plush Captain's cabin. The spacious quarters had been ransacked by DaRoga, with him taking the obvious valuables, uniforms, clothing & logbook. Several personal items remained like a decorative framed portrait of a young woman with extraordinary beauty. The large hand carved oak desk sat to the rear, close to the stain glass stern portals. Eli carefully went through all 8 of the drawers only finding useless papers & bills of lading. Opening the thin center drawer, he noticed something peculiar about it, it was far too shallow for such a massive desk. As he pulled it out farther, he saw two small chain lengths on either end attached to a second hidden drawer.

In it was an 18-inch-long wooden box. To his amazement was a set of shiny brass seal stamps, the kind used for official documents by kings & high-ranking members of government. Usually choosing red melted wax, the seal would be pressed into the center confirming its authenticity. Eli inspected every one of the detailed stamps showing they were from: British, French, Spanish & Dutch Crown. The other 3 were from: East Indies Trading Company, Dutch East indies Company & Royal Shipping Lines Company. He paused a moment, smiled a said out loud, Oh My God! Darin's gonna love this"! Deeply thinking more, he started to wonder why this sea captain had such a valuable set like this. A quick search of the papers in the desk revealed the name, "Captain Benjamin Winslow".

Benjamin was first cousin to Lady Winslow, the wife of Viscount Ervin. He had been a trusted employee of the Royal Shipping Line for well over 15 years and was a respected member to court. He was married to his teenaged second cousin, Belinda Winslow, a ravaging beauty, assuming the portrait in the cabin was her. Combined with her vibrant stunning looks & zestful ways, she was a favorite of the Crown, especially at court functions. Even though her mother, Duchess Freda of Mecklenburg, was of German descent. Belinda's one drawback, she was presumed barren since she had produced no children in their 3 years of wedlock. Eli remembered the Winslow name from his journal as he etched Belinda's name deep into his mental notebook along with the others associated with Ervin.

Eli eventually found the false seat compartment DaRoga had discovered the valuable iron lock box in. He searched inside the dark void seeing it was empty. Just as he was closing it up, he noticed a solo shiny object wedged in the wooden crease at the far corner inside. Gently working it out, he held in his hand a wore old Spanish Piece of 8. Remanence of coral spotted the edges showing it had been submerged for several years. Minutes later he gathered up the crew on deck to show them what he had found. Impressed with the box of seal stamps, Noah was more intrigued with the gold coin. He recognized the marking from a few others he had seen over the years saying reverently, "This is a Spanish Treasure Fleet Doubloon"! The same one lost in the historic wreck of 1715 off the southeastern coastline of Florida. The question now was, how did Captain Winslow come about it?

Going back into the cabin, they shuffled through the bills of lading in hopes to find a hint. One of them showed the Ketch purchasing 30 bunches of bananas down in Haulover 2 months before. Another was for 20 barrels of coffee in Havana, 3 days prior. But this was only one coin, he could have bought it from someone in any of these ports. What they didn't know was all of the gold coins DaRoga had taken in the iron lock box were mates to this one. Nevertheless, it was something to think about while they relaxed to a well-prepared meal onboard the Miss Fortune. Fabrice began to share his new ideas inspired by their demasted prize. Initially he had drawn up plans for a 100-foot brig with a cargo capacity of around 300 tons. But after seeing firsthand the capabilities of the less useful Ketch, he knew it was possible to build a bigger, better brig, especially now that he had more than ample quality materials to do it. He added, "It will take a lot more time though but if I'm right, we have time on our side". Glancing over at each one of his intent looking brothers, he turned to Wolf and asked, "What do Ya know about crafting mortars"? Smiling slyly.

The following morning the Tripoli sailed south to Charleston, anxious to see the look on Darin's face when he would get the box of seal stamps. The Rover headed back to Brunswick with the Ketch's name plank aboard. They had roughed it up to appear the ship had been destroyed. Just before they entered the harbor, it was dropped over the side allowing the incoming tide to eventually wash it ashore. By late afternoon, a local fisherman carried it to the British harbor master. His port log read," May 31st, 1757, wreckage found this day from Lady Fortune, presumed lost at sea". The port business was slow when the Tripoli docked that evening with the 4 men reunited at the Studman house. Darin was truly amazed at the 7 stamps, remarking, "I've never known of anyone to have a set like this. You realize the power this box possesses"? They brought Darin up to speed about Miss Fortune and everything she yielded for them now, including the rare gold coin.

As he listened intently, Darin continued to carefully examine the brass beauties inside the black satin lined box. It seemed the set was newly crafted & never put to use. Flipping the cypris wood box over he saw a small, embossed emblem in the lower right-hand corner. A 3-pointed shield with a Fleur de Lis at its core. A scroll topped the shield with a single word, "Mieux" translated in French meaning the very best. Over the years, Darin had heard tales of a master craftsmen named Emele Meilleur who was world renowned for his minuet detailing with jewelry & precious metals. His last name in French also meant best or greatest. In his younger years he was commanded by the kings of Spain & France to fashion unique necklaces for their queens, including an ornate one made solely of emeralds that was presumed lost in one of the Spanish Treasure Fleet ships in 1715. Emele had long since retired to a quiet life in the small town of Chalmette, a few miles southeast of New Orleans. If Eleme was truly the creator of this seal set it made it even more valuable, especially to whoever contracted him initially.

While all this was transpiring, it seemed the air was beginning to fill with something new & advantageous for the 8 men, pigeons! Rosie received the first flight from a carrier pigeon that Hans's wife had trained. It seemed Ursula had a knack for turning the ordinary birds into homing ones. This linked up Port Bath with their farmer 20 miles away. Her goal was to eventually extent the ariel routes to everyone concerned, thus cutting needed information time from several days down to a few hours. By late-July the carrier routes were complete: Ursula to Rosie to Marino to Ruth as the last leg into Charleston. To be safe they worked up a code system in the carried notes in case a bird fell into the wrong hands. Eventually the flight path would be added in Griffin Cove.

Fabrice had the reworked plans complete for the brig. She would be 133 feet long, from stem to stern, including the long boat fixed to launch from the outer aft of the raised quarterdeck. An efficiently slim down deck of 30 feet wide & set only 3 feet below the broadside railing. This allowed a much larger cargo space below to accommodate almost 500 tons. The main & fore masts would be fitted with square rigging sails, as the aft tacking sail would be attached to the main mast. Forward on the bow stem would be 3 foresheets as needed. Below the quarterdeck was cabin space, 30x30 feet to comfortably fit up to 9 men, since it was agreed there was no need for an elaborate captain's cabin. The detailed plans showed she would be sleek, fast, sturdy & powerful. The deck had more than enough space to fit up to 24 cannons that would have slide away gun ports making them undetected till they were ready to fire. 2 cannons could be set at the bow angle with 2 more flanking the stern at the rear of the quarterdeck. Fabrice had more powerful plans but had to work out the details with Wolf & Tohru. With everyone in full agreement he proceeded to get to work on the hull & keel, joined now by Marino & Everwyn as much as they could.

Wolf had already made the cannon mold from the worthless British 8 pounder and was redesigning it into light weight potent piece of devastating art. The mold would eventually produce a six-foot-long cannon, with a smooth rifled bore. It would fire a 12-pound ball shot and be ignited with his own creation, a flint lock trigger rather than the dangerous & undependable black powder fuse. The outer layer was smoothed from breech to muzzle, eliminating any unnecessary decoration, thus making it considerably lighter. He added a thick iron cast loop atop the breech housing used to thread rope through it. This stablished it during recoil, making it easier to roll on its wheeled carriage & reset faster.

If Hans was correct about his stronger long leaf hemp he was growing, that could be used to manufacture the heavy rope harness for the gun carriages. Via carrier pigeons, word got to the Ruth that the hemp crops were a few days away from harvesting at Hans farm. There was an established mill in Charleston that turned out quality materials for clothing, canvas & rope. The Tripoli sailed for Port Bath to work up a deal for the needed hemp, and a sweet 16 birthday side trip for Eli.

July 31st, 1757. They arrived at the small dock Hans had built a few months back near the thriving farm. Hearty greeting from the German family for the Tripoli crew as they boarded their wagon for the half mile ride to their home. The corn & wheat they planted, had already been harvested & sent to market making them a substantial profit. They spent the night as guests of the Wilhelm's and amazed at the progress they had made including they all were speaking broken English a lot better. Noah told Hans the unique hemp strain he was growing would bring a sizeable price down at the mill in Charleston once they see the difference from the usual one grown in the colonies. They agreed to evenly split the profits and making all the Wilhelm hemp exclusive to them. Hans had already doubled the hemp planting for next harvest, including adding in several acres of Tobacco. They spent the follow day loading up all the hemp the Tripoli could carry, as Ursula sent word by air to eventually get back to the Rover crew to come get the remaining harvest. That evening the crew docked in Port Bath to celebrate Eli's birthday. At the Crimson Garter, Rosie had prepared something special for the birthday boy, as two petite oriental beauties flanked him in the decorated parlor. Soon Me & Chew Yu curled up tight against him whispering, "Happy Birthday Mister Stud". Eventually, the 3 strolled up the staircase to the dim lite bedroom so he could thoroughly enjoy unwrapping his far east gifts. That night Eli learned a new French phrase, "Menage a Trois"! An learned it repeatedly too.

The trip back to Charleston was brisk with the Atlantic winds of August kicking up as usual this time of year. They laid over a few extra days while the mill owner tested out the German hemp. The aged Irishman had heard of the rare strain but had never seen it in use firsthand till now. Noah explained this was just the product of a first season crop. The following season would bring much more if they could come to a deal. The owner was clearly impressed with the hemp wanting exclusive rights to it all. Noah agreed with one added stipulation, "We get the wholesale price on your rope & canvas as needed". They came to an accord with the overall selling price of the German hemp bringing almost 35% more than the existing hemp would. The mill owner could see this deal would make his factory an enormous profit as word got out about the greatly improved products he would be creating. Rope that was stronger, canvas much more durable & lighter, clothing that would last longer. Combined with the port's production of indigo, he could really benefit from this, possibly enlarging the existing factory to add in sail making and a paper mill. A few days later the Rover arrived with the remaining harvested hemp, much to the delight of everyone concerned. Within a week Hans was delighted by the return of the Rover carrying his substantial share of the profits. Jingling the large leather coin pouch Hans sang out with glee, "Money makes da world go round"!

Meanwhile the Tripoli was on her southern run as they pulled into St. Augustine with supplies. The port was low on any export cargo, so they decided to venture down to Haulover and pick up some bananas. It was midafternoon on August 13th when the last of the bunches were loaded aboard & they sailed out to head north once more. Within an hour they found themselves bucking a strong headwind & ever-growing choppy water. They decided to come about and ride out the nasty weather back in Haulover, but before they docked, the ship was caught up in a growing storm as the sky grew dark gray. White caps emerged off the Atlantic side slapping hard against the hull thus pushing the Tripoli farther off course. Rain pelted the flapping sails making it difficult to steer with any control as they grew dangerously closer to unknown shoals.

At the bow Eli saw an inlet coming up fast dead ahead as he yelled it out to Noah at the helm. Thunder roared up with crackling lightning flashing out close behind. Just then the helm gave way, wildly spinning uncontrollably as the rudder cables had snapped. Suddenly the ship came to a crashing halt, throwing the 3 men forward. They had found one of the numerous coral reefs gashed deeply into the port side amid ships. Luckily no one was injured as they franticly worked to free the ship off the pointed reef. Water was pouring into the gaping hole below but thankfully they were in shallow waters & only about 20 yards from the beach. Harsh waves were smashing into her stern, one after another, till the force of Mother Nature finally pushed them loose off the reef as it cracked, leaving the remains in the water filling cargo hole. A few roaring waves later the Tripoli had washed ashore several yards on the beach. The men quickly grabbed up mooring lines to secure their ship to nearby palm trees. Insuring they all were ok, they huddled into a nearby sand dune to ride out the storm best they could. Gray sky turned to clearing stary ones a few hours later with nightfall upon them. The beach fire they made revealed the Tripoli leaned over to portside, wounded & silent. With makeshift torches they inspected the damage done. A 3-foot high, 8-foot-wide gash had been made with most of the culprit coral still filling the hole. Inspecting the stern rudder cables revealed the ropes had snapped from wear & tear but could easily be replaced with temporary ones. The few rips in the sails would take no time to mend well enough till they got to port. The major problem was the hole.

After a few hours of sleep on the beach the morning had them hard at work to repair the Tripoli with all haste. First priority was to clear out the large cone shaped coral mass still sitting in the hole it caused. Several reef fragments had washed ashore, scattered across the sandy beach. Tohru picked up one of them, the size of a melon, noticing something unusual in it. Crusted over was a small glint of gold peeking through the jagged white coral. Noah & Eli stopped what they were doing to watch him chip away at it till it revealed a familiar looking gold coin. The same type of Spanish piece of 8 found on the Ketch weeks before. 3 mouths sat wide open in amazement till Tohru broke their silence, "Holy Shit"! Using him hammer, Noah broke open the rest of the coral block to show at least 2 more buried coins embedded. Knowing now they accidently stumbled onto some of the 1715 wreckage, Eli recommended they gather up whatever remains on the beach before the tide washed it back out to sea and put it in the cargo hole for now along with the enormous chunk in there. They shoved the heavy cone shaped block deeper into the hole as Noah said," ok, let's get her fixed up now, we can play treasure hunter once we get the hell out of here". Several dozen pieces were scooped up and stored as the 3 eager men got back to work on the Tripoli.

Fashioning a temporary patch from the deck planking, they nailed it to the outside of the hull. Inside the cargo hole they attached a second patch in place and wedged in spare canvas around the edges. It took no time at all to rethread the rudder cable with rope and secure it enough to get them going. By nightfall they sat on deck sewing up the tears in the sails. Knowing the morning tide could get them off the beach, they unloaded the water-soaked cargo of bananas to lighten the load. Grabbing a few hours of sleep on a rotating watch, they woke to the sound of waves slapping the hull as the sun came up. Noah & Eli detached to mooring lines from the beach as Tohru reattached the onboard ends from the bow to the stern. The 2 men waded into the shallow waters with the lines secured around their waste while Tohru maned the helm. Slowly the hull began to slide into the ever-deepening waters as Noah & Eli swam back to board the ship. Gently the Tripoli bobbed freely in the shoals as the tide gradually carried her out. Eli & Tohru raced into the cargo hole to see if the patch was working, with Noah at the helm now. Quickly they emerged with an elated thumbs up when Noah ordered out, "set sail boys... let's get the hell out of here while we can". Once the canvas was up Eli headed to the bow, using his keen eyes to help steer them through the reef to open sea. Tohru kept a close watch on the patch below and securing any leaks that would pop up. Turning due north, they headed carefully to the nearest port, keeping close to the shoreline as best they could since they had no idea how far south the storm had pushed them.

4 hours into the trip, they started to recognize the coastline knowing Haulover was about 10 nautical miles or so ahead. Around noon they limped into the village. Using the time in the small port to seal the patch with tar they gathered up, then getting something to eat & needed sleep the crew resumed the run the next morning. Everything was going fine, they decided to bypass St. Augustine & Savannah. Aching to dig into the cargo below, they thought it best to wait till they got it safely to Griffin Cove. A day later the ship arrived in Charleston as Darin was told all about the terrifying experience & unexpected find. He had Ruth send an ariel message to the crew in Brunswick to rush to the cove at once. Provisioned once again, the 4 men sailed the next morning to the hideaway to link up with the rest of the crew. The Rover was docked when the wounded Tripoli came in around dusk. As they unloaded the unexpected cargo, the tale was told about the Tripoli's frightening experience. Once in the well lite cave, the sounds of chiseling echoed off the walls. Wolf & Tohru started in on the base of the large cone shape coral mass that was easily 4 foot in diameter. The rest were chipping away anxiously on the other reef fragments hoping to be the first to discover treasure. Everwyn hollered out, "I got one"! As he revealed another piece of 8, proving this had to be one of the 1715 wreckages. One by one, they uncovered more of the coins including short lengths of thick gold chain. But the most astounding find wasn't made of gold, it was case in bronze.

Wolf & Tohru slowly started to see a large thick circle appear as they picked away at the coral base. Knowing that familiar shape & size, Wolf spoke, "I think we have a ship's bell here boys"! Ears perked up as everyone stop chiseling and gathered around to see what they had found. Chunks thick white coral quickly fell away revealing an ornate molded bronze bell used on board ships to sound out the times on the hour. Using his knife, Tohru carefully carved away at the rim till it clearly displayed the ship's name, "Senora de la Regla".

Fact: The Senora de la Regla was named for the patron saint of Cadiz, Spain, also known as the Lady of Rule. The ship was one of the larger Spanish galleons that sank in the 1715 disaster. She was built in 1678 as part of the treasure fleet, making several successful trips from Panama & Havana back to home port Spain. Strong & powerful she carried 70 guns with a crew capacity of 400 seasoned sailors. When she went down on the evening of July 31st, 1715, with 10 other treasure ships, she was carrying 200 passengers & a full complement of crew. In her holes was 1,200 tons of gold & silver bars including 120 tons of gold coins. Rumor had it that on board was the precious Emerald jewelry intended for the Queen of Spain.

8 pair of eyes glared intently at the detailed name, dumbfounded to the point of speechless silence. Their minds all thinking the same thing, "Oh My God"! It took several moments for anyone to regain their senses when Noah broke the hush," There's gotta be more here, I can feel it"! He was right too.

The remaining scattered pieces yielded another 12 coins including 9 more broken sections of what was once a long thick golden chain. They all started in on the huge sections left from the coral that housed the bell as they tirelessly worked thru the night till dawn's light shined in on the cave entrance. Moving the work outside for a better look, Tohru stopped long enough to make them a large pot of hot coffee while they all paused briefly to grab up some smoked meat. Bellies refilled the brothers were back at it in a flash. With every passing minute of careful chipping the count grew till all of the massive pieces of coral reef that ripped open the Tripoli was reduced to white powder on the ground. It produced an additional 27 coins varying in size & weight. A few more lengths of the matching gold chains were found as well, linking it all together, it came to 41 inches.

Everyone was so overcome with excitement they forgot about the inside of the 18-inch-wide bell. Tohru chipped away gradually from around the rim as pieces fell away enough to wedge his chisel in a gap and began to pry at the core. Hearing the coral crack, a sizable chunk split from the base revealing a portion of the bell clapper. Cutting around the bronze ball, the other side of the coral released from the inner wall of the bell as he gingerly wedged it out. I small hint of gold appeared from one of the fragments, but this obviously wasn't another coin or chain. Breaking it away bit by bit the golden edge of the object started to show a dark green color that reflected off the bright sunlight. Moments later his meticulous patience finally paid off to show a jeweler's masterpiece, a detailed pendant encircling a magnificently cut pear shaped emerald. Almost in unison they all gasped, "Holy Shit"!

In 1714, King Philip V contracted a gifted young craftsman to create a one of a kind set of gold & emerald jewelry for his green-eyed beauty, Queen Elisabeth Farnese. That jeweler was Emele Meilleur who was establishing himself in the growing French colony of Mobile. Gently cleaning off the back of the egg sized pendant was the inscription,"por la joya de mi corazon", translated meant "for the jewel of my heart". There in the lower right corner was the tiny trademark crest of Emele. The original pendant appeared to be the center of an elaborate necklace fashion to cascade the queen's bust from shoulder-to-shoulder with breathtaking smaller emeralds incrusted in detailed gold inlays. The short bits of thick chain they found was used to link the creation together. 3 of the smaller pieces of the jeweled necklace were also found in the remaining coral as they cleared the rest away. For several minutes the 8 men sat there astounded, hands covered in white coral powder from cutting away nearly 300 pounds of reef that days before ripped open their ship. Now that jagged chunk of Mother Nature had been transformed into a rich bounty for them all. Breaking in with his ever-growing humor, Eli smiled saying," All this hard work wasn't for nothing... at least we got a ship's bell out of it"! The crew burst into open laughter as they relaxed in the morning sun. Putting the jokes aside for the moment, Eli added it would be a great idea they use the bell for the Brig as a sort of tribute to all their efforts. Noah agreed saying, "who knows it might bring us continued good luck too".

They began deciding what to do with the newfound treasure, since the coins had no real added value due to their minting less than 50 years ago. Darin nodded saying, "It would be better we melt them down... this way no one knows or suspects where we got them from". Wolf agreed and included the chain pieces get melted down too. "What about the emerald pieces"? Asked Marino. Everwyn suggested they hold on to them as is for now, "Just in case we need a backup of money". Tohru volunteered to make a bar mold for the molten gold so it could be sold as a presumed mined ingot, adding, "We can even stamp it with one of da seals Ya got Darin". They got around to bringing up the Tripoli to the beach and started in on a proper repair of her hull. By evening the experienced brothers had her fixed good as new while the tar seals dried overnight. Gathered on the Ketch, underneath the clear stary skies, they sat on deck enjoying a delicious dinner Tohru had prepared for everyone. Barreled ale kept in the cool waters of the lagoon added to the feast. Their minds were still filled with treasure as it would be for anyone, including Eli. He had not thought about revenge for several days with everything that had transpired. With all the coins & chain pieces safely put in a leather pouch, Wolf bounced it around in his hand guessing there was at least 4lbs or more of the precious metal in there. Sold for British pounds in any of the larger ports would yield well over 400. Money was coming in pretty well for each of them, so it was agreed whatever was made from the gold would go into the brig, such as strong rope & sail.

Production on the hull was slow but going better than Fabrice had suspected. The keel & frame had been laid with the strong inner ribs sprouting up more with every passing day. Since everyone was working steady jobs from both ports, time spent at the cove was minimal at best. All things considered, they still felt everything was progressing quite well. More than ample materials had been amassed, supplies & provisions well stocked. What was still needed to finish the brig was already set in motion to be obtained. As for the progress of Eli, he's expanding education had far surpassed those twice his age. The seven he called brothers become more than family to him, they were his mentors, his instructors, his professors. He could fluently speak 5 languages now. His mathematical skills riveled any proficient navigator on the high seas. Physically he stood more than capable with sword & pistol in hand, growing stronger at every passing lesson. When time permitted, he would read of the great sea commanders, absorbing strategy & tactics they perfected. He knew to be forever grounded, retaining the facts of basic common sense at the forefront of his mind. He was learning to use the God given gifts of his dashing looks & a masculine body to his advantage in the bedroom as well. All this and more were eternally center around one echoing word...Revenge!

Before they sailed out of the cove the following day, the gold was smelted into a solid bar weighing 4lbs 1oz and stamped with the seal of the Royal Shipping Lines Company. Everwyn, dressed & disguised as "Sir Johnathan Smyth", special envoy to Viscount Ervin, arrived by horseback a few days later in Charleston. Once he got his forged papers, documents & gold bar from Darin, he headed to the textile mill for a private meeting with the old Irish owner, Patrick Cohen. Easily in his 60's, Patrick had established the mill in Charleston back in 1750 but had to totally rebuild it after the devastating hurricane of 1752 that put him in serious debt. He was almost caught up on it when the rare hemp arrived to help boost his sales, but he needed cash immediately for his expansion plans.

The documents proposed that the gold bar was an offer of investment into the expansion of the mill, knowing the aging Cohen wanted to add sail making to his factory. Explaining that the bar came directly from Viscount Ervin with specific instructions that the investment be kept strictly private between them, using Sir Smyth as the go between. The Mill would receive a 4-year tax exemption from the crown effective immediately upon the agreement. In return, the Viscount would receive 10% of the net profit from the mill to be paid quarterly to Sir Smyth. In addition, any written orders of purchase from the Viscount via Sir Smyth be free of charge, not to exceed 100 British pounds (wholesale price) per year for 4 years. Cohen jumped at the offer without question, signing the forged contract as Everwyn sternly repeated, "Remember, this is to be kept in the strictest of confidence, you are to deal with me and me alone. Any breech of our agreement & the deal is off"! Seeing the old man's face filled with a mixture of excitement & fear, he knew the deal would be seen through to the letter. Before leaving, Everwyn mentioned he would be checking on the progress of the new additions to the mill, especially the sail making section, adding, "I'm curious to see how well you put good use to the better strain of hemp you have now". Shaking hands with the befuddled old man, Sir Smyth got on his steed and rode off. Thinking to himself, Cohen wondered how in the hell did he know about the hemp?

With more immigrants arriving in the colonies monthly, the larger ports like Charleston, Brunswick & Savannah grew even more. Farmers, craftsmen, sailors from all over Europe were fleeing from the raging war there to find a better life in America. Generations of colonial born children were coming of age as the settlers expanded westward. Educated & talented people were making their mark bringing prosperity & knowledge everywhere. One such example was Luka Rotundo, an Italian tailor. He brought his family to Brunswick from the small seaport of Calabria. Along with his new bride Sofia, the 21-year-old man quickly setup a small shop in town to sell his quality clothing. Both were artistically gifted with their knowledge of wool, linen & silk, felling this talent would be better suited in the new world then remaining in southern Italy scared with civil war & feuds. Both of their families had been caught up in the crossfire several months before, leaving the couple the only ones to survive. After selling off whatever properties they had they married and used the money to start a new life. It took no time for them to pick up the language in Brunswick with the help of a newfound friend, Marino. Eventually he introduced the young couple to the rest of the crew, including Noah, Tohru & Eli, who now had a new language to learn...Italian.

In early October 1757, the Brunswick harbor master contracted pneumonia and eventually passed away. Word got back to Darin by carrier pigeon as he knew a replacement was quickly needed since there was no apprentice there. He sent his qualified partner Jacob West to act as temporary master till another was provided by the crown. Before leaving Darin talked with Jacob & wife Ruth about the possibility of them moving permanently there. The couple agreed knowing they had a trusted friend who could take over the fish market & tend to the homing pigeons in town. Of Scottish decent, Gloria was a middle-aged widow who befriended the couple a few years before. Darin sent off a letter on the first ship bound for England, recommending to the king that Jacob West be appointed Harbor Master of Brunswick immediately. By mid-December, a message arrived confirming the official position be filled by Jacob. Ruth enjoyed the Christmas holidays with her husband in their new home in Brunswick as Gloria quickly took her place in Charleston. Introduced to the Rotundo couple, Ruth & Sofia quickly became friends. The tailor shop was prospering now & in need of help. Ruth had some experience in sewing so the Italian couple hired her on shortly after the first of the year. The crew now had a firmer foot hold in both Charleston & Brunswick. Even though Jacob & Ruth were still unaware of Griffin Cove, they could still be trusted with their present tasks at hand.

January 1758 proved the investment in the textile mill beneficial. Sir Smyth received the first quarterly payment of the agreed 10% in the amount of 141 pounds. The new stronger ropes & canvas were selling better that Cohen had expected so he was more than happy with the arrangement. The addition of sail making was in full operation as the old Irishman enjoyed his first prosperous Christmas in 5 years. Sir Smyth gathered up his supply of free sails & rope totally well under 50 pounds wholesale. Loaded on his hired wagon he drove it back to Brunswick to be shipped to the Cove & stored. Since the canvas was now made from a much stronger fiber, it could be milled into a thinner sail, thus making it lighter on the masts. The same went with the hemp rope as it was weaved tighter with less strands needed then the normal ones.

Wolf & Tohru found time at the cove forge to turn out the first cannon for testing. Setting it up on smooth rock platform just off the edge of the lagoon they fired it for strength & accuracy using a 12-pound projectile. Targets were setup across the wide lagoon at 100, 200 & 300 yards. After making adjustments to the wheeled carriage the ball hit its mark every time. Firing it over 50 times, the new flint lock trigger performed perfectly without fail. They thoroughly checked the bore and barrel for any wear or cracks and found none. They reset targets for distance and discovered that the 12-pounder had a range of just over 400 yards with good accuracy at its maximum elevation of 30 degrees. Using the canvas sown load, they were able to fire 4 rounds in one minute with just the 2 of them manning the weapon. Over the course of testing, they also used a variety of different loads; chain shot for destroying masts, grape shot to take out crew, & fragment shot for shredding sails & lines. All the loads were packed the same way with a canvas jacket. They noticed that occasionally canvas would ignite causing the targets to burst into flame. Tohru had an epiphany as he shared it with Wolf, "What if we load wood pieces in loose black powder"? After testing out several varieties they came up with successful fire shot that torched a 20-foot-wide target from 100 yards. The only thing left was perfecting the carriage to allow varying elevations for a much more accurate hit.

The winter months found business slow at the shipyard in Brunswick, so Fabrice had more time at the cove. Between short cargo runs, Marino & Everwyn assisted him in getting the hull closer to completion. It took more time than normal to ensure the keel was even & balanced. Fabrice shaved the base to a fine edge allowing the keel to cut through the water cleaner with minimal resistance. The strong hull ribs were treated, then curved identically before they were wedge bolted in place. With the frame completed, they could start in on layering the fitted hull. Following the plans of the master craftsman, every plank was treated, cut & fitted to match the next one, the same way a jigsaw puzzle would. Working from the bottom up, each length was then secured to the ribs, starting at the curved bow till the horizontal layer reached the stern. It was time consuming but well worth it.

With every ariel route reset, the carrier pigeon messages we arriving without a glitch. The second crop of hemp was harvested & delivered in Charleston, much to the delight of the old Irishman. By early March, the Wilhelm family had planted the next crop of hemp expanding its production by almost 50%. With tobacco, corn & wheat growing well the farm was now thriving as they went into their second season. A message flew in from the farm that read, "40 white gifts ready for U"! The last of the precious white oak was cleared and eventually picked up by the Tripoli & Rover. Hans was amazed at the fantastic turnabout in just over 12 months, with a little help from some friends.

The holiday festivities at the royal court presented a long overdue sight, Lady Belinda Winslow. The widow was making her first appearance to family & friends since word of her lost husband, Captain Benjamin Winslow arrived 6 months before. Shedding the mourning black, she dazzled the court in a brilliant red gown that only the spectacular beauty could do. Her numerous friends were elated to see she had finally overcome the grief & was on the path to living her life again. Among the many attending the annual Christmas ball at the palace was the Ervin family which included the viscount's eldest son, Lord Ervin II. Recently given the title lord, he was accompanied by his charming wife Lanora & their ever-stunning youthful daughter Elinore. Like so many men in court, Lord Ervin II had always fancied Belinda, but there was something more in his eyes now she was widowed, a burning lust. It seemed the hot wandering loins ran deep in the Ervin men, obviously starting with the viscount. Even King George II found her appealing, but his majesty's erotic tastes were more for the young virgin ladies in waiting, after all it was Good to be the King! There were countless attractive ladies all about at the palace ball, but the widow just seemed to stand out as she always would. Lord Ervin II eyes followed her throughout the night, desperately trying not to make it obvious. But Lanora was well aware of it, saying nothing to avoid making a scene.

Over the following winter months, he would occasionally find an excuse for a chance meeting in public with Belinda. Always cordial toward his passes, she generally would sluff them off as she did many a men's advances. The lord trumped up some phony papers for her to sign regarding her last husband, as she was asked to meet with the lord at his office. Not suspecting anything, she promptly arrived per requested at the Royal Shipping Line office. Once inside his large office the two began to talk. Noticing they were the only two in there at the time, a sense of restlessness came about her. After a few moments of useless chatter, he rose from his chair, heading for the closer door saying, "I can only imagine just how lonely it must be for you now... if there is anything I can ever do I am totally at your service", as she heard to door lock. Seated still with her back to the door, she suddenly felt his hands firmly embrace her shoulders while whispering in her ear, "There is so much I can do for you if you'll let me, after all... We are Family"! As his sweaty hands moved down to cup her full breasts. Launching out of her chair enraged she gathered herself and declared, "Do you take me for a common Stumpf? How dare you put your hands on me like that, family or no family, if you Ever try anything like that again I will let the King know of it, not to mention your faithful Wife"! As she stamped toward the door. Her threat hit the mark as he walked quickly to unlock the door in dead silence. Leaving in a huff, she turned briefly saying, "Good day ma Lord"!

Belinda knew all about the shady affairs of the Ervin family, both in & out of the bedroom. Benjamin had shared all the sorted details with her. He & his elder cousin, Lady Winslow was close, going back to his childhood days. She found comfort in sharing some of the horrifying tales about her less than reputable husband with young Benjamin. Prior to departing on the last voyage of his life, he told Belinda of the mission, including the secret side trip to New Orleans. She long since knew her husband was the main privateer Captain for the company that was mostly kept from the crown. He assured her this voyage would be the last one as she recalled his words, "With what I plan to bring back, we will be set for life... so don't worry... be happy". He went on to tell her he had already informed the viscount of his resignation upon completion of the mission. The more she thought about it all, the deeper her anger got for the Ervin men, especially after being treated like a cheap street whore.

Even though her petite physical stature was barely 5 foot tall, the raven-haired beauty possessed a gigantic temper when fueled, primarily due to her lineage. Being half Welsh from her father and half German on her mother's side. The Mecklenburg-Strelitz name had a checkered past. They fought their way up into the royal ranks the hard way starting out as commoners till Belinda's grandmother broke the barrier and married into royalty. The British court knew this, admiring her for it and the way she regally carried herself while maintaining that ravishing orra. But what Ervin II did cross the line, days later, her head filled with vengeful intent, Belinda sat down in her study and began a diary starting with everything her late husband shared to the most recent incident. Keeping it locked away from prying eyes and trusting no one... A least until the right person came along and fortune smiled again.

CHAPTER 5

Easy to be Hard

With every passing day, Eli felt himself changing, physically, mentally & especially emotionally as almost everyone his age would go through. He had spent his entire life surrounded by adults with no one his age to compare to. Everything he had learned from his elders; Eli never regrated a second of his 16 plus years. Instead, he compared himself with those men & women closest to him, how they thought, how they reacted, how they dealt with life. Much of which displayed a strange sense of hard heartedness. But rather than felling remorse, he embraced the cold emotion with certain degree of self-pride. Was it from habit? Was it from not knowing any better? Was it from the fiery burn of revenge deep in his gut? His only thought of any faith in God was the repeating question... Why him? He had killed a man at age 11 without a moment of hesitation or reservation. Reflecting back on it, there still wasn't an ounce regret in his heart. Instead, there was a sort of morbid feeling of accomplishment, even joy that he had succeeded in eliminating an enemy to his family. For now, he had no time to ponder his future other than the steady day to day tasks at hand for himself & his self-adopted family. That's what mattered most to him, the 7 men he had grown to respect, admire, and yes, even love, if he truly understood what that word really meant yet.

Responding to the message from Hans, the Tripoli added the farm to its cargo route northward from Charleston, with stops at the cove & Brunswick first. After dropping off provisions of rice, corn & potatoes they sailed into Brunswick to make the usual cargo exchange before heading to Port Bath. There was some good & bad news awaiting them, it seemed the Rover was showing its age. The old pinnace's keel was beginning to rot away with repeated leaks popping up from the cracks that were spreading. Fabrice told them repairing her would be a futile, "Let's face facts, she's had it, even a complete overhaul would be a worthless effort". He paused then gave them the good news. 10 days before, a Caravel came into port for some minor repairs. After inspecting to 41-footer, he could see the 10-year-old craft was more than seaworthy, unfortunately the owner/captain wasn't. His 3-man crew had left him when they arrived and signed on a larger ship bound for England. The British captain had a history of hard luck or as the mariners called it a "Jonah". He drank too much, he was a lousy card player, he was a poor navigator & was pathetic when it came to trade. After several attempts to gather a crew with no success, he buried his head in a bottle at the wharf tavern. "Sounds like the captain needs a change of luck", murmured Eli with a sly grin.

Everwyn was elected to talk with him while the rest slowly ambled in one by one. Sitting alone at a table with an empty mug, he gradually raised his head from it when Everwyn spoke, "Looks like you could use a drink". Blurry eyed he finally focused in on the man standing before him. "Sure... why not". He muttered. Knowing he was near to penniless from the tab he owed at the tavern and the 10 pounds still owed for the repairs, Everwyn wasted no time cutting straight to the heart of the matter. "I understand you have a crewless ship here. I was looking over her before". The drunk asked," You interested in signing on"? Smiling he popped back, "No... I'm interested in buying her"! The Jonah's ears perked up at the unexpected offer. He sat upright, adjusting his wrinkled jacket then replied, "I might consider selling her if the price is right".

That was the response Everwyn was waiting for as he slowly pulled a piece of paper from his pocket and read it. "Seems you have some debts here that need to be paid... 10 pounds to the shipyard for repairs, 3 pounds for food, lodging & drink here, 2 pounds dock charges to the harbor master. That's 15 pounds and the longer you stay the more it will mound up". Everwyn paused as he sized up the intoxicated Brit adding, "And frankly, I don't think you got a brass farthing to you name...nothing personal of course"! It was clear to both men that Everwyn was spot on in his assumption. Brow beaten, the man asked meekly, "what's your offer then"? Folding up the bill he replied," I will pay all your bills here & give you an additional 15 pounds. That is more than enough for you to make a fresh start...elsewhere"! Pausing a moment to collect his soaked brain he countered with, "make it 25 pounds". Quickly back Everwyn sternly said," 20 pounds, take it or leave it"! Begrudgingly he pulled out the folded ownership papers to the Caravel and said, "Deal". With everything officially signed over to Everwyn, he dropped a coin pouch on the table, counted out 20 pounds and stood up saying, "we are done here & so are you. I strongly suggest you find another line of work, elsewhere"! The drunk saw Everwyn paid his tab at the tavern before staggering out, never to be seen again.

The crew gathered up minutes later at the dock to survey their new addition. Jacob walked up smiling, as the harbor master simply said, "Congratulations... that will be 1 shilling docking fee. Shall I put it on your tab"? As everyone burst into laughter. Fabrice chimed in, "And I suppose I'll add this to your tab too, I swear you guys are gonna put me in the fuckn poor house"! As the laughs got louder. The following morning, they sailed the 3 ships to the cove to overhaul the new addition using the Rover's sails & rigging that were in much better shape. The 7 stayed on to get the Caravel refitted so both could sail together to Port Bath. Things were a bit slow in Brunswick for Wolf & Fabrice as they joined Marino & Everwyn on the newly named Caravel, "Hard Luck". Since the only thing left of the stripped Rover was the hull, it was broken down for firewood & eventually turned into charcoal for the furnace.

The addition of Hard Luck gave the 2 ships a combined cargo hole better than 100 tons. The Caravel could easily be maned now with 2 to 4 men depending on the length of the runs. As they sailed into Port Bath, everyone was pleased by the way she handled smoothly in a secure watertight hull. With what the 2 ships sold from their cargo, it almost paid for the Hard Luck on her first trip. Hans' oldest son Kurt was in town picking up supplies for the Wilhelm family when the crew saw him. "Damn boy you have grown since I saw Ya last", remarked Fabrice as he griped the strong hand of the 12-year-old lad. After a few moments of greetings, they told Kurt the crew would be at the farm's dock in the morning. "I'll tell my folks, mom will have breakfast ready for Ya'll", the boy replied as he headed off in the wagon.

The town was pleased to have a traveling carnival that arrived the day before to entertain the people with actors, singers, acrobats, & a variety of sideshow novelties. Among them was "Professor McKracken the Great" as he was billed. His show combined magic tricks with elusions rarely seen by the dubious colonials. His finale to his performance was taking a volunteer from the audience & "putting them in a deep trance of hypnotic somnambulance", as the masked professor would say while waving his hands across the volunteer's face. After a few moments of proving he or she was in a deep sleep, he would quickly snap his fingers at their face as they suddenly awoke, not remembering what had happened.

Everyone weas amazed at the mystical gifts the wizard possessed. What they didn't know was story behind the flim-flam man. *Born Hardy McKracken, a second-generation Irishman, his grandparents migrated to the new world at the turn of the century and settled in the area of northern Pennsylvania.

Being among the first white people seen by the long-standing Iroquois & Shawnee Indians. By the time Hardy was born in 1726, the small colony had grown to live in peace & harmony with tribes, sharing food, cultures & knowledge through their understanding languages. As a young boy, Hardy befriended the tribe's medicine man who taught him the use of various roots & plants. One combination was using lavender flowers with valerian roots in a green tea mix that made a powerful sleep potion.

As he grew older, he perfected several healing remedies and illusional tonics that would astound the average person. By the time he was 17 he had his fill of rural farm life and set out on his own. He spent several years in growing Philadelphia, learning all he could about chemistry & medicine. Eventually he opened a small remedy shop there that was struggling to stay open. By the time the traveling circus came to town, he was near penniless & decided to join them as Professor McKracken. But 3 years of this charade was boring him senseless as he felt a change had to come & soon. With the experience, knowledge & education he had acquired could easily be a pharmacist, possibly a doctor, but Hardy craved more. He longed for adventure in his life before he was too old to enjoy it.

During the finale, Tohru caught a whiff of a familiar scent, something he hadn't smelled since he was a boy in Okinawa, valerian root that grew wild there. He knew now why the professor was wearing a mask during his performance, and it wasn't for theatrical effects. Later while the 7 enjoyed dinner at the tavern, Tohru shared his discovery with them. Just then Hardy came in, this time not wearing professor's mask, as no one recognized him. Well, almost no one but the perceptive oriental. Telling the rest who he was, they decided to invite him over for a drink. Tohru walked toward Hardy who was seated already and quietly said, "Valerian root if my guess is right"? Hardy smiled replying, "Very good, you're the first to pick up on it'. After accepting Tohru's invitation, Hardy joined the rest of the inquisitive crew.

Eli watched closely as Hardy's eyes stared deeply into each man's face as everyone introduced themselves. After a few minutes of idol chat, mostly complimenting his performance, Hardy sat back in his chair with a confident look about him and spoke, "I must admire, you all are a rather unique lot; Japanese, German, French, Dutch, Spanish, English & if my guess is right...Welsh", as he glanced over at Eli. Smiling slightly Eli asked, "How'd Ya guess"? Hardy pointed at his bone handled knife on his side, "Roe or maybe red deer bone I'd say". He was right too, his grandfather made it from a red buck he had killed. "Very perceptive of you professor, I am impressed', said Noah as he asked," So what in the hell are you doing with a cheap carny outfit like this"? Hardy laughed and replied, "Ya know, I been wondering the same thing lately... maybe it's time for a change"!

The informative idol chat seemed to turn quickly into a much deeper probe from both parties as the crew slowly felt they may have a new addition for their latest ship. Noah was the first to ask, "So just what is it you're looking to do with your life now"? Hardy looked about at the 7 pair of eyes eagerly awaiting his reply. One word emphatically came out, "Adventure"! Seeing their reaction, he continued that he had spent most of his adult life bouncing from one thing to another. "I guess I'm destined to be a jack of all trades, but one thing has been steadfast... knowledge. I learn enough to appease my desires & make enough money to satisfy my needs...with a little left over for some fun". Eli could relate to that as he said, "Fair enough Professor, maybe it's time you better understood our unique lot, as you put it".

He explained that some of them were fulfilling a creative dream they have had for a long time. Some had finally found a place they could be accepted for who they are and truly belong. While others had a darker purpose in mind. Marino continued for the young lad," It's true we do well enough together and want for nothing, but if your main goal is money, then I suggest you look elsewhere for your new adventure". Hardy soaked it all in as he smirked & plopped a healthy coin pouch on the table saying, "Making money has never been a concern for me for years". Seeing a relaxed look come over the men, Hardy went on saying, "It's obvious that each of you have something unique to contribute to one another. Assuming that's the least you expect of me". He went on to give them a brief synopsis of his learned past. The men listened intently to his tale, when he finished, they cast a judging eye to each other with a nod. Noah stood up and said, "Let's get your gear Professor, I think it's time to start your new adventure". As everyone rose from their chairs, he firmly shook hands with Noah and said, "Just call me Hardy"!

They all walked to his circus wagon while Hardy quickly gathered up his belonging in a large chest. Seeing this the Carnival leader asked where he was going. As they all headed for the docks, Hardy turned and replied, "It's time for me to move on"! Once his gear was stored aboard the Hard Luck, they decided to spend a night of delight with Rosie & her ladies at the Crimson Garter. Looking around at the lusty decor adorned by the erotically dressed ladies of the evening, Hardy's face beamed with delight. He took a deep breath then sarcastically proclaimed, "Momma told me not to come"! After a night of overdue debauchery, the crew got an early start for the short voyage to Wilhelm dock. It gave everyone a chance to bring Hardy up to speed on the relationship they have with the German family. The 2 ships bells rang out their pending approach to the small homemade dock as Hans hitched up the wagon to greet his dear friends and meet the newest one. On board the flat bed was 10 of the 40 logs the crew was there to pick up. They finished off the rest of cargo load in no time and headed back to the farm for a hearty breakfast Ursula had prepared for them all. Pulling out his leather shoulder satchel from his chest, Hardy dawned it as he was the last to climb aboard the wagon.

A large makeshift table & chairs were setup outside the front door of the farm as everyone sat down to a delicious morning meal. In between devouring Ursula's excellent preparations & jovial chat, Hardy was surveying the terrain, especially the open ground surrounding the farmhouse. The soil was moist & rich prime for growing almost year around. He asked Hans," I was wondering if I could borrow a small piece of ground behind your house"? The rather curious question had everyone perplexed for a moment till Hans smiled replying, "Sure...I guess". Hardy reached into his satchel and explained his plan. He pulled out a couple of small pouches filled with unusual seeds, valerian root, & lavender. Ursula perked up being familiar with lavender from when she was a child back in Germany.

Hardy noticed small patches of wild mushrooms growing in the backside of the house as he briefly explained the acid that can be extracted from them is called theanine. The right combination of those 3 ingredients would produce a very strong sleeping potion, especially if it's put in green or herbal tea. Within a few hours they plowed up & planted alternating rows of lavender & valerian root in a short 50x50 foot section. Hardy explained the simple process in order to extract the theanine from the wild mushrooms and how to store it. He pulled out 5 pounds in coin and attempted to hand it to Ursula. She pushed his hand back saying, "No... your money is no good here, we are Family"! The crew spent the day helping out all they could including hunting down a sizeable deer. That night they comfortably bedded down in the Wilhelm's new barn before sailing out at dawn the next morning.

They sailed side by side with a heading for the cove giving Hardy time to get his sea legs and get familiar with basics of sailing. The crew had a chance to pass along their back stories while getting better acquainted with him. He figured since he was embarking on a new life, a new name would be a great idea. He decided on Hardy McKay. Once word got back to Darin, he would fix him up with a set of papers for his new identity. Like everything else he tried, Hardy was quickly picking up on the new roll of sailor by the time they sailed into the cove a day or so later. To his amazement, he was thoroughly impressed with the way Mother Nature had concealed the entrance in. Once they landed in the lagoon, he got a clear picture of what his new companions were all about and just how talented they are as a team. Once the white oak logs were all unloaded & stacked, Hardy had a chance to explore Griffin Cove. He was intrigued with the unique rock formations surrounding the beach line, especially around the backside of the waterfall. The mixture of minerals with plant life had produced some unique growth he hadn't seen since he was a boy. When time permitted, he would investigate deeper, for now it was back to the daily chores at hand.

Across the Atlantic Pond, the routine for Royal Shipping Lines had run into a snag for Viscount Ervin. The good news, he was able to pay back the 35,000-pound debt to the crown within the 12-month allotted time. The bad news, only 22,000 was collected from the phony land deeds & taxes. He had to come up with the balance out of his own pocket by selling off portions of his land in Wales. With the war in Europe hanging over the company, demand for additional supplies from the colonies had heightened. The ships were doing everything possible, but quality of crews combined with aging vessels made the trips across the Atlantic slower with every passing voyage. Even with bringing on slave laborers, the viscount was still having trouble making ends meet. His father had acquired large partials of land in Pyle, Wales at the turn of the century for damn near nothing and was homesteading it out, well more like force labor. The production was, at best, fair from most of the farms. When his father died, things didn't get any better with Ervin taking over. Crops & harvests from the bulk of the farms became less with every passing season as did the money from taxes. That was when he secretly hired the bandit raiders to take what wasn't being given. After years of plundering with little or no success his only alternative was to try and sell off some of the unproductive partials for whatever he could get. Eventually word got back to Darin in Charleston about the land sales in Wales, when an unscheduled visitor docked, the British Crown tax collector.

Arriving at dawn, May 15th, 1758, a Royal Shipping Line Carrack docked to be in port for at least 4 or 5 days before sailing north to Brunswick to collect taxes there as well. Bulletins were posted all around town immediately informing everyone the collections would be made starting the following morning in the town square. A rider was sent to Brunswick to post them there as well with the proceedings to commence on or about May 21st. Luckily the Tripoli crew was in port at the time and got an aerial message to the crew in Brunswick for everyone to meet up at the cove as soon as possible. Darin informed his new assistant to get everything setup for the tax collector while he took care of crown business in Brunswick adding, "I'll be back in time tomorrow morning for the start".

At sunset, both crews gathered at the cove to hear a plan Darin had in mind. After informing them of the land sales going on in Wales by Ervin, he proposed they send an unknown buyer to check out what's being sold there. Darin unrolled a detailed map of the coastline, pinpointing a river called Kendig Inlet on the southwestern corner of the Atlantic. Everwyn perked up as he spoke, "I remember that area when I was younger, my uncle & I use to duck hunt there". He when on to explain the winding narrow river was flanked mostly by marsh land till it ended about a mile inland. Assuming it was still mostly uninhabited, they all thought it would be a great second hideaway with Bristol about 60 nautical miles to the east. The idea intrigued everyone, especially Eli who could easily in vision their brig working her magic there. This plan would cost some serious money, but Darin had a plan for that too.

Knowing they had the talent & materials; they would mint up heavy iron-based coins dipped in a mixture of gold color lead paint. Hardy had the formula for making "fool's gold" that would pass as the real thing to the average human eye. The plan was to have him disguised as a rich nobleman & book passage on the Carrack in Brunswick. Once at sea he would swap out the collected taxes with the phony coins before they arrived in Bristol. "The only problem is time", added Darin. Was it possible to mint up enough coins before the ship sailed in about 10 days or so? Darin would instruct Jacob, in Brunswick to transfer the final count of collected taxes from pounds & schillings into the larger valued gold crowns, thus needing less coins to mint and carry.

Everyone wasted no time starting in on the plan while Noah, Eli & Darin sailed back to Charleston to be back before dawn and the start of the tax collection there. By daybreak, they had the molds made and were turning out the phony coins at a good pace. Back in Charleston, Darin was working with the tax collector recording every payment in the town ledger book including the taxes for John Smith's property lot 133 (Griffin Cove) & covered the taxes for the textile mill. Later that evening he forged up some identification papers for Hardy's new persona, Richard van Harden, Dutch nobleman with a royal lineage. Darin finished it with the Dutch royal stamp.

His back story if asked was 2nd generation descendant from the royal family with his grandfather being Baron van Harden. He was born & raised in the new world due his father squandering his inheritance and forced to migrate. After his parents died, he sold their plantation and invested the money in several businesses in Boston & New York that proved highly profitable. He is looking to find a secluded piece land in Wales to enjoy the rest of his life. With that story, combined with the stamp sealed papers, Ervin should probably jump at the opportunity to sell him any area he wants in Wales.

With all the collection completed, Darin joined the tax collector as the ship sailed to Brunswick on May 19$^{th.}$ He told the crown representative he wanted to ensure the new harbor master got the books right since this was his first time assisting in the collection procedures. Impressed with his dedication to the king, the tax man & Darin enjoyed a safe quick trip as they docked in Brunswick the following afternoon. Later that night the Hard Luck quietly came in with everyone but Tohru & Wolf who stayed behind at the cove incase more coins would be needed. The Tripoli was there to give them a lift when ready. Darin met up with the men passing along Hardy's official papers and let them know the collection in Charleston was 1,250 pounds. He had already changed it into 125 gold crown coins and estimated the Brunswick total should be at least another 1,000 pounds.

Hardy had with him 300 forged coins they had produced so they figured that should be more than enough. Everwyn & Marino sailed back to the cove the following morning to pick up Wolf. Just to be safe, he turned out 30 more and passed it along to Hardy when they returned to Brunswick. Everything was set in place before the collection came to an end 3 days later. Jacob & Darin exchanged the 1,120 pounds collected into 112 gold crowns from the Brunswick treasury to add to the rest of the money the tax man had. With the minimum of 237 coins needed, Hardy was ready to make his first appearance as nobleman, Richard van Harden.

Darin introduced him to the captain & tax representative the evening before the Carrack was to sail back to Bristol. Impressed with the Royal Dutch seal documents, they were honored to have him aboard and was given the spacious cabin next to the captain's one. The vessel was also carrying 9 other passengers who were getting off in Waterford, Ireland, including 3 British officers who were being transferred there. As far as everyone on board knew, Richard was sailing back to Europe on crown business. With his locked traveling chest loaded in his cabin safely, Richard assumed the role as a snooty rich nobleman while he carefully watched everyone's daily tasks at sea. Every evening he was invited to dine at the captain cabin with the rest of the ship's officers including the 3 British infantry ones.

Over the next 2 weeks at sea everything was going fine as Richard would occasionally show interest in how the meals were prepared by the ship's cook. Using the excuse, he had been intrigued for years with the culinary field. 2 nights before they were to arrive in the Irish port, he shared his old family recipe for a delicious stew with the cook. While his back was turned Richard added his own special ingredient to the pot & left unseen into the mist on deck. He had waited till the ship had sailed into a dense night fog to pull off his plan with the entire crew enjoyed the meal including everyone at the captain's cable.

Minutes later, Richard slowly watched his table companions pass out in their seats as he faked it himself before the captain & a few others dropped off. Once assured everyone was out, he raced to his cabin & grabbed up the pre counted box of phony coins and returned to the captain's cabin. Figuring they all would be asleep for several more minutes, he quickly grabbed up the key around the captain's neck and opened the heavy locked chest hidden away right where Darin said it would be. Making the exchange for the real 237 gold coins, he stashed it safely away in his chest & returned to his fake sleeping position at the table after replacing the key. Noticing the ship was slowing down while he waited for everyone to awaken, he smiled knowing the bulk of the crew was knocked out as well.

Minutes later the captain came to, shaking off his brief nap. First thing he did was check to see if the key was still around his neck, which it was. With everyone in the cabin still passed out he crept over to his stashed away chest to ensure the money was still there, which it was. Breathing a sigh of relief, he proceeded to try and wake up his officer's, then check on his crew. Richard was one of the last to come to, making sure everyone saw it as he shook his head saying "What in hell happened"? Once everyone had revived from their brief nap it was assumed that the eerie fog bank was the culprit of the strange sea occurrence. Making sure the crew didn't go into a panic, the captain agreed it was just a freak occurrence caused by the mist he had experienced once or twice before.

Two days later the Carrack docked in the busy Irish port to off load its passengers & take on provisions before they sailed the next morning for Bristol. Richard headed into town as if he was just browsing the shops until he eventually walked casually into the British bank. He exchanged 100 real gold crown coins for the equal amount into British pound notes. Using a few of the forged coins in various shops with ease, he eventually returned to the ship with his purchases. During the final leg of the voyage, he asked the captain for a letter of introduction to Viscount Ervin, which he did gladly. When they arrived in Bristol, the tax collector sent word to the best hotel in the city that crown nobleman Richard van Harden would need their best suite. A Royal Shipping Line coach carried him there, compliments of the company. Once settled in, Richard made his way to Bristol Bank of England where he setup an account of 1,250 pounds using 125 crown coins.

Shortly after they docked, the captain, accompanied by the tax collector arrived at Ervin's plush office to give him the good news about the productive voyage. Ervin II was present as well to count out & record the transaction. Seeing everything was in order, 237 crown coins were locked away in hidden company safe. The captain proceeded to inform the pleased viscount of a pending visit from Richard van Harden. The 2 men briefed father & son about the "well to do" nobleman as the captain said, "In my opinion he is clearly of royal blood... I assume he wants to talk business with you me Lord". Nodding in total agreement, the tax man added, "Yes, I carefully watched him throughout the voyage, this man is definitely of noble birth from head to toe". Delighted with the additional news, Ervin turned to his son and instructed him to personally invite Richard to luncheon with him.

It was just prior to noon when Ervin II met up with Richard at his palatial hotel suite. Obviously impressed with his look & regal mannerisms, the two men boarded the viscount's coach to join up with him at a lavish impromptu lunch in his office. After enjoying the delicious meal, the viscount asked politely, "Sir Richard, what is it I can do for you"? Smiling he replied, "I like a man who gets to the point". He explained that he might be interested in purchasing some land in Wales to retire on. "I seek something quiet, secluded & peaceful. With so much conflict & unrest happening everywhere I want to build a home far from it all". Ervin brought out his map of the properties he owned in Wales as the two men began to survive what was available.

Looking through several prime areas, Richard noticed that the desired section in the southwest corner was up for sale still. "Tell me about this acreage here off this inlet", Richard inquired. Forgetting himself and his usual conniving ways, Ervin quickly replied truthfully, "This is mostly marsh wetlands, not even capable of any agricultural resources. For years, it has been uninhabited with maybe the occasional spot for hunting & fishing". Moments after he spouted out the truth, he realized his selling mistake, but it was too late. They discussed a few more areas when Richard suggested he sail over to see it firsthand. Ervin agreed replying, "I will put a sturdy vessel at your disposal for the journey, compliments of Royal Shipping Line". At dawn the next morning, Richard sailed on board a small, hired sloop to get a better look at the potential new hideaway for his colonial brothers.

Far winds carried the fast ship to the mouth of the southwest inlet by late afternoon, as they traveled a few miles farther into the narrow winding river till they were in sight of the mouth. Richard brought along a sketch pad to roughly etch out a better view of the terrain to eventually share with Darin & the others. The navigator helped to mark the depths, range & distance of various landmarks before they came about to return to Bristol. When they docked in the wee hours of the morning darkness, he thanked the captain & his 6-man crew by handing them a bonus of 10 pounds in gold coin. Knowing they weren't part of the Royal Shipping Lines, he copied down the captain's name saying, "I may be in need of your services in the future, thank you captain". Delighted to accommodate the nobleman he saluted replying, "Anytime me Lord, anytime"!

Later the following afternoon, after cleaning up & resting, Richard returned to Ervin's office to try and finalize the deal. Richard got right to the point as he indicated on Ervin's map the sections of land he was interested in from the Atlantic inlet to the river's end. The terrain encompassed well over 5 square miles or 4 sections the viscount had for sale. "If this is truly what you want Sir Richard, I'm sure we can come to terms on a reasonable price. I was asking 300 pounds for each section there but since you want all 4 adjacent ones, I can make you a deal for 1,100 pounds for them all", offered Ervin. Richard reached into his elegant coat pocket & placed several British Bank notes on the table saying, "Let's round it off to 1,000 pounds sterling Viscount, that's my best offer". His eyes lit up at the sight of the sterling notes and agreed saying, "I will have the papers drawn up immediately for you to sign", as they shook hands on the accord. "One more thing Viscount, this is to be considered royal property now, thus not subject to taxation of any kind", Richard emphatically added. "Oh yes, Sir Richard that goes without saying", Ervin meekly agreed.

With official documents well in hand a few minutes later, Richard left with a smirk on his face thinking to himself, "What a dumbass"! He found out there were no ships sailing for the colonies out of Bristol for at least 2 weeks but there was a British Naval vessel docked in Plymouth bound for Boston within a few days. Before leaving Bristol, he withdrew his 1,250 pounds in British notes from the bank, hired a coach, and headed for the popular port to book passage. Using his forged royal documents, he was heartily greeted by the captain of the large frigate. They were to make one brief stop in Cork, Ireland to off load a garrison of troops before making the ocean crossing. Normally the captain wouldn't carry passengers, but after seeing Richard's official papers he made the exception with him being the only civilian on the voyage. It also helped that Richard handed the captain 50 pounds in gold coin to help seal the deal & secure a spacious cabin aboard.

Once the garrison disembarked the ship in Cork, Richard knew he had a few hours to shop before they set sail again. Finding the port bank, he when in to exchange the remaining 90 phony gold crown coins for British pound notes. It never ceased to amaze him just how gullible people are, especially when they see that royal seal. For a country who boasted they ruled the waves, their common-sense was less than a beached whale. He had purchased more than enough land his colonial brothers had wanted; lived it up like a real nobleman; and was returning with well over 2,000 pounds in legal British notes. He laughed out loud as he strolled back to the ship thinking, "well, I wanted adventure & I sure as hell got it with room to spare"!

It was a brisk 3-week voyage when the frigate arrived in Boston on July 21st, 1758. Keeping his noble disguise Richard got a room at the port Inn then went to see if any ships were heading south. Fortunately, a Dutch merchant sloop was leaving for Port Bath in 2 days. He talked the captain into letting him catch a ride, well after he handed 5 pounds to him. He browsed about town window shopping till he came upon an apothecary shop. This was a great chance for him to stock up on some needed potions & ingredients. He was amazed at the rare mixtures the old German shop owner had, including a potions book that came from Prussia. Only one problem, it was written in the old Prussian language that ceased to be spoken around the turn of the century. He bought it anyway in hopes that Wolf or Hans could translate it.

A Pigeon flew into Ruth's coop at Brunswick with a message reading, "Hard at Rosie fetch me". She laughed & relayed the message to the crew in Charleston. The timing couldn't have been any better for everyone since it was just about harvest season at the Wilhelm farm. Everyone was anxious to find out what Hardy had accomplished over the last 2 months, especially Darin. Things were slow in port, so he told his assistant to take over for a few days while he was gone on official British business. They sailed out that evening on the Tripoli to meet up with everyone in Port Bath as the crew of Hard Luck was well on the way there. Meantime, Hardy had no choice but to accept the overnight accommodations at The Crimson Garter, bath included.

All 9 men were finally reunited when the Tripoli docked on July 28th and sat back to relax at the port tavern. "Sorry for the delay, we hit some rough head winds getting here", said Noah. With the crew being the only customers there, Hardy felt safe enough to share the news with his brothers as he first produced the sketch he made of their new property in Wales. "I saw the whole area firsthand... it's perfect! The river is more than deep enough all the way to the mouth", as Hardy pointed it out and continued. "The shoreline is all marsh & wetland till Ya get to the end here, with solid land for a dock and more". He showed them the land deed that included the no tax clause since it is now classified as Royal Property.

The crew was beaming with delight at the purchase their brother had made as the news continued on. Hardy told them the successful story how this timely fog bank showed up long enough to explain why the entire crew was knocked out for a few minutes. Shortly after he made the coin switch, he raced up to stern of the quarterdeck and tossed several smoke bombs overboard. When they ignited & mixed with the misty weather it created an eerie fog bank as the oncoming winds eventually engulfed the ship. "As for the phony coins, I exchanged them all in 2 different Irish ports, this way if or when they were found out it could never be traced back to me". Hardy saved the best news for last as he told them he bought the land for only 1,000 pounds. He then reached into his jacket pocket and pulled out a bulging leather wallet. Slapping it on the table over the land deed saying, "Gentlemen we can also add 2,050 pounds sterling to our bank now... sorry it couldn't be more, but I had to spend a little of it to get back", as he laughed. The faces at the table were in absolute awe at the amazing accomplishment their new brother had pulled off. Eli eased back in his chair, smiled & said, "Now we are 9"!

With another round of ale ordered they passed along to Hardy what they had done for the last 2 month. The work on the Brig was progressing well, the hull was completely assembled as the deck was being laid out. 6 new cannons on their custom carriages were finished, tested & stored away. All of the new rope needed had been gathered with about 75% of the customs sails and about half of the lignum rigging blocks were made ready. Marino removed the female bust figurehead from the Ketch and was altering it to resemble his sister Rosie. Noah broke in with some interesting numbers, "With the 2,050 pounds Hardy brought us we have close to 3,500 in the bank, not counting the 4 emerald jewels. I vote we take a break tonight & celebrate Hardy's successful return at The Crimson Garter"! Smiling all around the vote was unanimous as the 9 headed for Rosie's place. Rosie sent off an aerial message to the Wilhelm farm that the 2 crews would be docking at their place first thing in the morning.

It seemed every time they showed up at the farm it grew bigger & better than before. All of the fields had been harvested including the expanded acres of hemp & tobacco. They built a small blacksmith forge between the barn and new smokehouse. The hemp crop was the largest Hans had produced to date as they loaded it up almost filling both ships. Most of the crew headed off on a short hunting trip and returned a few hours later with 2 deer, a few rabbits & a rather fat wild turkey. As for the herb garden in the back of the house it was growing great. Ursula had several containers of ingredients ready for Hardy. He helped plant a few more rows of some new seeds he picked up in Bristol, Cork & Boston.

Eventually he sat down with Hans & Wolf to see if they could decipher the Prussian potion book. Hans had not seen the old language since he was a boy; his grandfather had spoken the extinct dialect fluently. Hans suggested the book be left with him saying, "This will take some time for me & Ursula to translate but I think we can do it". Hardy agreed telling him, "I can't thank you enough my friend... there's no rush. You all got your hands full here so please take your time". How right he was too, within 2 seasons the Wilhelm farm was now utilizing over 75% of their acreage. Thankfully his sons were old enough now to help in the fields from planting to harvesting.

By the time Eli's 17th birthday rolled around the crews had off loaded their hemp cargo in Charleston and were back at their respective ports. Everwyn dawned his Sir Smyth persona to collect his quarterly share from the textile mill and gathered up another supply of free canvas sails. With the onset of the storm season at its height the sails were quickly stored away at the cove with the rest of the provisions. Even though there weren't any severe hurricanes along the Carolina coastline, there were several days of torrential downpours thus hampering their usual trade routes. This gave the crew more time to work at the cove.

Using the spare canvas from the Ketch, they rigged up an overhang tarpaulin above the brig hull allowing them to continue work on the deck. Fabrice knew what he was creating had already exceeded far beyond his wildest expectations. Yet, there was this concern that the build was taking over twice as long as he originally planned. Noah saw the haunting frustration seep through his passion to complete his dream. Finally, he spoke up, "Never think any of us are expecting you to finish this tomorrow or even next month. We all have decided to give it our best... no matter how long it takes. Just remember each of us has time on our side, especially Eli"!

CHAPTER 6

The Family of Man

Like many times in past history, this one had more than its fill of toil and strife. Carving out a new life in a new land was no easy task, dealing with the elements mother nature had produced for centuries. Clearing land to live on while fighting off sickness, disease and the ever-present creatures who prowl without any concern. In some remote areas, there were the native tribes whose ancestors roamed the land freely long before the white man came. Yet, with all that man had fought through it and managed to survive even though the cost was high. Families hung together to build a better life for themselves and their future sons & daughters. But as progress started to rear its head from the ashes, another obstacle appeared in the form of taxation from abroad. They knew the time would come when they would have to battle that as well. But this fight had to be waged with brain more than the brawn.

The once illiterate colonial immigrants from all over Europe, South America, Asia & Africa were giving birth to a savvy breed of off springs. Taught by their parents to endure life with basic common sense & the education of the mind. With each generation the families of the new world grew to respect the accomplishments of their forefathers, vowing to defend it at any price. Revolution was growing stronger with every passing year and so was America. With the war at its peak in Europe, the countries involved (primarily England) focus their military might on it rather than the colonies. For many Americans, it was a time to try & unite together as one, politically at first. But for some, it was a time to better their own lives any way they saw fit, such as the 9 brothers.

Individually they each had their own personal reasons for coming together. But no matter what it was, a unique bond had formed without anyone realizing it. Most had no living blood kin to speak of, yet there was unspoken respect, faith & trust that became the catalyst to made them a family. Strangely enough the unseen leader would eventually be a rather remarkable young lad that every man knew would be the best at it. Eli was absorbing the talents & skills from every one of his brothers thus reaping the benefits from their years of experience. Not everyone was as lucky, a prime example was the slaves laboring in the factories & fields from Massachusetts to Georgia. Better known in the trading circles as, "from molasses to rum to slaves".

Fact: Dating back to the early 16th century, the trade route of molasses, produced in the colonial sugar cane fields in the south were exported to distilleries in Boston & New York to make rum. The liquor was then shipped to ports in west Africa, traded for captured slaves and sold off in the new world. Over a million African natives were imprisoned on overcrowded ships with better than half of them perishing before the ships even arrived in the colonies. Those who survived were sold off as forced laborers in sweat shops & plantations.

Royal Shipping Lines was one of many companies who reaped the benefits of the slave trade which included using them on farms in Wales for decades. As Ervin sold off farmlands there, he would include the option to the new owners to buy the laborers there. The slaves that weren't bought were shipped off to the colonies with him making money off them again. When one of the ships docked in Port Bath in mid-October the Wilhelm family was in town for supplies as the auction was going on. They bought a family of 4 farm slaves for 25 pounds. Zachery, his wife Polly and their two boys Isaiah & Joshua, ages 11

& 9. On the wagon ride back to the farm, Hans informed the family they would be staying in the barn till a house could be built for them. They would be treated as hired help, not slaves working for meals & housing to begin with till harvest season came around again. Delighted at the unexpected turn of events Zachery replied," Thank Ya master, we will serve Ya well". Hans told him," I'm not your master Zachery, you all work for me so just call me Hans. By the way do you have a last name?" "No master...I mean No Hans". Ursula laughed saying, "well we will have to fix that"! By month's end they got their name, Carpenter as Hans found out Zachery was good at farming but better at building. Their house was finished in no time and the family finally had a comfortable place to call home.

When the first chill of November rolled around the crew had a finished hull, treated, sealed & painted. The deck, including forecastle & quarterdeck were done as they slid the brig into the waters of the cove lagoon. Tied up at their dock would make it a lot easier to construct her masts & riggings as well as mounting the deck cannons. The ketch was moved over & tied up on the brig's port side, this way the crew could move easily from one to another. Fabrice had built two 6x6 foot removable cargo hatches on deck just a few feet fore & aft of the main mast. These were normal sized & positioned for most cargo vessels, but the clever Frenchman had an additional use for them.

The December quarterly bonus from the Charleston textile mill was the best Sir Smyth had seen to date being 170 pounds. He picked up the last of the free canvas sails needed for the brig as it was eventually stored away with the rest at the cove. Everwyn made a call on the Rotundo tailor shop in Brunswick to place a rather special-order for some ship's flags, including a unique rectangular one with a 3-point end. Using the design Darin had created awhile back the golden griffin. With everything progressing well the crew decided to take a few days off for Christmas and spend it in Port Bath.

Word was sent days before by pigeon to Rosie and the Wilhelm farm that the 9 brothers were on the way to share the holidays with them. On board the 2 vessels were a plethora of meats, cheeses, fruits, wine & ale for a Christmas eve feast at the Crimson Garter as well as Christmas day bounty at the farm. Plus a few unexpected gifts for some well deserving folks. They docked midafternoon on December 24th to a busy port who was preparing for the awaited holiday festivities. Rosie and a few of her girls arrived in her carriage to greet them and help unload the supplies for the coming feast later that evening. She posted a sign on the ornate door that read, "Closed for Christmas, will reopen December 26th". She gave her girls the holiday off for those few who had family, the remaining 10 ladies were overjoyed to partake in the 2-day planned party.

The dining table was overflowing with delicious treats prepared by Tohru and the girls, from French onion soup to roasted turkey, duck & venison, to baked potatoes, corn on the cob & green beans. The dessert trays were loaded with fresh apple & blueberry pies, cherry tarts as well as a wide variety of cookies & candies. Truly a feast fit for kings & queens as they all reveled in it till, they couldn't eat another bite. They gathered around the massive tree decorated from top to bottom and lite with dozens of tiny white candles. Beneath it sat an abundance of beautifully wrapped gifts for everyone. The brothers had something special for the ladies of The Crimson Garter, the Rotundo tailors had made up 20 pair of fancy dark red garters with the golden initials "CG" embroidered in the center. From her brother Marino, Rosie unwrapped a small hand carved wooden jewelry box. Inside was 18 gold crown coins and a note reading, "Happy Christmas to our lovely sisters... from: your 9 brothers"!

The ladies had one more gift for them, a hat filled with room keys. Each man was asked to take a key and retired to their room. Minutes later they were joined by one of the girls. 30 minutes later, Rosie rang the bell, as the girls left to join another room. This continued, nonstop until every girl took care of every one of the 9 rooms until, they all eventually collapsed to sleep amidst their erotic holiday bliss. When dawn broke, the brothers enjoyed breakfast in bed until it was time to dress and head out to the Wilhelm farm, some in the 2 ships, the rest in the carriage. Rosie sent off an ariel message to Ursula saying, "Add 20 on the way". The German hosts had setup a canopy tent out front of their farmhouse anticipating a full crew for Christmas dinner. Thankfully the weather cooperated with it being sunny and a brisk 48 degrees. With the addition of the girls from the Crimson Garter, Zachery and his boys got to work fast putting together some sturdy makeshift chairs for the additional guests. Within a couple of hours everyone had arrived and was preparing the lavish holiday meal. 29 friends & family sat down to a bounty of perfectly made dishes that enhanced a day of giving. Among the gifts exchanged, there was one in particular the touched everyone's heart.

A month before, Darin got a message from Hans requesting some official papers be drawn up. Hans stood up and spoke," I have one last gift to give, this is for the Carpenter family". As he opened the document, "On this day December 25th, 1758, it is proclaimed that Zachery Carpenter, Polly Carpenter, Isaiah Carpenter, & Joshua Carpenter are free citizens of the human race. Signed Sir Darin Cavety, authorized representative to King George II, England". Stamped and sealed with the official British crown emblem. A roar of applause echoed from everyone as the Carpenter family sat there stunned with tear filled eyes. Handing the documents to Zachery, Hans explained that they all were now free to come and go as they pleased. Without a moment of hesitation, Zachery firmly shook his German Brother's hand and said, "If it's ok with you, we want to stay on here, this is our family now".

When winter hit shortly after the first of the year, snow had covered the bulk of the eastern seaboard well past Charleston. The cove saw its first real effects from Jack Frost with everything coated in white including a cascade of ice icicles adoring the surrounding rock formations. Even the waterfall was slowed by the freezing temperatures. With it too cold to do any work, it gave Wolf & Fabrice a chance to draw up plans for a unique mortar for the brig. The idea was to build a sturdy carriage fixed firmly to the keel with an iron cast mortar attached to sit just below the ship's deck. The circular base would be capable of a full 360-degree turn with a maximum muzzle elevation of 45 degrees. This way it would conceal the 2 deathly weapons with the deck cargo hatches till it was time to fire them.

Wolf figured he could make a 6.7-inch 36-pounder using an explosive shot that would have a range of almost 1,000 yards. Anything bigger would put too much stress on the keel plus this weight would be about 150 pounds per mortar including its mound. If rifled, the accuracy would be greatly increased even at long range distances. With a smaller sized weapon & carriage it would still allow cargo to be brought through the holes comfortably. The addition of the 2 mounted weapons would reduce the brig's cargo capacity by roughly 20% but it still gave her more than enough to suffice the brother's needs. When the winter chill ended, Wolf would get started on the casting since he needed his furnace hotter than ever for these two devastating guns. In the meantime, they went on to the construct the foundations and carriages.

Much of the remaining winter allowed them time work on the rigging harnesses, blocks & tackles. In between they would set time aside to perfect their skills with pistols & swords, made for each of them by Tohru & Wolf. Even Darin found time from his harbor master job to get in some practice with shipping slow in Charleston. By the time March rolled around, the dawn of an early spring was a welcome sight for everyone, including the arrival of European trade ships. One unwelcome vessel was the Royal Shipping Line Carrack with the tax collector aboard for his annual visit to the port. But this one was new to the job as he explained to Darin shortly after they docked.

Back in December, it was discovered that over 2,300 pounds of gold coins were forgeries when Viscount Ervin attempted to deposit them in the Royal Bank of Bristol. The old tax collector was charged with embezzlement and forgery then sentenced to death. 2 British officers who were stationed in Ireland were imprisoned for conspiracy to aiding and abetting when the same phony gold coins turned up there. Even though Ervin was reimbursed by the crown for the full amount lost, he felt there were watchful eyes creeping down his neck, he was right too. A squad of handpicked British troops were now assigned aboard the Carrack to oversee & protect the tax collector in Charleston & Brunswick. Darin knew this collector would be left alone, but he had plans set in his head for their return the following year.

Over the next few months, the 2 cargo ships managed to pick up a good size profit from some supplies that had been sitting on the docks too long due to the heavy winter. The Tripoli & Hard Luck grabbed up a sweet deal in Savannah by hauling cotton bails to the textile mill in Charleston. On the last run Sir Smyth was onboard to pick up his quarterly profit and grabbed up some cotton cloth to pass along to the Rotundo tailors in Brunswick. It was an added thank you for their fine work they did on the flags including the unique Griffin one. Stored away in the brig's gear locker was ship flags from England, France, Spain, Netherlands, Ireland, Scotland, as well as company pennants from Royal Shipping Line, Dutch Indies Trading & East Indies Company.

Business was picking up for the tailor shop, so Luka hired on a local young man whose talent included leather working in clothing & shoes. Franz Oberman was a second-generation Holland cobbler who was born in the new world along with his wife Heidi. They both had experienced hands that impressed Luka when they arrived in Brunswick at the start of the year. Eventually he added on to the growing tailor shop to accommodate the new leather works. In no time the venture was paying off from the shoes, boots, vests, belts, etc. that the artistic Hollanders were creating.

Marino was being his creative self as he had finished redesigning the figurehead of his sister Rosie and was now working on the second one for the brig, the winged griffin. He & Fabrice had set up the base of the bow point to easily make the ship's figurehead interchangeable even while at sea. The same went for the vessel's name plate on the stern. The idea was for the brig to change appearance close in as well as from a distance. 24 False gun ports were made from light weight 2x2 foot wooden squares to resemble 12-to-16-pound cannons. Once attached to the brig's broadside, any ship in the distance would think she was a heavy corvette or even a frigate.

Hardy mixed up a variety of paint colors for the hull to add to the changing disguise as needed. In their spare time he & Darin put their artistic talents to work on the square jib sail that attaches to the bow sprit. They would hand paint an official emblem on it, like the ones used on British Crown vessels and so forth. Eventually they would have a full set made for every country including the ones used for the prominent shipping lines. As for the golden griffin sails, they were being hand sown at the Rotundo tailor shop with painstaking detail. The brass ship's bell from the 1715 de la Regla wreckage was cleaned and polished up before mounting it on the quarterdeck. A little more each day the brig was coming closer to her completion.

During the very profitable runs in Savannah, the brothers noticed a disturbing sight, the increasing abuse of slave labor. Over worked and underfed they would toil in the cotton and sugar canes fields from dawn till dust. Entire families would be forced to labor endlessly, those who resisted would be whipped and shackled mercilessly. Royal Shipping Lines had taken over control of the numerous plantations there about 2 years before when the colonial owners couldn't pay the increasing taxes. Ervin had more than doubled the slaves, most of them coming from the farms in Wales he once owned. His ships would import them in and export the cotton and molasses to be sold in Boston & New York. It's true that this had been the normal routine for over 100 years, but the excessive cruelty and abuse was far beyond human toleration in the minds of the brothers. Something had to be done.

The crew put together a plan to free at least some to start with. Darin had forged up some orders for Everwyn, Hardy & Marino to impersonate 3 British field officers with the rank of Colonel, Captain & Lieutenant respectively. Once outfitted with the uniforms from the Rotundo tailors, they traveled by horseback to the British outpost at Fort James about 40 miles north of Savannah. Orders read they were to dispatch 3 wagons from the fort accompanied by drivers and a platoon of infantry to complete a highly classified mission. The orders were signed & sealed by Major General James Wolfe under the orders of King George II personally. Provisions for 10 days was loaded aboard along with the troops as they left heading north.

They spent the first half of the day slowly circling west till they were well clear of the fort and proceeded due south to the first plantation on the outskirts of Savannah. That night they camped by a river a few miles from their destination. After being fed, (Captain) Hardy treated the troops to an unexpected keg of rum he brought with him. A rather special blended mixture that knocked them out within minutes. The 3 stripped them, then tossed 30 unconscious bodies in the swift flowing river. With all the uniforms, gear and weapons safely stored away it was time to proceed to the second phase of the plan as they were now joined by Noah, Wolfe, and Eli. They had anchored both ships in an inlet about 5 miles from the prearranged camp sight. Tohru stayed with the vessels to safeguard them till they all returned. The 3 additions found uniforms to fit them as they took over driving the wagons to the large plantation. Just before dawn they arrived to be greeted by the old plantation owner. Everwyn saluted him and said, "Colonel Kanard of his Majesty's Dragoons at your service sir". He handed the sealed orders to the old man. It read that he was to hand over at least 60 slaves for temporary assignment to assist in the construction of an undisclosed British outpost. He would be given full replacements of slave labor within a fortnight, plus for the next 3 years he would be given a tax-free bond for all his property. The Colonel handed him the forged bond document saying, "Compliments of King George II sir"!

He added that when the outpost was completed his slaves would be returned to him. "I would prefer any slave families you may have sir, since we will need them to farm as well as build". The old man was more than satisfied with the offer since the planting was done in his fields. He immediately ordered his foreman to load up their wagons including offering an additional wagon of his own for provisions. Before they left the Colonel emphasized once again that this was a highly classified mission, "Not a word is to be said to anyone about this, the fate of this British advancement south is in your hands sir"! The owner firmly shook the colonel's hand and said, "You can count on me Colonel Kanard, I'm honored to help the crown anyway I can"! As they rode off, the uniformed brothers started laughing under their breath at the continued gullibility of the English man. "What a bunch of Dumbasses"!

Pulling the same stunt, they intentionally headed south for a few miles then turned northeast to meet up with their ships hidden safely at the coastal inlet. Late that afternoon they arrived much to the delight of Tohru who was waiting for them. Once they unloaded the 66 passengers those who were shackled or chained had them removed. Food provisions and fresh water was handed out as Everwyn explained to them what was going on. "We are not British soldiers; we are free men of the colonies here to help you all have a better life. Our ships will take you all to a safe place where you will be free to recover and live without slavery or pain. Those who wish to head out on your own, will be given enough food for your journey". As they all sat there filling their bellies in shock, they look about one another till one large black man spoke up, "I can speak for us master, we want a go with you"! Everwyn smiled saying, "That's fine, but from now on you all have No Masters, I'm Everwyn, this is Noah, Eli, Wolf, Marino, Hardy & that's Tohru"!

They unhitched the horses and put them down. All 11 were skinned & gutted for the meat then the remains tossed in the river. With the wagons emptied they rolled them into the water till they had sunk as the loaded down ships sailed off bound for the cove. During the late-night voyage everyone got acquainted with one another. The brothers learned there were 10 families totaling 41, with children ranging from 8 to 13 years old. The remaining 21 men & 4 women were single for one reason or the other. Over half of them had past experience at sea including the large black spokesman they all called Abel. Almost all of them had been farm laborers in Wales till they were sold off to the plantation. The men who had ship experience were part of press gangs aboard a Royal Shipping Line vessel till they were sold off. Whether they realized it or not, every one of them had a common enemy, and his name was Viscount Ervin.

Even though they had been underfed and physically abused they all were young strong survivors. Abel was the elder, roughly about 30 years old as best as he could recall. It seemed the rest sort of looked up to him for his years of experience, it also helped he stood well over 6 & a half feet tall and was built like a bull. Most had been on the plantation for a little over a year clearing the land, tilling it and harvesting. Those who had shipboard experience was used primarily as deck hands or cooks. It seemed the brothers got a lot more than they bargained for with the 30 uniforms, rifles, bayonets, and ammunition. Add the personal effects of a few pocket watches and around 15 pounds in loose change. The troops were all packing the usual camping gear that would come in handy for the families till they could get some shelters built.

Just after dawn they arrived at the cove to the wide eye amazement of the newcomers. Noah pointed out the sturdy walking bridge the brothers had built several months before. The long rock ledge that was on the water's edge rose up gradually to a smooth flat plain about 10 feet off the ground. From there the wooden bridge worked its way up to the top of the stone cliffs some 50 feet high to the abundant ground where the brothers would hunt. The land was literally covered with tree and plant life with fertile soil all around, especially near the freshwater stream that flowed down into the waterfall below. Fabrice was there working on the main mast for the brig as he was introduced to everyone. He told them they were welcome to setup temporary camp on the backside of the beach till they got better settled in. They had free reign of the area including all the supplies there but the treated lumber and materials to be used for the brig.

66 thrilled people immediately went to work putting together a safe place to sleep. Using all the captured tents sown together they put up a large canvas shelter in the rear of the beach area. Cooking

from the iron stove on the ketch, combined with a couple of pit fires, the women started preparing a long overdue hot meal for everyone. Since the horse meat was the freshest, they quickly turned it into a tasty stew with potatoes, carrots and corn the brothers had stored there. They stretched out the 11 horse hides to dry so it could be used to make some decent clothing and shoes, especially for the children. The brothers stayed on for a couple of days to ensure their new residents were ok. With the added muscle the main mast was finished and mounted on the brig. Abel let the brothers know he would oversee everything, and they all would be fine as the 2 ships sailed out.

A week later they returned with provisions in both vessels. Rice, corn, wheat, carrots, beans, apples, sugar & salt was a welcome sight along with several bolts of cotton & linen cloth. The Tripoli was also carrying the iron cast stove from the Studman house to give the cove an additional one to cook from. But the most welcome sight was the astounding production they had made in just 7 days. Clearly rested and getting stronger the 66 had put together a half dozen huts on the upper level using the stone overhang as the base foundations. Their plan was to build all the housing there allowing the fertile soil free for tilling & planting. They looked considerably cleaner & healthier with every one of them beaming a smile from ear to ear. The salted meat & fish barrels were kept filled as the men setup a daily routine of hunting and fishing. Using the bows & arrows the brothers left for them as well as fashioning some deadly spears on their own. With the perfect weather of May the cove was growing by leaps and bounds.

Back in Charleston, a rumor had spread like wildfire about a large garrison of British deserters, led by several turncoat officers who had abducted over 150 slaves from a Savannah plantation. Word had it that the renegades were terrorizing their way south into Florida to link up with Spanish sympathizers. Fact of the matter, the 30 bodies that were tossed in the river eventually wound-up traveling into a dense swamp infested by hungry alligators. As the tale moved north it grew into legendary status, sparking the revolutionary minded even more. Ideals are peaceful, it's history that is violent. Ain't it amazing what a little white lie will do!

The summer of 1759 was a very productive season with the cove thriving with growth for the newcomers. Once all the huts were finished, they turned their energy toward bettering themselves by turning out decent clothes & shoes. Furrows were tilled and planted with corn & winter wheat in the upper areas. Coops and pens were built on the beach area to accommodate a batch of chickens, roosters & pigs the brothers had shipped in to add to the menu. Wooden traps were made and dropped over the lagoon side of the ketch for gathering up the abundant blue crabs. 3 of the women had grown up on a plantation near Biloxi. Their mothers were cooks there learning the spicy Cajun seafood recipes and passed it along to their daughters.

The brig was shaping up faster now as both the main and fore masts were secured in place with a little help from some strong friends. For Fabrice it was down to setting up the rigging for the sails. Wolf & Tohru had tested and completed 16 cannons as they were set into their spots on deck including 4 swivel guns mounted on the quarterdeck. The next job was to forge out 2 mortars, that was going to take some time and about 400 pounds of cast iron. Luckily Wolf had a basic pattern to get the mold started then added whatever modifications needed. As they were testing the cannons Wolf & Tohru would take the time to train some of the men who had past sea experience. Taking them through the basics load, aim, fire & reset till they could do it in their sleep. Using the 21 single men with the intent of adding them to the brig crew when she would be ready for sea. The German explained, "You all would be part of our crew, not force labor so you would be paid a crew's share like any other sailor. The choice is yours"! Abel spoke up, "Do that mean we free men if we join da crew"? Wolf quickly replied back, "As far as we all are concerned, every one of you here are free now, all we need is the papers to make it official".

A week later, the 9 brothers, including Darin, gathered at the cove for a meeting with everyone there. Comfortably assembled on the beach Darin addressed them. "Ya'll have been with us long enough to know we want to help get you started on a better life. For some it might be a chance to freely farm for yourselves. For others it could be a chance to earn a good living at sea. No matter what you decide the point is your free now to choose. I will put together official papers for each of you stating your free men & women, but we have to change your names so there is no chance any of you can be traced back to your former slave owners. So, take your time, talk it over and let me know what new names you all want, including your children". One by one they got with Darin as he wrote down their choices. He told them it would take a few weeks to complete, but it would be done.

Fact: Slavery trade had been going on for over 100 years in the new world, but as civilization evolved with colonies being firmly established, more and more white European immigrates began to see the cruelty of it. Of the original 13 colonies, only 4 were still pro slavery by 1760. The majority of the slaves who had been given their freedom were still shunned and considered second class citizens. Unaccepted in most of the schools of higher learning as well as ignored in the business community. Those who managed to get a proper education beyond the basics, were primarily self-taught or privately tutored. Whatever race a man was born into there is always that select few who have the innate ability to rise above the rest. Driven by a passion to excel no matter what the reason may be.

While clearing off some of the heavy foliage on the upper level at the cove, a small cave was uncovered emitting a strange pungent odor. When the brothers returned, they were led to it discovering a heavy deposit of raw sulfur. Hardy spoke up, "Holy Shit! This is fantastic"! He wrapped a handkerchief around his face telling everyone to do the same. He explained that this can be used for so many things but mainly to produce gunpowder. The yellow mineral was literally covering walls of the cave that had been there untouched for God knows how long, Hardy thought. All he needed now was potassium combined with charcoal & sulfur to produce the gunpowder. "I know where we can get your potassium and a lot of it too, in Haulover"! Replied Noah. "Looks like everyone is gonna be eating bananas for a while"! Laughed Eli as they planned a cargo trip south.

Hardy stayed to oversee the safe extraction of the yellow mineral and explain the process of extracting the potassium from banana peels. With gunpowder their weapons would fire safer with better accuracy producing less smoke compared to standard black powder that would be best used for smoke bombs and such. They started carefully mining the sulfur while producing the charcoal for both to be stored away. Within a week the Tripoli returned with a full load of bananas. As they gradually ripened then consumed the black peels were extracted of the needed potassium. In no time, the cove was manufacturing barrels of gunpowder in abundance, and everyone was enjoying a healthy overdoes of the sweet fruit.

August 2nd, 1759 found everyone celebrating Eli's 18th birthday at the cove which included a large, delicious banana flavored cake. Now sporting a full beard and standing well over 6 foot tall, the young one had officially shed his adolescent age for manhood. Among the many gifts was a custom pair of black leather knee boots or better-known as buccaneer boots as the maker, Luka had called them. Tohru had created a unique black handled sword with a matching sheath. The grip was fitted for his hand resembling a fencing handle, but the long blade was that of a samurai sword. Forged & folded with no less than 150 layers of razor shape steel. Engraved into the base of it was the winged griffin emblem Darin had created. When the remaining gifts had been opened, it was time to present some gifts to the 66. Darin handed out official papers to each one of them declaring they were now free men and women under their new chosen names, stamped and sealed by the British Crown. He assured them the documents were legal and binding as he kept a full list of every one of them if they were ever questioned. He added, "Any children born by you all will also be considered free of slavery". The brothers felt it was time to let them in on the proposal they had talked about in length now that the brig was close to completion.

Noah stood up and said, "Captain Eli will explain it to you". A shocked look engulfed Eli's face as his brothers stood to attention and in unison barked out, "Captain"! Seeing this honor, the 66 stood as well in respect. It took a moment to gather his emotions, then smiled and said, "Everyone please sit down". After taking a deep breath he explained the offer to them. "We own a very large piece of land in the southwest corner of Wales. Most of the area is wetlands with a river winding through it. But there is fertile land as well. More than enough for each of you to settle on and build a good life there. The land is completely tax-free too". As he showed them the map of the area as well as the documents of ownership. Hardy added, "I personally saw the land there, it's filled with wildlife, deer, rabbit, duck and a great area for fishing. There's plenty of trees to build strong homes & farms. As for others there you would be at least 10 miles from the nearest farm".

Eli continued that they all would live there free of charge for as long as they liked. Abel stood up and asked, "Captain, how we get there"? Eli replied, "When the brig is finished & the ketch is refitted, we will sail them both there. The ketch will be left for Ya'll to live on till you have your homes built. We will stay as well to help get Ya settled in and with more than enough provisions till your farms are up and running. As for those who wish to sail with us on the brig you will continue to be trained in every aspect of a free sailor and considered part of the paid crew. Our plan is to make it our second hideaway. We will be keeping this cove as our base in the colonies". He went on to tell them they had plenty of time to decide since they weren't planning to make the Atlantic trip for at least another 6 months when the weather was favorable. One of the cook's stood up and said, "Captn' if you is finished, we got a heap a hot food gettn' cold so get Yō butts over here and eat it"! As she grinded with everyone laughing.

After everyone was fed, Abel gathered up the men who were learning everything about the brig. A few minutes later the 21 men walked over to the brothers who were sitting together eating. The large leader spoke, "Beg pardon Captain, we talked it over and decided we want to crew with Ya". Eli stood up, smiled and shook his large ebony hand and simply replied, "Welcome Aboard men" as he went down the line shaking every man's sturdy hand. Since the rest of them had everything else at the cove well in hand the 21 were now assigned to work on the brig's completion and train in between. This included daily practice with pistols. Rifles, swords and gunnery. 5 strong women, using the launch worked on clearing & dredging out the last of the passable side of the inlet sandbar to ensure the brig could sail through it with ease.

Once they made the usual run up to the Wilhelm farm for the hemp harvest then delivered it to Charleston textile mill, both ships kept close to the coastline with the oncoming storm season upon them. Luckily the only hurricane of the season close to them was in September down in Havana that disrupted the southeast Florida currents. It was a choppy voyage in early September when the Tripoli made another run down to Haulover for bananas and drop off some needed provisions to the small village. Profitable enough to more than break even. Thankfully the quarterly drop from the textile mill was a good one with Sir Smyth gathering in 160 pounds plus a free load of rope & sail for the ketch's eventual rebuild. With everyone paid including Hans' share the brotherhood treasury was almost at 4,500 pounds.

A pigeon message arrived at the cove in early October that a large shipment of wool was sitting on the docks at Port Bath. An Irish cargo Bark was forced to unload everything due to serious hull damage taken from the trip across the Atlantic. The wool was slated for delivery in Boston, but the vessel had to pull into the nearest port before it sunk. Strapped for money the Irish captain was selling the cargo for whatever he could get. Noah sent a message back that the 2 ships would be in Port Bath within the next 2 days or less. With both vessels emptied they left out of the cove with two extra crewmen on board including Abel.

Picking up a good tail wind they made it into Port Bath about 36 hours later and wasted no time seeking out the Irish captain. After cutting an excellent deal, both ships were fully loaded as they headed off the spend the night at the Wilhelm farm. As a thank you, the crew gave a load of wool to them to be eventually turned into some warm clothing for the upcoming winter months. The black crewmen got a firsthand chance to meet everyone and see just harmonious life was there on the farm. While they sat down to enjoy a hot meal, Hans could see a hint of curious apprehension in the black crewmen's eyes. He began to weave the tale, "A few years ago these men came to our rescue when everyone else turned their backs on us. They helped us get the farm on its feet with no questions asked. Look around... this farm grows and thrives more & more every season". Zachery continued to explain that a year ago his family was enslaved till they became part of this family of man.

Hearing the deeply sincere stories, Abel and the others would relay this on to the rest back at the cove ensuring that the 9 men they put their faith in was well placed. The following morning, they set sail for Brunswick. Hardy had reloaded with a full pouch of herbs along with a stack of gifted tobacco for them to enjoy. Plus, the potion book was translated into English for him to read now. They carried some new seeds for planting, wild peppers, onion, basil, parsley etc. This would delight the cooks to be able to add a little zest to their recipes. It never ceased to amaze the young captain that little things like simple seeds could make such a positive impact on someone who, a short time before had nothing to look forward to but pain and despair.

The Hard Luck docked in Brunswick to sell off its load of wool at a premium price, more than doubling what they paid for it. They took care of the Rotundo tailor shop by selling to them at wholesale cost as a small token of thanks for all they had done. The Tripoli docked in the cove to unload more than enough wool to comfortably cloth everyone for the winter and drop off some special seeds for planting. The remainder was sold to the textile mill in Charleston for a sizeable sum. The run yielded them a net profit of over 250 pounds with everyone paid their share including the black crew. Smiling wide Abel shook his hands in his pockets saying, "Been a long time since I heard that sound"!

When the chill of November rolled in the cove was rocking with work. The final touches of the brig's rigging were set in place. The two mortars had been tested with complete success at a maximum range of almost 1,000 yards. They were then mounded into the hidden carriages on board and tested again to see what stress it would put on the hull and keel. It seemed the calculations Fabrice & Wolf had made were spot on. The final touch was added by Marino, affixing his sister's figurehead to the bow and bolting in the fitting name, "Sea Rose" to the stern. The hull was given a 2-foot-wide crimson stripe that stretched just below the cannon line from stem to stern. The newly built 27-foot launch was secured in its block & tackle harness off the stern's quarterdeck that flanked the ship's running lanterns.

On the bright crisp morning of November 11th, 1759, the Sea Rose sailed out of Griffin Cove on her short shakedown cruise. With the crew aboard, they took the brig through her paces in the open waters of the Atlantic. Running a varies of drills to test out the crew and their lady. After 2 days of testing her speed in the southeastern stream they found out she could cut through the calm seas at almost 15 knots at top end. That was 5 to 6 knots faster than any other ships of her size. The gun crews drilled on the 14 deck cannons till the speed and accuracy was honed down to near perfection. After several tests of the twin mortars, fired at various angles, the Sea Rose took the effects with the greatest of ease. With a few minor adjustments back at the cove, Captain Eli knew she was ready as was his crew, First Mate Noah, Second Mate Marino, Navigator Everwyn, Gunnery Mate Wolfe, Shipwright Fabrice, Ship's Doctor Hardy, Chief Cook Tohru & Boatswains Mate Abel Strong. She was now born to the family of man.

CHAPTER 7

The Show Must Go On

The crew wasted no time once they docked back at the cove to get the ketch refitted and ready for sea. The Tripoli & Hard Luck crews went back to their normal routine while rotating 4 black crewmen for every run. Hardy stopped by the Rotundo tailor shop in Brunswick to pick up a new suit of clothes he had ordered. While he was waiting, he noticed a few sketches Luka had brought with him from Italy. They were duplicates of several royal medallions & seals including those from Sicily, Malta, and Pantelleria. The detailed drawings focused on a familiar duel headed eagle crest used for regal emblems of, not only Italy but France, Germany and Prussia from time to time. When asked where he got them, Luka replied, "Decades ago my grandfather was asked to make some uniforms for an Italian sea captain who was from Pantelleria".

Pantelleria was a small island east of Tunis in the Mediterranean Sea. Hardy recognized the name from some delicious, sweet wine he had a few months ago when he was in Boston. The tavern keeper said the wine was the last of a rare batch that came in a year before from an Italian merchant ship. It got the clever man thinking about it as he eventually passed it along to his brothers. They needed all the information they could gather about the island, its resources as well as who ruled over it. Hopefully Luka or Sophia might have more to share about Pantelleria and its history. Darin said he would check his records at the Charleston town hall if there was anything about the island. But for now, the prime task at hand was to get the ketch ready for sea.

November weather was mild at the cove as everyone got busy to get the ketch ready for the upcoming voyage across the Atlantic. All of the families decided to take the brothers offer and make a new life in the safety of southeast Wales since the crew would be gone for an extended time. As they worked on the refitting, barrels of provisions were filled and stored including salted fish, & meat. With the chilly December temperatures, staples like rice, corn, wheat & fruit was kept fresh before crating it up for the trip. Just prior to the Christmas feast at the cove, the ketch was completed including 8 of the original cannons installed. Now ready for sea this allowed the brothers to estimate the departure around mid-January during the usual cold & foggy weather. Everything was going as planned till Darin informed the brothers of an unusual arrival.

January 8th, 1760, a Royal Shipping Line merchant ship docked in Savannah to offload slaves and fill its cargo holes with cotton and sugarcane. His informant there let Darin know the ship would be in Savannah for at least 4 to 5 days for repairs and hopes that it could pick up an armed escort. It seemed the voyage from west Africa took its toll on a British Naval Bomb Ketch forcing the unarmed merchantman to sail solo into Savannah. There was something unusual about this particular run. In the past, harbor masters in British controlled ports would have estimated arrivals and routes prior to them docking. When the ship docked its captain immediately contacted the Savannah garrison commander to post troops alongside the vessel while in port. Darin gathered up the brothers to inform them of this and decide what to do. Once together they figured they had about 2 days to work up a plan to take the helpless merchantman without being detected.

Wearing his British Dragoon uniform (Captain) Hardy rode out on horseback from Charleston the following morning to hopefully arrive in Savannah by that evening. His orders read he was to escort Captain Ferrell of the merchantman "Royal Sea Hawk" to a predesignated area to meet with its escort, "Sea Rose" of the British Royal Navy. The orders were stamped & sealed by Viscount Ervin in the name of King George II. When Captain Ferrell saw the orders, he was elated to know the remainder of his voyage was well protected. In the privacy of the captain's cabin, Hardy added, "We are to proceed immediately once your repairs are completed captain. I am well aware of the secrecy of this mission you're on and the viscount is anxious for your safe arrival".

The next morning tide had the ship at full sail bound due north to link up with her escort. Once at sea the weather turned cold and overcast as they slowly followed the course Hardy had told the captain to stick to. Just before dusk, a signal bell rang out from a silhouette just off the starboard bow. It was the code signal Captain Ferrell was told would be the rendezvous point for his British escort ship. Peering through his telescope he was relieved to see the British Union Jack flying from a heavily armed brig as he quickly counted her 28-gun ports. The crew had attached the fake gun ports to give the appearance of a second gun deck. As the two ships crept within 300 yards, Noah bellowed out from his quarterdeck, "Ahoy Captain Ferrell I'm Captain North of his majesty's ship Sea Rose"! He replied, Ahoy Captain North this is Captain Ferrell I'm so happy to see you sir".

Hardy instructed him to come to a halt as a long boat from the brig would come along side. Night fall and a cloudy sky made the brig hard to clearly see from about 100 yards away as the long boat approached the merchantman. Dressed in his Colonel uniform Everwyn boarded the unsuspecting ship to help navigate them north to Boston. Wearing British uniforms, Eli & Marino rowed the launch back to the brig as the 2 ships slowly sailed off. Everwyn told Ferrell to sail ahead with the Sea Rose staying close a stern and within sight. The rendezvous was about 10 miles north of Griffin Cove giving the brig time to watch for their pending prey before launching their plan. Having both ships turn into open waters, clear of the coastline Everwyn & Hardy knew it was time to act.

Once inside the confines of the captain's cabin Hardy walked behind the unknowing captain and pressed a saturated handkerchief to his face quickly knocking him out. The 2 men headed up to the deck where the sparce night watch was. Carefully knocking out the 5 unaware crewmen, Hardy headed below to the crew quarters who were asleep and dropped in 2 smoke bombs to ensure they stayed asleep. Using the stern running lanterns they signaled the brig to come along side. Within minutes both ships were still in the calm waters as the brig crew went to work. They stripped the 33 unconscious men then using the slave shackles left below in the merchantman they bound their hands and feet and tossed them overboard leaving only their captain left aboard.

Several minutes later Hardy helped him wake up as the bastard found himself naked and clapped in the irons, he had ordered so many slaves to wear over the years. Ferrell was renowned for being a ruthless captain particularly when it came to the treatment of slaves. He had been Ervin's top skipper for almost 10 years and his most trusted too, especially when it came to the west African runs. He was always given the command of the newest vessels the Royal Shipping Lines would get, including the Royal Sea Hawk that was only a year old and on her fourth voyage. The ship was built for one purpose only, hauling human cargo and the occasional provisional ones. That was why she carried no cannons to help maximize the space and speed at sea. She usually traveled in a fleet for protection, but this trip was so secret it was believed better to have only one escort from west Africa to Savannah to Boston and home to Bristol per Ervin's orders.

When he finally came to his eyes focused in on several men surrounding him saying, "What's the meaning of this! Release me immediately or I'll have your hides for this"! They burst into laughter as Noah replied, "Captain Ferrell the only hide you need to worry about is your own nasty one! Your crew is dead, and you are about to join them. We just wanted you to see who your executioner was before you got what's coming to you. Abel he's all yours"! From the gathering the tall black man emerged with a devil's revenge look in his eyes that terrified Ferrell speckless. "You don't remember me captain but I sure as hell remember you. Ya chained and whipped me years ago when I was boy. Ya beat starved & killed my family before we even got to a port"! As the massive boatswain mate picked up the trembling man with one hand. Eli opened the stain glass stern portal as Abel spoke, "Now it's time to meet your maker and my God have mercy on your soul Ya Son of a Bitch"! With one mighty thrust he tossed him out into the black waters and disappeared.

They left enough crew aboard to safely sail her as both ships slide undetected into Griffin Cove just before dawn broke. The merchantman was too wide and deep in the water to get her around the sandbar barrier, so they anchored her at the face of it. After docking the brig, they used the Tripoli & Hard Luck to unload the cargo of cotton and sugar cane to eventually sell whatever was left after what they used themselves. All the clothing, shoes and gear were washed and set aside for use later as needed. They divided up the share of the money gathered from the captain and crew which came to over 500 pounds mostly in gold coins from Ferrell's cabin alone. The remaining 150 plus shackles & chains were eventually melted down to the joy of everyone at the cove. But there was one more thing aboard the ship they weren't expecting as Eli read excerpts from the captain's journey.

It seemed the ship had another stop to make before sailing into Bristol, the Belgian port of Antwerp. Reading the log carefully, it seemed the ship was in port in South Africa for about 2 weeks before sailing west to Savannah. An unusually long stay in port with no recorded reasons why. The only thing logged was the day they sailed out as it stated in the journey, "All personal cargo aboard and accounted for, we sail on the tide". The brothers had already gone through the captain's cabin with a fine-tooth comb and found nothing unusual. So, they decided to check it once again and if need be, take it apart piece by piece. After dismantling the bed, cabinets, clothing locker and desk there was still nothing. They checked every plank in the floorboard to see if there was a hidden compartment, nothing appeared.

While Tohru was on his back checking the underside of the desk, he noticed sunlight cutting through stain glass portals. The reflection angled off one of the overhead beams that split in a weird way. He climbed on a chair to get a closer look and discovered a thin seam that ran along the top of the beam between it and the overhead. After looking over the other beams Eli saw that this one was sectioned in short 3-foot lengths, unlike the much longer ones that supported the overhead. As he slowly moved his hand across the top, he found four small latches that triggered the short section to drop down. They carefully lowered it to the desktop and pried it open to find a truly wonderous sight. Inside was a large leather bag filled with uncut diamonds.

Several months before, Ferrell had heard a rumor about a hidden excavation going on a few miles from the African port where they were buying the slaves from. He told Ervin about it when he returned to Bristol who immediately scheduled Ferrell for a return trip. With phony documents from King George II in hand, Ferrell was ordered to bring back positive proof of the diamond mine no matter what it took. Both Ervin & Ferrell felt it best to make the run as inconspicuous as possible by having only one escort especially if the rumor was false. This way they could at least profit from the usual slave trade.

The look of astonishment was nothing short of epic on the brothers faces when they gazed down at the bag of glimmering gems. It was one thing to have a rare egg size emerald, but this was far beyond their wildest dreams. Eventually the silence was broken as Eli smiled saying, "Well, we know now why they were headed to Antwerp". The Belgium port was world renowned for its diamond trade and expert cutters. Belgium was also an independent country at the time and free of any taxation on goods including rare gems. Piecing the puzzle together it appeared that Ervin was trying to cash in on this without the consent of the Crown. Darin examined the orders Ferrell had and was convinced they were forged signatures of King George II including the poor quality of the royal seal.

Two days later the brothers gathered up in Charleston to decide their next move. One thing was certain now, the concern for money was eliminated. If they split up the diamonds equally every man was set for life. Eli gave his brothers a sincere look and spoke, "I know this may change things for some of you. I would completely understand if you wanted to take your share and move on. For me, I see this as an opportunity to finish off this son of a bitch once and for all". He paused a moment then said, "Whatever you decide is fine with me, none of us will ever think less of you". Abel stepped up saying, "I can speak for the crew Captain, we maybe newcomers but we have a home and purpose now...we sail with Ya to the end"! It was then that each brother stood up in agreement placing their right hand on the table. Eli's face beamed with a broad smile and proudly said, "Now we are one"!

It was decided that they continue on their normal routine to avoid any unnecessary suspicion. A few bails of the captured cotton were sold at the textile mill in Charleston before both ships sailed to Brunswick to make a deal with Luka at his tailor shop. The sugar cane was left at the cove for the families to process it for the upcoming trip to Wales. The bunch at the cove was instructed to strip the merchantman's galley of everything including the 2 cast iron stoves and store it on the brig & ketch. Darin instructed his assistant to take over for a few days while he was on a business trip to Brunswick. He had done some research in the town hall library about Pantelleria, and he wanted to discuss it with the Rotundo family.

Fact: The 32 square mile Pantelleria Island sits about 70 nautical miles east of Tunis and 100 miles west of the tip of Sicily. At the time it was sparsely governed by King Ferdinand III who took over as ruler of Sicily in October of 1759. The small island originated from an extinct volcano several hundred years before. The chief resources were capers, olives, lemons and most recently a rare blend of sweet wine from the zibibbo grape that only grew on the island. The fishermen nicknamed the island "The black pearl" due to the abundance of the unique colored pearls found in the oyster beds. Pantelleria was only 1 of 3 known places to find the valuable black coral that grew from the centuries of cooled volcanic ash in the clear blue waters that engulfed the island. At the time there were about 1,500 Italian speaking inhabitants, most of them farmers and fishermen. Scattered ruins spotted the upper hills and mountain areas presumed to date back to presents of the Carthaginians in the 9th century.

What they were not aware of yet was the conflict in the bourbon family between Ferdinand III and his three younger brothers. It seemed the reason he was crowned King of Sicily was due to the fact that he had a portion of his inheritance left. The 3 siblings had squandered theirs before the age of 18 thus making the entire bourbon family leery of their ability to rule a donkey cart let alone a country. Needless to say, King Ferdinand III was struggling to keep his kingdom from going under economically. Thankfully Italy or Sicily was not involved in the war at the time, since neither had much of an army to speak of or the funds to amass one.

Things were a bit slow in Brunswick when the 2 ships arrived on January 15th, 1760. Luka could see from his shop window a hearty group of friends heading his way as he greeted them at the door. After a round of hot coffee to take out the winter morning chill they got down to business. Luka joked saying, "Ok... I can see you all are up to no good again, what's it gonna cost me this time"? They all snickered as Eli answered the jovial Italian's question, "Such a deal we got for you today my friend. How would you like to have 4 bales of prime cotton free of charge"? He smiled then replied, "Did Sofia put you all up to this birthday joke"? They soon discovered it was Luka's birthday, so they just went along with it. Noah spoke up, "Well Happy Birthday Luka, but this is no joke, you have been very good to all of us we want to give you this as our gift of thanks". The 30-year-old tailor was in tears from their generosity.

They persuaded him to close the shop early as they all gathered at the tavern later that afternoon for a massive lunch in the birthday boy's honor. During the meal they shared the information each had about Pantelleria Island as well has what the Rotundo's knew of the bourbon family. Wolf asked Luka if he could borrow the detailed sketches he had of the various Italian crests and emblems. Darin said he would make copies as well for his "collection". Eli was admiring the color sketch of the officer's uniform, clad in gray with deep red and gold piping. "I want you to make me this outfit but with a few variation". Luka happily agreed and said they would get right on it since business was slow at the time. The more they all thought about it the more it seemed a great idea for all of the brothers to be measured for the Italian uniform. Luka & Sofia was given a complete rank list of each man to coincide with their job aboard the brig. After all, the show must go on!

The Tripoli sailed back to Charleston the following morning with Darin aboard anxious to get some new documents printed up starting with "Count Ricardo Maschione" aka Eli. Meanwhile, Wolf got to work on the royal dual headed eagle insignia as Hardy mixed up his special batch of fool's gold to add that regal touch. Marino spent most of the time at the tailor shop helping with the officer's boots and hats. As for Fabrice, he told his employer at the shipyard he was taking an extended vacation and to find a replacement as soon as possible. Wolf explained to his assistant at the blacksmith shop he was going to be gone for a few months and to take care of the place. The ketch was completely refitted and ready for sea including a total face lift with new paint on her hull and her new name plate, "Miss Fortune". The families had setup birthing areas below the deck of both ships a week before to get everything comfortable for the long voyage across the Atlantic. The brothers split up evenly with Noah at the helm of the ketch and the crew equally distributed as they set sail on a crisp clear morning in early February. With Darin the only one staying behind they caught a brisk tail wind as the 2 ships headed for Wales. The black members of the voyage were in high spirits the entire way thinking it was a far cry from the last time they crossed the Atlantic.

Late afternoon of March 1st, the vessels came into the entrance of the winding river in Pyle. An hour or so later they anchored at their destination as everyone settled in for the evening with a hot meal and rest for the upcoming days of work ahead. When morning broke, they wasted no time to get supplies and provisions unloaded as the brothers' surveyed the land for the best possible spots to have them build their new homes. Small teams headed off to hunt and fish for needed fresh food. Hardy had made the perfect choice in purchasing this area. A freshwater stream ran through the soft slopping land that was fertile & ready for planting. The ponds & river was full of fish ripe for the catching. Plenty of sturdy trees everywhere to build a strong community and not a soul in sight for miles around. The woods teamed with red tail deer & rabbit as the sky would resound with duck, pheasant, and a variety of birds great for eating.

Smiles abounded from everyone as they happily worked to get their new home created. Within a week they had fields plowed and planted, pens were made to house the chickens and pigs they brought over from the cove. Some of the brothers hiked the 10 miles to the nearest farm and purchased several horses and wagon to help the effort. Hardy rode into town one day to have a talk with the local magistrate. After presenting him the deeds to the land that was signed by the king, he informed the official that several free slaves were now homesteading the land under his control. He noticed a slight look of disapproval on the old man's face as he firmly said, "I hope there will be no problem, these people all have crown documentation of their freedom and have been hand-picked by me to work my land as I see fit... I would hate to have to go to King George II if there was a problem"! The look of disapproval immediately turned to cowering agreement as the magistrate quickly replied, "Oh yes sir me Lord, I will personally see to their safety"! As Hardy walked out, he muttered under his breath, "My god what a dumbass"!

With everything running smooth, the crew sailed out on the 10th of March, assuring everyone they would see them in a week or so on the return trip from Antwerp. As they hit the open waters and headed south the brig was transformed into the "De La Regla" flying her custom gray & crimson crossed Pantelleria flag. The plan was to sail into Antwerp with all to see a royalty ship from Pantelleria Island in order to get the gossip going. The black crew was dressed in their mariner uniforms and instructed to remain aboard and say nothing to anyone. Hopefully those who see them from the docks would assume they were Tunisian sailors. The brothers, wearing their custom-made gray & crimson uniforms would accompany Count Maschione to the port's diamond trading house to take care of some business in style. The more they made a visual statement the better.

They timed their arrival at the peak of the busy day on the wharfs as the impressive brig docked with all eyes on her. The harbor master, along with an honor guard met the Count as he slowly walked down the gangplank that was flanked by his officers standing at attention. The black crew stood erect alongside on deck with Abel at the center towering over everyone with a stern look in his eyes. Noah was closest to the harbor master standing on the wharf as he spoke, "Allow me to introduce Count Ricardo Maschione, heir to the royal bourbon family of Pantelleria". The honor guard snapped to attention with a unified salute as the harbor master bowed saying, "Antwerp is privileged to have you honor our humble city your Grace, I am at your command". Eli stood there looking over his head with a royal aloof expression. Speaking English with a heavy Italian accent he replied, "Thank you, I am here on official business with the diamond trading house. My ship will be in port for today only and my crew has orders not to allow any outsiders aboard during my stay"! The harbor master quickly replied, "I thoroughly understand your grace I will have the honor guard posted here to ensure your orders are carried out... please allow me to escort you to the trading house". Flipping his hand forward he said, "Proceed"! The count's officers followed behind in formation as they made the short walk to their destination. Once inside he was immediately greeted by the elderly Belgian owner as they made their way to his plush office.

Eli sat down with his officers in line behind him. Noah presented the owner with the count's royal documents as Eli spoke, "I am here to open an account if the terms are suitable with me". Everwyn opened the leather satchel he was carrying and produced an egg sized uncut diamond and handed it to the wide-eyed owner. He put on his loupe to get a closer look at the large gem. Seeing the magnified clarity he muttered, "Magnificent quality, I've never seen a purer gem this size before. May I ask where did it come from"? The count replied, "It was discovered in the volcanic remains on my Island of Pantelleria". The owner called in his top inspector to test the purity and carat size to determine the value of the diamond. After a few minutes it was calculated to be 54 carats of the highest quality worth almost 9,000 pounds sterling.

To prove to the owner there was more, Eli had Everwyn pull out 4 more smaller ones from his satchel and placed them on his desk. He quickly noticed one of the many papers there had the British Crown seal on it signed by King George II. He silently made eye contact with Eli to see it for himself as the count caught on immediately. While the owner and inspector looked over the 4 other stones Eli, spoke up, "I assume since you have accounts here with other members of royalty, I will be accorded the same premium benefits as they receive". Looking up the owner said, "Most definitely your grace, I will be adding your name to the exclusive list immediately". He summoned his chief accountant in to record the count's name and coat of arms as he was informed that this will be passed along for various court invitations in the future which included British Royal Court.

Once the account was opened in the amount of 16,600 pounds sterling the brothers left and headed back to the brig. The ship had been provisioned with more than enough fine food, fresh water and several kegs of the town's best wine & ale, compliments of the harbor master. By now all the town was buzzing about the splendid royal brig as several had gathered on the wharf to bid them a fond farewell and safe voyage. Once they entered the harbor and unfurled the coat of arms sail, a cheer rose up from the watchers in port echoed by a 9-gun salute from the Belgian fort. The entire crew was smiling, waving and laughing under their breath as they all thought the same thing, "What a bunch of Dumbasses"!

The deposit of the 5 stones in the safety of the Antwerp bank was a minor amount compared to the remaining precious gems left in the brothers' possession, but it served a very valuable purpose. They all knew word would spread like wildfire throughout the land especially in England. They sail under the Pantelleria colors for a few days till they eventually turn south bound for the curious little island to see it firsthand for themselves. With the navigational expertise, Everwyn had them dead on course as they slide through the Straits of Gibraltar and only a day or so from Pantelleria Island. Calm seas and perfect weather helped them along her 8-day journey as she transformed now into a sleek Dutch merchant brig, they named The Sea Stallion.

On the beautiful afternoon of March 25th, 1760, the brig pulled into the quiet port surrounded only by the numerous colorful fishing boats. The port trading house was thrilled with the unexpected arrival of needed goods they had to offer up. Cotton bales, sugar cane, rice and indigo were all welcome sights to the trade owner. He worked out a beneficial deal for the island's exports of capers, olives, lemons and mostly the rare wine that only Pantelleria could produce. By nightfall, the ship's cargo hole was loaded with everything including needed provisions. The entire crew spent a relaxing evening at the town tavern including the black crewmen. Pantelleria was so close to Tunis, so the towns people naturally assumed they were from the North African area and never gave their color a second thought since many of the fishermen there were dark skinned as well. They spent the next day exploring the 32 square mile island while gathering information about this tiny island paradise including who exactly governed it.

The town mayor Josephi Antonio was especially helpful as he explained to Noah & Eli that even though the island was legally under the rule of Sicily, they acted as an independent state. Spain had relinquished its control several years before to the bourbon family with the stipulation of allowing Spanish free trade there. Thus, there were no taxes collected for now from commerce or trade by Sicily. As for Ferdinand III he had visited the island only once just before taking over the crown. The mayor went on to tell them that the king was much more concerned with the troubling economy of Sicily so the last thing on his mind was the welfare of Pantelleria. Josephi laughed adding, "If someone had enough money, they could probably buy this place for next to nothing"! The men thanked the jolly mayor and assured him they would be back in a few months with more needed supplies for them. Firmly shaking hands, he said sincerely, "Grazie... you are always welcome here"!

It seemed Abel & Tohru did some exploring of his own at the wharf. The abundance of various fish caught their eye, including large rock lobsters and oysters by the bushel. One of the fishing crews were seated opening up oysters and invited the curious duo to join them. After 3 or 4 failed attempts Abel & Tohru got the hang of it quickly. A few dozen successful opening, Abel was treated to a surprised inside one of them, a perfectly shaped black pearl. The group smiled as Abel went to hand it to the boat's captain. The Old man waved his hands signaling no, "You found, you keep". As Tohru was looking about the nets scattered over the deck, he picked up a small piece of black coral lodged in the net. One of the crew tried to explain that it sometimes gets caught up and rips holes in the net. The amazed oriental offered to pay for it but the captain said it was a gift for him.

Tohru had seen the rare black coral before as a boy in Okinawa. Once it was cleaned shaped and smoothed it became a valuable commodity in jewelry making. The sale of it in large markets like Tokyo would bring a sizable profit, enough to feed a family for months. As for the black pearls, they were an adornment only the very rich could afford much like diamonds. A single pearl could sell as high as 500 pounds depending on the size & quality. The rushed back to show Eli and the others what they had been given. Minutes later they returned as Eli spoke Italian to the captain showing interest in the coral and pearls. He was a bit confused at first about the worthless coral but told them to follow him to his house near the wharf. Inside he produced a small wooden box, in it was over 50 pearls of various shapes, sizes and colors including several black ones. Eli reached into his pocket and sat 5 gold crown coins on the table explaining to the old man they were worth 50 pounds sterling or roughly 5,000 Italian liras.

The fisherman was astounded at the offer and accepted it gladly. Before the day was done, the other fishermen in the village sold their stock of pearls with many of them literally gifting whatever black coral they had aboard their boats before trashing it back into the sea. When the brig sailed out the follow morning much to the happiness of the fishing community, she was carrying 3 crates of black coral and over 300 pearls including 133 black ones. One luxurious pink one the size of Abel's large thumb nail stood out as the ultimate catch of the day. And for the next 2 days the crew feasted on fresh boiled rock lobster till they were all gone. More importantly, they knew word would eventually get to Sicily about a rich Dutchman named Elijah Studman.

10 days later, now the De La Regla, they sailed back into Antwerp greeted with the same pomp and splendor as before. Count Maschione instructed the harbor master to have his ship provisioned for sea

the following morning including a new case iron stove due to the failure of the old one during the long voyage. Eli figured the families in Wales could use another one. He ordered Marino to give the harbor master 5,000 lira to cover the cost of the supplies as he headed to the trading house. With the port honor guard posted alongside the brig, the dock workers began loading her up as ordered. Eli speaking Italian, turned to Abel standing erect like a statue on deck and said, "Boatswain, No one is to come aboard without my permission"! Abel knew what to reply, "CeCe Mio signore"! As he saluted and passed the order to the crew standing there.

Once inside the office of the owner they sat down to bargain once again, this time with something new to offer. Everwyn placed a small leather bag on his desk, inside were 25 black pearls as the Count explained, "This is just a small sample of what I can offer you from my island. Like the diamonds there is much more to be uncovered in time". The owner was thoroughly impressed with the quality and quickly summoned his gem expert to see them for himself. He looked over them and confirmed all 25 were of the highest caliber, adding, "finest I have ever seen". After a few minutes of calculating the pearls were estimated to value, 5,400 pounds sterling varying from the size & shape. Eli signaled Everwyn to proceed, as he pulled out 6 uncut diamonds to be added to the ever-growing amount. When all was done the total in the account read, "33,400 pounds sterling".

During the transaction at the diamond trading house, Marino was at the export trade company supervising the trade of the capers, olives & lemons withholding the bulk of the rare Pantelleria wine for a more needed port. He purchased a batch of fine lace, linen and silk that had arrived a few weeks before from the far east. He knew Luka would be delighted with the splendid cloth and put it to good use. He learned from one of the traders that there was a call for the black coral in London due to the numerous jewelry makers in the city. One particular craftsman who catered to the tastes of the court. It seemed a quick trip to London was in order for the brothers and a chance to help spread the word a bit more about Count Maschione of Pantelleria.

During the half a day voyage to London, the crew gathered to discuss what plan of action they would take while there. It was important that everyone put on just the right show since they would be under the eyes of the British crown for the first time. Once in port the black crewmen would remain silent while on deck giving the illusion, they were Tunisian slaves. Only Noah and Everwyn would leave to seek out this jeweler to the crown carrying a few samples of pearls & the precious coral. Assuming word had already reached London's court about the count the idea was to show the town of his regal aloof manner by not being seen on such a brief meaningless visit. Everyone agreed whole heartedly as the ship arrived just before evening fell.

It took no time to find the craftsman who was just about to close up shop for the night when Noah & Everwyn arrived. He was impressed and delighted to see the samples they had with them inquiring how much did they have to sell to him. Everwyn replied, "I am authorized by Count Maschione to sell you 1 crate of black coral weighing 60 lbs. for 600 pounds. As for the pearls I can offer you 50 white pearls and 20 black pearls for 6,000 pounds. The elder jeweler thought for a moment, knowing he could create dozens of elaborate pieces with this offer making over 5 times the amount paid. A year ago, he had fashioned such a necklace for Lady Belinda Winslow for the sum of 12,000 pounds. It seemed Belinda had a particular fancy for the color black since the loss of her husband. The jeweler agreed on one condition, that he be made exclusive to the precious materials. They came to an accord, with the exchange being made the following morning when the bank opened.

The next morning Eli joined Noah & Everwyn to complete the deal after hearing the familiar name of Lady Winslow, the radiant goddess in the portrait he had gazed at to memory. Since the old man was close to her and the court, he knew his mere appearance would be just enough get the name of Count Maschione spread even more in the palace ranks. Eli made it obvious of his interest in the well-known beautiful widow who's painting he had hanging now in the clothes closet in his cabin. They shook hands with the count assuring the craftsman he would be the only jeweler in London he will continue to deal with as there will be more rare materials brought to him in the near future.

After departing London, they headed to the settlement in Pyle to see how the families were progressing. Once they hit open waters of the Atlantic and turned northward, they reverted back to The Sea Stallion before docking into Pyle in mid-June. Delighted at the splendid dock they had built with everyone cheering them as they tied up. The ketch was no longer needed for shelter as the brothers gazed at the community, they had built in 2 months. Strong houses for every family, barns, smoke houses, even a blacksmith setup and rich fields of growing crops. They even had time to clear an inlet to stow away the ketch safely that could hardly be seen from a distance. They unloaded the new case iron stove and enjoyed a delicious hot meal that evening with everyone. Hardy had passed along several varieties of seeds to the farmers to use as they saw fit. Eli made a gift of 500 pounds to the community so they would be able to purchase whatever they needed.

The following morning, the entire crew joined by the men of "Liberty" as they named their village, set out for a hunt for game. A few headed to the ponds that were teaming with fish. Everyone knew it would be a while before the brig would return so they wanted to insure they left Liberty well stocked with whatever was needed. It seemed the land was fertile in more ways than one as 3 new members were born with 4 more on the way. To the delight of the brig crew Liberty was well on its way to becoming a productive and safe haven for them all.

A few days later, on June 16th, 1760, as the Sea Rose, sailed out on a west-southwest course for Griffin Cove where they would transfer the cargo of Pantelleria wine to the Tripoli & Hard Luck and sell to the colonial ports. The trip was swift with them arriving 24 days later at the quiet confines of their hideaway. Fabrice and most of the crew stayed on to take care of any minor repairs and adjustments needed on the brig. Both small vessels left out for Brunswick with their cargo holes filled with wine, lace, linen & silk to have some new outfits made from the Rotundo tailors. Once there they sent an ariel message to Darin in Charleston, that they were back and would see him in a day or so. The Tripoli wasted no time setting sail to meet up with their brother and pass on the news of their productive journey.

July 12th, 1760, they slid into Charleston to glee of its harbor master as they reunited with tales of what had been going on for the last 5 months. After Darin was told everything, he had some rather startling information as well. It seemed Ervin was clamping down harder on the colonial taxes with a 10% increase. In early April his tax collector arrived in port with an armed contingent of British regulars as a show of force. He said they did the same thing in Savannah, Brunswick and as far north as Boston. He also added that he had word of another slave shipment due to arrive in Savannah within the week. "This one has a British Naval escort too"! Darin emphasized. That meant only one thing, uncut diamonds.

Eli thought for a moment then told Darin to send off a pigeon to the cove and to Brunswick, to have them start work on the "HMS Princess Royale" immediately. "Have your man in Savannah contact you as soon as they arrived and in what ships", added Noah. Within a few hours after the messages were sent out the replies returned confirming all was being made ready. The Tripoli sailed out to join the rest at the cove and work out a plan of action depending on the information they would hopefully get in time from the Georgia port. By the time they arrived, the hull had been repainted resembling a British war ship of the line. Marino had time to carve the HMS nameplate for the stern and mount it. The crew checked their naval uniforms to insure everything was set. Hardy had mixed up the finishing touch with a flesh tone powder for the black crews face and hands, giving them the appearance of white sailors from a distance.

Two days later the ariel message they waited for arrived. The large Indiaman merchant ship docked in Savannah to off load the slaves and take on a full cargo of cotton and sugar cane. Her escort was a British 28-gun frigate who had dispatched an armed platoon of soldiers aboard the Indiaman who carried only 8 guns on her deck. A second pigeon flew in moments later with more information. The 2 ships were scheduled to depart Savannah at dawn the following morning bound for New York to pick up another escort along the way before returning to Bristol. The recognition signal code was, "A C F", using the signal pennants. With the entire crew gathered to hear the messages, Eli laid out their plan of attack with every man knowing his job.

The brig sailed out of the cove just before dawn and slowly moved south to hopefully sight the small convoy. At noon about 20 miles off the coastline the crewman aloft in the crow's nest yelled out, "Ship Ahoy off the port bow"! Eli ordered them to man their posts and get ready for action. The black crew quickly applied the flesh tone powder and moved into position. As the brig closed within 500 yards they hoisted 3 signal pennants, Alpha, Charlie, Foxtrot on the port side halyard. With the frigate closest to them they watched the counter signal raised on her stern rigging. As they came closer Eli yelled out, "Ahoy Captain, HMS Princess Royale at your service, we are here to assist you as escort to New York"! A happy reply came back, "Ahoy Captain you're a welcome sight please take position on the starboard flank of the Indiaman"! Eli replied, "Aye sir we will come about now"!

The 2 ships slowed enough to allow the brig to swing around their sterns in order to move into place on the outside flank. This was what Eli was hoping they would do. As the brig turned to port, she closed within 200 yards of the frigate's exposed stern. When they had the right angle, Eli yelled out, "Port side FIRE"! The 7 guns when off simultaneously and destroyed the frigate's ass end in the blink of an eye. Eli commanded, "Mortars FIRE"! At point blank range 2 explosive rounds hit their mark as one of them drove through the deck into the powder magazine. What was left when the smoke cleared was nothing but burning rubble as the British war ship was gone. All this happened within a matter of seconds to the astonished eyes of everyone on board the remaining ship who still had her stern to the powerful brig.

Eli slowed and yelled out, "Captain, you have a choice, surrender now or I will do the same thing to you! You have 10 seconds to reply"! He quickly yelled back, "We surrender Captain", as the ship raised the white flag. "Captain we are coming along side, if one shot is fired, I will not hesitate to sink you where you stand". Within moments they eased along the starboard side of the helpless vessel and boarded her. The platoon of British soldiers was ordered to drop their weapons along with the crew of 30 sailors as the heavily armed brig crew gathered up the rifles and swords. Eli slowly walked up on the quarterdeck and relinquished its captain of his saber and said, "Captain you and your crew will be spared if you follow my orders without hesitation". The seasoned skipper looked close at Eli and replied, "Holy Shit! You're just a boy"! He quickly placed the tip of his razer shape blade at the insolent man and replied with a smile. "This BOY just blew up your escort and captured your smelly ass, now shut the hell up and listen"!

He instructed his crew to gathered up everyone on deck. Half went below to insure they all were accounted for. Moments later Abel emerged with 3 crewmen hiding and 18 slaves who were chained below. He ordered them to be unshackled and put aboard the brig to be taken care of. Eli turned to the assembled men and ordered the cargo be put aboard the brig immediately along with the 8 cannons she carried on deck. Under the watchful eyes of the brig's crew, the captives quickly transferred everything as commanded. While this was happening, Eli turned to the disgraced man and said, "Now captain tell me where the diamonds are"! He paused then replied, "What diamonds""? "Mister, you are wearing my patience thin I'm gonna ask you politely one more time, where are the diamonds"? With a smirk the man said, "I don't know what you're talking about"! Eli reared up and backhanded the smartass across the mouth. "You're rapidly pissing me off you son of a bitch! It's time you see I mean business"!

Noah put his pistol to the head of the Indiaman's first mate and pulled the trigger splattering his brains all over his insulting captain. The captive crew stopped for a moment to witness this as one of them yelled out, "tell him captain or we all die"! By now all the cargo had been safely put aboard the brig as the 8 cannons were hoisted over. "Ok mister, have it your way, Strip" ordered Eli. "What"? Asked the man. Eli put his blade to the top button of the bastard's coat and popped it off and repeated for him to strip. Around his neck was what Eli was looking for, the key to a chest hidden somewhere aboard. He took it and tossed it to Marino and told him to check the captain's cabin.

When the last of the cannons were put aboard the brig the soldiers and crew were ordered to strip as well. When they had finished, they were taken below to be shackled and chained. The smart mouthed man turned to Eli and said, "You're nothing but a nigger loving bastard"! As he spit on Eli's boots. Eli looked down then wiped the saliva off on the bastard's bare leg and said, "For some ungodly reason I hate that word! Actually, I'm just a man who appreciates human life and despises anyone who takes advantage of it... like You"! Eli ordered the naked man to be shackled and put aboard the brig while he went below to see how Marino was doing. Joined by Noah and Hardy they sifted through the cabin, gathering up the ship's log and papers. Eventually they found a 2-foot-long box hidden under the captain's bulk that the key fitted into. Inside was what they been looking for, a leather sack the size of a cannon ball filled with the uncut gems.

With all the naked captives securely chained below, the brig crew went through the ship one last time to make damn sure they had everything they wanted, including a better stove for Tohru to cook on. With all the clothes, gear and weapons put aboard their ship, they cut the Indiaman loose to drift away. Once they were about 50 yards off Eli looked down from the quarterdeck and said, "Mister Wolf, it seems there's a flaw in that ship's water line please fix it"! The chief gunner smiled slyly and replied, "Aye Captain... Port side, Fire"! A stream of 7 heavy round projectiles sliced the water line open like it was gutting a fish as they watched her sink to the briny deep. "You fucking murderer, you said we would be spared" exclaimed the bound & naked captain. "I lied! Now join your crew asshole and may God NOT have mercy on your worthless soul"! As Eli pushed him overboard and watched him disappear. He turned to his hearty crew and ordered to set sail for the cove. The show was over, for now!

CHAPTER 8

Liar

During the short voyage they all made sure the 18 male slaves were well fed and taken care of. Only one of them spoke a little English as Abel and the other black crewmen tried to explain what was going on. By the time they docked at the cove several hours later, the new members had a good idea of the situation to feel comfortable enough to explain their tale. Several of them were slaves in the diamond mine in west Africa before it caved in a few months before. Hundreds were killed in the catastrophe as the mine was closed due to the lack of decent manpower and funds. The diamonds on board the Indiaman represented the last to be excavated for the time being until another mine was discovered. The problem was there were no funds now coming from the Royal Shipping Lines Company. Ervin had sunk all his private holding into the African mine and when it collapsed so did his private venture there. And to add insult to injury, he would soon find out this last voyage he funded was sitting at the bottom of the Atlantic Ocean. It appeared to Eli and his brothers that they had the viscount by the balls, it was time now to squeeze them dry.

After a hot breakfast the next morning, the crew transferred the captured cotton and sugarcane to the idol Merchantman anchored at the base of the sandbar. They quickly installed the 8 cannons they took off the Indiaman and within 2 days the vessel was ready for sea. The name plate was left basically the same purposely as Marino carved out the name Royal leaving it called now the Sea Hawk. The plan called for only the brothers to sail her down to Spanish held St. Augustine and sell everything outright including the ship. The Tripoli would follow maned by Hardy & Tohru arriving a few hours later. The remaining 6 brothers would be the skeleton crew with Marino posing as Spanish Merchant Captain Mendoza who was down on his luck and forced to dump everything. Abel and the black crew would remain in the cove to look after the still weakened new men. They had one simple task, strip off the British Naval colors from their brig and reset her as the Da La Regla once more.

The trip was slow going mostly due to the lumbering vessel that handled like a "wet sponge" as Marino nicknamed it. Eventually they docked in St. Augustine the afternoon of July 20th to a quiet port with only a few local fishing boats scattered about. After unloading the cargo and selling it at the trading house Marino began to put the word out that his ship was for sale to the highest bidder. The harbor master suggested an auction be held in 2 days to give prospective buyers a chance to gather. He agreed as riders were sent out to nearby villages and towns about the ship sale. Later that night, the Tripoli came in basically undetected and waited to see what would happen.

People started coming in from the neighboring towns of Fernandina, Haulover, St. John and more to have a look at this large merchant ship that was up for bid. The morning of the auction at dockside was teaming with onlookers and buyers that included the Spanish captain of the guard at the city's fort. The harbor master spoke out, "Up for sale is this fine 800-ton Merchantman ship complete with 8 10-pound cannons and a watertight hull. She was built 6 years ago and has plenty of life left in her. I will start the bidding at 3,500"! A moment of silence pushed over the crowd till the fort Captain yelled out, "3,500"! Slowly others joined in as it rose quickly to 4,500. From the back of the onlookers rang a familiar voice, "4,600"! Eli had a tough time not busting out laughing at Hardy's bid. It was overtaken quickly till it reached 5,400. "Going once... twice... Sold to Captain Hernandez for 5,400 pieces of gold"!

With the transaction completed Marino handed the harbor master his 10% for conducting the event, thanked him and signed the forged papers of ownership over the Spanish officer. "Good luck Captain you got one hell of a bargain, she's a fine ship", uttered Captain Mendoza. The new owner shook his hand replying, "Thank you Captain the Sea Hawk will be put to good use I assure you"! As the large crowd disbursed and evening fell the brothers quietly gathered at the Tripoli and beat a hasty retreat from St. Augustine. When they sailed out of the harbor and headed north, Marino laughingly said, "Ya knows, I can get use to this lying thing especially when you're dealing with Dumbasses"! They all burst into laughter as they marveled at almost 5,500 gold pieces that included the splendid sale of all the cotton and sugarcane.

There was one important underlying benefit to this sale far beyond the money. Over time, the once owned Royal Shipping Line Merchantman would be recognized. Thus, the loss of her, the Indiaman and her frigate escort would be attributed to the Spanish navy as was the ongoing rumor of ketch presumed sunk years before. The brothers had covered their tracks again as the next step was about to be taken, this time in Ervin's own back yard. What concerned them now was what to do with the addition of 18 slaves. Most were young enough to eventually recover from mistreatment & malnutrition and either be productive sailors or possibly farmers at Liberty. Their ages ranged from about 15 to the elder they called Sage who was at least 40 at best guess having the beginnings of gray hair and beard.

Sage spoke a little broken English as well as fluent French being from the area around Guinea as a boy till, he was sold into slavery. He had worked in the fields for several years before being sent to the mines. It seemed the aged man had a talent for wood crafting primarily the ability to turn it into amazing art forms. When the brothers returned to the cove, they noticed him sitting on one of the rocks at the water's edge whittling on a 3-foot slender piece of white oak. He was carving out what appeared to be a walking cane and at the tip was a clean-cut detailed wooden diamond for the grip. Using the rock formation, he was sitting on he had rounded and smoothed the arrow straight shaft to near perfection. As he put the finishing touches to it, he looked up and handed it to Eli saying in French, "pour Vois Monsieur". Eli was touched by the gesture as he thanked the craftsman and told him, "Merci beaucoup Sage". He stood the man up and shook his hand as he could see the deep gratitude in elder's eyes.

With everyone cleaned up and in better clothing they were looking stronger every day. The black crew had taken great care to make sure they were well fed and rested while they made the change over on the brig. Marino sat to talk with Sage about a project he wanted to do with the newfound artist, to make a new figurehead for the brig, a stallion's head with a fiery look. As for the other 17 arrivals they would be given their freedom along with Sage, as soon as Darin could work up the documents for each of them. The brothers explained a couple of options they could have, either as members of the crew or join the growing farm village of Liberty when they returned to Wales in a month or so. If they felt, they wanted to head out on their own they would be able to do that as well.

The regular Tripoli crew sailed out to Charleston with the information about the 18 new men to pass along to Darin. Everwyn, Hardy & Wolf took the Hard Luck into Brunswick to gather up the new Dutch uniforms and gear from the Rotundo tailor shop while Marino & Fabrice stayed behind at the cove with the rest of the crew to take care of some last-minute work on the brig. The 2 ships would pick up the needed supplies of rice, corn, grain & indigo for the brig's upcoming trip. Once Eli brought Darin up to date on everything, he told them it was about time he retired from the harbor master trade, "I've decided to take up the sea going life, my job is finished here". He left a letter addressed to King George II to be sent out on the first British ship. Enclosed was his official letter of resignation. With all his gear stored in the Tripoli they sailed out with a full cargo load back to the cove.

The following day all the brothers were back at the hideaway preparing for one last run up to Port Bath. They loaded up several cases of the Pantelleria wine in the 2 cargo ships as the brothers instructed Abel to take over at the cove till, they returned in a few days. Darin handed the 18 men their papers of freedom with their chosen names officially documented and sealed by the crown. 4 of them, including Sage decided they wanted to live their life as farmers once they arrive at Liberty. The remaining 14 chose to become part of the strong crew on the brig. Abel would spend the time to train them while 14 new births were setup in the crew's quarters in preparation of the long trip across the Atlantic.

Arriving on a rainy morning on Eli's 19th birthday, the brothers carried some special wine to Rosie at her lusty palace. Her and the ladies were thrilled to see the long overdue brothers as Eli sat down to offer the madam a splendid proposition. Her lavish bar would be stocked with 18 cases of the expensive wine compliments of Count Maschione, of Pantelleria Island. He knew over time her, and the girls would spread the rumor of a dashing young Italian who appeared in port one night in a spectacular brig. And just like that, vanished back to sea before the morning tide. It was also the brother's way of thanking her for all she had done over the years. So, one last wild party was set for the night, compliments of The Crimson Garter. And for Rosie, it would be her final lesson to be taught to the birthday boy. She called it, "How to bed a woman without touching her"!

A pigeon was sent off to the Wilhelm farm informing them of the brother's arrival the next morning. The crew said so long to their sexy friends as they sailed to the Wilhelm dock at daybreak. By mid-morning they were greeted by Hans and his growing sons as they boarded his wagon to the farm and a hearty breakfast spread. Over the past year the farm had flourished with the help of the Carpenter family. Almost every square acre was put to good use as crops were growing and harvested as far as the eye could see. The brothers informed Hans it would be quite a while before they returned and to start selling the hemp out right from now on. They loaded the 2 ships with hemp & tobacco while Hardy gathered up the last ingrediencies from the herb garden. Eli handed Hans 500 pounds, shook his hand and said, "Thank you my friend for everything you've done for us, we will see you again sometime"!

August 5th, 1760, they returned to Griffin cove to the cheers of their crew. Sage had a surprise for the brothers as he showed them his finished work. Standing almost 6 feet tall was the bust of a raging stallion he had stained in black to resemble the steed on the new Dutch Studman flag. From Darin's design, Luka had hand stitched a silk two-point pennant with the Studman crest in the corner. Behind the reared up black stallion was a burnt orange lightning shaped "S". The flag was striped in alternating shades of navy blue and beige. The officer uniforms matched in navy blue with burnt orange and beige piped trim for "Count Elijah Studman" and his crew. Abel showed them the finishing touch with the brig's additional name plate, "The Sea Stallion" Sage had ornately carved out and painted in the matching coat of arms colors.

With all of the supplies and provisions stored aboard the De La Regla, they securely beached the 2 small cargo ships that had served them well over the years. Under the cover of darkness, the following night they set sail for Liberty. The 14 new crewmen spent the long voyage going through their paces as deck hands and riggers. In between they practiced with sword, pistol & rifle as well as running daily gunnery drills under the supervision of Wolf & Abel who had become quite the marksman himself. The 4 men who decided to stay on to farm at Liberty, assisted Tohru in the galley and helped out with any minor carpentry work needed aboard. Sage had them building new stern lanterns to change out from one appearance of the brig to another. The paint locker was completely stocked with the matching colors needed to change her hull look to coincide with her various identities.

Mother nature was favorable to them with only a few days of rainy squalls before they arrived in Liberty on the third day of September. The small village of Liberty was now a growing town with everyone overjoyed to see their dear friends. They enjoyed their first full harvest there with everyone looking healthy and strong including 3 newborn arrivals. They made the 4 new men welcome and assured them they would have homes of their own built as soon as possible. It seemed the 4 unattached females there quickly took a fancy to the newcomers as it was made evident at the lavish feast the town put on for the brother's return. They unloaded the needed supplies of exported corn, rice, wheat, hemp & tobacco while the town made sure the ship was well stocked with its own provisions. Before leaving Eli added another 500 pounds to the town treasury much to the glee of everyone there.

Before they sailed out Eli assured them, they would be back soon as the brig set sail 3 days later for a return to Antwerp. They left out of Liberty under an overcast night to ensure no unexpected ships would see them till they hit open waters, especially since they were so close to Bristol's shipping lanes. After making the turn eastward in the English Channel a few vessels were sighted on their usual merchant runs as each one hailed and salute the obvious royal brig. It seemed the lie they had planted months before was paying off better than they had imagined. As they pulled into Antwerp to a cannonade salute from the town fort and the honor guard awaiting them at their birth on the dock along with the ass kissing harbor master.

Dressed in their new regal crimson uniforms, Count Maschione was timidly greeted by the harbor master, "We are so thrilled to see you return to our humble port your grace, I am at your service for anything you may need". Giving him a brief look, the Count snapped his fingers as Darin stepped up and replied to the man, "We require these provisions immediately since we will only be in port until tomorrow morning"! As he handed the man the list of supplies Darin added he wanted to meet with the town's cartographer about some mapping information. Darin and Hardy headed to the map makers office as the rest made their way to the Diamond exchange.

Once seated in the office of the trade owner Eli wasted no time having Everwyn pull out a dozen small uncut gems to be inspected and added to the growing account. Over the last few months their account had compounded interest bringing the total now to over 34,000 pounds sterling. As the diamonds were inspected an additional 18,300 pounds was recorded making the total 52,300 in his ever-growing bank account there. The owner then produced a royal sealed letter that had arrived a few months before from King George II. It was an open invitation to court at the palace to meet him and his royal family at his earliest convenance. The lie was working the brothers thought, as he smiled and told the owner, "I am honored and grateful sir. Before I leave, I will have my personal secretary give you my reply to King George with my deep respects".

A few hours later, Darin had the letter composed and sealed for the British monarch as he handed it to the exchange owner with specific instructions it was to be delivered to his majesty as soon as possible. Inside it specified that Count Ricardo Maschione's vessel should be arriving in London within 48 hours of the dated letter and is greatly looking forward to the honor of attending his majesty's court. The letter left by ship within hours as the entire crew of the De La Regla was treated to a delivered banquet that evening, compliments of the city of Antwerp. Darin & Hardy picked up some valuable articles while they visited the city cartographer earlier in the day. While Darin distracted the old map maker by seeking out a few maps of the expanding area, Hardy found his official stamp seals for Antwerp and quickly made a wax impression of them. Wolf would eventually turn them into metal stamps to add to Darin's growing toy collection.

The traditional 9-gun salute resounded from the fort as the ship slowly sailed out bound for London the following day. They intentionally took their time on the short trip across the channel as they all went over the upcoming charade to be played in merry ole London town. Just before sunrise they entered in the busy port as several onlookers watched the royal vessel dock at one of the main births. Per their instructions the crew remained aboard as an honor guard from the town was posted along her side. A coach was put at the count's disposal compliments of the harbor master. Eli ordered the remaining 2 crates of black coral loaded with him and Everwyn as they climbed aboard to take it to the familiar jewelry maker in town. Unlike normal species of sea coral, the black grew more like a leafless bush underwater with all the characteristics of wood. Once drier and carefully cut, shaped and sanded it could be polished into gleaming pieces of jewelry.

Arriving just as he opened his shop, they immediately began the exchange. "I brought you 2 crates of black coral this time along with 150 pearls including 80 black ones", the Count proclaimed as Everwyn placed them before the wide-eyed craftsman. As he browsed through the exquisite gems and opened crates, he began to calculate a fair price for the lot. From less than half of the last batch the Count brought him, he had fashioned and sold several detailed items to ladies of the court for well over 30,000 pounds. With this shipment more than doubled from the last one, he would make a fortune from it. "I can go 14,000 pounds for everything sir", the man said. Eli quickly replied back with a determined look in his eyes, "I want 16,000, nothing less". The jeweler agreed as he opened his safe and counted out the agreed amount in sterling notes.

Also, from the safe he handed a sealed letter addressed to Count Maschione that came in over a month before. Eli & Everwyn quickly recognized the familiar seal of the Royal Shipping Lines Company and the signature of Viscount Ervin. Not showing any emotion Eli simply placed it inside his coat and thanked the owner for the transaction as they left. Once inside the awaiting coach he opened the letter and read that Ervin was offering him an open invitation to meet with him in Bristol to discuss some possible business. "I would deem it an honor to meet with you at your connivence of course". He signed it, "Your humble servant, Viscount Ervin". The 2 brothers smiled at each other and knew they had the asshole on the hook now.

When they returned to the ship a royal coach was waiting with the palace Captain of the guard inside. He stepped out, saluted and said, "King George II extends his personal greetings to your grace and requests your presents tonight at a banquet in your honor at the Royal Palace". Eli replied, "Please thank his majesty Captain, I would be honored to attend". Eli turned to Hardy standing at the gangway and ordered 2 cases of wine be brought up and loaded on the royal coach. Moments later it was done as the officer saluted again and said the royal coach will pick him up at 5 o'clock sharp. As for his officers and crew they would be treated to royal feast aboard ship later that evening.

Eli had waited for this opportunity for years as he carefully prepared for an evening of elbow rubbing with royalty. Making sure he was smooth clean shaven to continue the look of a youthful Italian member of regal decent. He adorned the never wore white linen and silk waist coat and form fitted pants that were stripped down the sides in crimson & gray. The coat was trimmed in matching pipping to accent his family crest, the solid gold double headed eagle medallion over his heart. Attached to his shining black knee-high boots was a set of regal silver spurs Wolf had made for him a year before. His long dark chestnut hair was neatly pulled back into a classic ponytail style of the time. His hands were covered in a pair of white officer's gloves. The finishing touch was his hand carved diamond headed walking cane that was now deeply stained in solid black giving the appearance it was possibly made of black coral. Just before the palace coach arrived to take him to the banquet, a half dozen wagons rolled up to the ship's gangway to deliver the De La Regla's feast. Once the crew carried it all aboard, they sat down together below deck to enjoy the best food and drink London had to offer. The last order Eli gave before he departed was to insure no one was to come aboard and no one was to leave the ship. The night watch was posted as it was alternated every 2 hours with at least 2 of the officers taking part as they had rehearsed on the trip there.

As Eli entered the historical palace most of the usual court was already there, anxious to get their first look as the mysterious count. The royal herald announced, "Lords and ladies please welcome Count Ricardo Maschione of Pantelleria". As he regally walked in, the bows & curtseys looked to him like a royal wave of humanity as he was escorted to the seated King & Queen on their throne. Once he approached them, he could hear the murmuring whispers from the onlookers of how young and handsome he was. When he reached the short steps before the throne he stopped and dropped to one knee, using his cane for balance and bowed clearly saying, "Your majesty I am deeply honored to be in your royal presents". He stayed there motionless till the king spoke, "Arise Count, we are pleased to finally have you here with us". The Queen then asked if his voyage was a safe one and that he & his crew were enjoying London. "Yes, your heiress the trip was a quiet one. My officers & crew are deeply grateful for the splendid feast your magnificent city has given them. By now I'm certain they are all fat and happy"! As a wave of laughter could be heard from the king & queen followed by everyone there.

With the royal formalities out of the way he was introduced to the rest of the court, many who were anxious to get a closer look at the dashing young Italian. Eventually a stout wrinkled faced man stepped up and extended a limp wristed hand, "I'm Viscount Ervin sir, it's a pleasure to meet you". It took every bit of strength Eli had to maintain his composure as he replied, "the pleasure is all mine sir". Ervin then introduced his elder son Ervin II who said, "Welcome to court sir may I present my wife Lady Lanora and my daughter Elinore". Lanora was dressed in a low-cut light blue gown that accented her large breasts enough to be seen clearly from across the crowded room. As she slowly curtsied, Eli's eyes were fixated on her lusty cleavage. He softly grasped her gloved hand and kissed it. Without anyone seeing he placed his thumb in the center of her palm and gently circled it. Looking into her eyes he could easily see she picked up on the flirtatious gesture as she slyly winked at the young stud. He then turned to the attractive teenage girl who was still in a deep curtsy as he took her hand to lift her up then quickly kiss it as a formality then turned away to greet the next person. Eli knew his first target was the mother, the daughter would eventually come much later.

Minutes later a familiar face stepped up to be introduced to the count. Dressed in a glittering crimson and black gown with a most unique matching necklace made of small diamonds adored by black coral and lusty black pearls. Her escort, a British Captain spoke up, "Count Maschione may I introduce Lady Belinda Winslow". The portrait of Belinda did her no justice, she truly was a ravishing beauty with cascades of raven black hair that enhanced the face of a goddess. It was obvious to Eli she truly was the standout of court. Kissing her silk black gloved hand, his eyes were torn between her captivating dark blue eyes and her youthful plump breasts. In a song like voice she spoke, "Your Grace, it is my honor to meet you at last". "The honor is truly all mine Ma Lady" as he added, "And such a stunning necklace you are wearing", as he slyly smiled at her. She softly laughed and replied, "I understand I have you to thank for the rare materials. This is now my favorite piece", as she quickly winked and walked away.

The long line of greeters had finally ended with everyone now seated at the long dining table to enjoy a feast truly fit for a king. Everyone's glass was filled with unexpected wine given by the count, King George rose from the head of the massive table and tossed his honored guest. With everyone delighted at the taste of the rare wine he added, "And we have Count Maschione to thank for this magnificent wine he brought from his island paradise. I must say it is some of the best I have ever had". Eli smiled and replied, "thank you your majesty, I guess I will have to bring more on my next visit". Much of the idol chat during dinner was directed at the count. From the rare wine to various other questions about Pantelleria Island.

The younger Ervin was seated several people from Eli who asked the question most of the flirtatious ladies were wondering, "You're much younger than I had expected, may I ask how old you are"? Not looking up from his plate of roast pheasant, he paused to clear his throat of food and replied, "I'm young enough to learn and old enough to know better"! As the entire table laughed and applauded the wise and gracious retort including the queen. From the corner of his eye, Eli saw a disapproving look cut toward ill-mannered young Ervin by the king who then turned it toward the older one. Soaking all this in a clear picture was forming about the opinion King George II had toward the Ervin family. It seemed the only reason they were still allowed at court was the money brought in from the shipping company, but all that was about to drastically change.

As the dinner was coming to a close, the orchestra began to play in the massive ballroom adjacent to the banquet hall. Lead by the king and queen everyone slowly moved into the music filled room and began to dance. The viscount walked up to Eli and quietly said, "Please forgive my son's impertinence sir, he has a tendency to forget his place from time to time". Eli replied in an aloof manner, "Think nothing of it, I have already forgotten about it". Ervin briefly smiled and asked if he had received the letter, he left for him at the jewelry shop. Eli acknowledged reading it as Ervin added, "I would be very anxious to discuss some business with you at your connivence of course". Lanora was close enough to overheard and politely stepped in smiling to say, "Count Maschione, do you dance"? He smiled back and said, "Yes Ma Lady it would be my pleasure". As he took her extended hand Eli turned to Ervin and said, "Excuse me sir it seems beauty over business beckons", as they all smiled at the gracious remark.

They slowly began to waltz in perfect time to the music while Eli smiled thinking how thankful he was to Rosie for the lessons on the dance floor. As more pairs joined in, their attention was turned away from the guest of honor. His hand firm yet gentle at her waist he guided the lusty woman with graceful ease. She peered deep into his dark hazel eyes and said, "You're a wonderful dancer Count I feel so comfortable in your arms". Eli began to slowly circle his thumb again in her palm as his other hand was massaging her waistline with his gloved fingers. "Thank you, Ma Lady, it's easy to look like an expert with such a beautiful partner in my arms", as they simultaneously exchanged winks only, they could see.

Quickly he peered around and asked, "I do hope your husband doesn't mind that we are dancing". Lanora slyly smiled replying, "I'm sure my husband won't mind a bit, if he was here to even care". Eli looked around quickly and asked, "Oh I see, he stepped away on business"? She giggled softy and said, "You might say that it's more like personal business if I know him".

That was the reply Eli was waiting for as he made it obvious to the desirable woman by increasing his firm grasp of her and said, "I'm so sorry to hear that Ma Lady, what a perfect waist lovely sensuousness and elegance". She blushed, batted her long eye lashes and said, "Oh my, you do have a way with words, I do believe you're flirting with me". He leaned in and whispered, "My dear lady, I do believe you're adoring every word rolling off my tongue... but it would be much better suited pleasuring you in other ways"! Winking again with a devilish grin beaming from his face. Lanora was speechless for a moment as he felt a shiver rush through her passion filled body. In her mind, her husband was a thousand miles away as every ounce of her being was erotically focused on the dashing viral young man. Then Eli said what she had on her mind and in her eyes, "There is chemistry between us Lanora, you felt it from the moment we first met, admit it". As if she was in a hypnotic trance the impassioned woman could only nod in agreement. He continued, "There is a fire lite inside you now, that hasn't smoldered for a long time, if ever. And it would be criminal to not allow it to ignite between us". All she could softly say was, "Yes... yes, I want you too Ricardo".

When the waltz ended, they resumed their regal manner, bowed and curtsied as he escorted her back to her father-in-law. Out of respect he danced with the young Elinore next and make it clear in her mother's eyes it was purely a protocol gesture on the count's part. After several dances with other anxious ladies, he noticed Belinda's dance card was filled as she glided across the floor with partner after partner. Yet, out of the corner of his eye, he could see the ravishing beauty occasionally looking over in his direction. But the attention wasn't geared for her this night, it was simply a night to tease her not please her. As the festivities began to wind down once the king & queen retired the court members would make their way to say good night to the guest of honor. Belinda walked up saying, "It was a pleasure to have you at court your grace, I do hope we will see more of you in the future". He kissed her hand and said, "Thank you Ma Lady I will certainly try, and I do regret not having the privilege to dance with you, maybe the next time I can be added to your dance card'. She smiled brightly and agreed.

When Lanora walked up to extend her farewell, she snuck a small, folded note into Eli's hand as he kissed hers. He firmly shook the extended hand of the inebriated viscount stating he would be in touch for that meeting in Bristol when time allowed. As for the younger Ervin he was nowhere to be found. It seemed he had a previous engagement with a loose lady in waiting who just couldn't wait anymore. Before Eli left, the palace Captain handed a seal letter to him directly from the king requesting the purchase of how ever many cases of the rare wine, he had available. He instructed the captain to meet with his cargo officer at the docks in the morning to picked 12 cases he had left on board.

Once inside his coach he read the note from Lanora as he returned to the ship minutes later. He told the driver he was done with him for the night as he drove off. Hardy & Darin met him at the gangway as Eli quickly explained he had to change into something less obvious for a rendezvous with target number 1 as they all laughed. As he was rushing into his cabin, he told them to have 12 cases of wine ready to sell to the palace captain in the morning. "And have one of the guards quietly call me a town coach". Within minutes he had changed into a smart looking outfit that was much more inconspicuous than the regal uniform. He boarded the coach and told the driver to take him to number 13, 3rd street Betty Court. It was a quiet ride to far side of town as the clock chimed 11 times in the square.

As the coach came to a stop at its destination Eli handed the driver a gold sovereign and instructed him to return in 2 hours or so. Thrilled by the payment he quickly replied, "Anything you say me lord I will be here"! Pulling his 3-point hand down and draped in his cloak he walked up to the door and quietly knocked. The door opened with Lanora hidden behind it as he walked in. Standing there in a silk full length blue robe she welcomed her young stud in while taking his hat & cloak. Her long cascading dark blonde hair rolled off her shoulders as she took his hand to escort him to the romantic dim lite bedroom. "I took the liberty of icing down some champagne if you'd like to open it for us my sweet", she said in a sultry tone. Eli slid off his dark brown coat revealing his open collar linen white shirt that accented his muscular chest and arms.

Popping the cork, he poured out 2 glasses of the chilled delight and handled one to his aroused partner saying, "May is say you look sensational darling". They took a sipe then he set both glasses down and moved in. Cupping his hands gently on either side of her face as his fingers slid through her silky hair and pulled her in to softly kiss her wanting ruby lips. Hearing her moan as the tip of his tongue moved across her mouth till, he gradually penetrated the opening and eased it inside her warm moist mouth. His hands crept down to her neck then moved across her shoulders as he felt her tongue begin to mingle with his. Pulling her into his tight body as his firm hands wrapped around her waist and slowly began to grind his growing erection against her moist mound. He could feel her large breasts heaving as her nipples hardened against his chest.

She couldn't resist her urges any longer as she peeled off his open shirt. She felt his hand untie her sheer robe as it dropped to the floor. He stepped back long enough to see Lanora was wearing a pair of heeled evening slippers, white silk thigh high stockings held up with fancy blue garters and nothing else. Eli was amazed at the body of the 33-year-old. For being a mother, she had kept herself quite fit and trim. She helped to take off his knee-high boots as she anxiously awaited what he had in store for her in his tight pants. She sensuously sprawled herself across the bed to enjoy the strip show as Eli slowly dropped his pants before her. Uncontrolled she murmured out, "Oh My God" at the sight of his thick fully erect massiveness. "I had no idea you were… that big… I want it All"! Eli smiled slyly and said, "Let's get you ready first"!

A curious look covered Lanora's face as Eli crawled in slowly like a tiger stalking his prey, he spread her quivering thighs and began to tongue kiss them. Inch by inch moving ever closer to her wet mound until he reach his target. Looking up into her eyes he said, "Lay back and relax, and enjoy"! Working his tongue in slow circular fashion he planted it over her throbbing clitoris and then gradually started to suck it in and out of his wet lips. Placing both of his thumbs over her lips he spread them as his mouth moved in to erotically devour her flowing juices. It didn't take long before she was moaning louder at every stroke of his educated tongue. Trying to speak between her cascades of extasy she muttered out, "No one has ever done this to me, Oh My God… more… more… More"! Eli was flooded with avalanche of her orgasm as her hips raised off the bed and her screaming out in climaxing pleasure. He smiled knowing he had her right where he wanted her as he gripped his hands on the cheeks of her butt and dove in deeper until she exploded again and again and again.

From that point on Eli knew he had the impassioned woman in the palm of his hands as he moved up lavishing his wet face between her large breasts. With her still recovering from the shutters of lingering orgasms she looked down seeing her magnificent stud ravaging her nipples with his mouth. He reached up and spun her over on top of him as he latched into her hips guiding them till his rock-hard erection penetrated her wanting wet opening. She eased down with her moans echoed off the walls of her private apartment. "Now let yourself go, every erotic thought, every sensuous desire, every wild fantasy, let them out Now"! Eli saw her eyes roll back as her hands began to fondle her massive breasts. Her hips thrusting back & forth faster as she pushed down deeper till, she had Eli completely inside her. His fingers buried hard into her ass cheeks as he pushed her harder saying, "Yes, now take it all my hot slut! Want it, need it, crave it! Say it... you want it all don't you my bitch"? Her voice could barely utter the words, "Yes... yes, I'm your slut bitch... I want it all"! Eli gave her a stern look and in a commanding voice asked, "Who owns you now"? She innocently spoke, "You do my lord"! He came back immediately, "I'm Not your lord I'm your Master now my nasty fuck slave! From now on you do exactly as I command you"! She knew he was right as she quickly replied, "Yes, my master, my life is yours to command"! That was what Eli was waiting for as he took her through one massive climax after another till see laid in the soaked bed totally spent.

The lessons at the Crimson Garter were paying off. Eli had penetrated the deep recesses of Lanora's sexual mind. An area that no one had even come close to in her 33 years. He knew all the philandering her husband had be doing was pent up inside her with growing frustration. Now she had a pleasurable way to let it all out while extracting her own special revenge. She curled up in her new master's arms as they relaxed with some champagne and pillow talk. With her face buried in his chest she softly & sincerely asked," Did you mean what you said before? Are you my master now"? He asked back, "Is that what you truly want? Think before you answer... and put your passion aside"! She was silent for a moment, adhering every word he said then spoke, "You opened doors inside me I once thought were strictly taboo. Now it's all I can think about, and I want to experience it all. Yes, you're my master now if you'll have me"! They both knew she wasn't speaking about love; she secretly fantasized about a life of pure sexual fulfillment and be the right man's sex slave, with no holds barred ever again.

She began to tell the tale of her life with Ervin II and how lecherous he was like his father. Because she was blood kin to the queen with her own title as Baroness Winston, both her husband and father-in-law were barely allowed to remain in court. She spoke of the possible arranged marriage the viscount was pushing for between his second son Reginal and her only daughter Elinore. Lanora was totally against it for several reasons, mainly because the 2nd son was a copy of his father and older brother. Her and Elinore had many intimate talks about it, so she knew her 15-year-old daughter hated him and the entire Ervin family including her father. There was something else as she hesitated to say it to her new master. She eventually revealed she knew firsthand that her daughter's sexual desires varied from other than men. Devouring all this information, Eli had a clear picture now of their situation. As much as she would relish divorcing the asshole she couldn't. Under British royal law, if she left him, he would retain everything including her estate and inheritance. Lanora would lose her title and privileges as a member of the royal court. Of course, there was the possibly Lanora could find herself in the same situation as the widow Lady Belinda Winslow. Eli planted the valuable information deep in the back of his mind for now as he learned more from his talkative wench, including why the viscount was anxious to talk business with the Count Maschione.

She explained that the viscount had a man on the inside in Antwerp and knew about the diamonds from Pantelleria Island and wanted in on it. Especially since the cave in disaster in West Africa combined with the attacks from the Spanish ships on Ervin's convoys. He had invested nearly everything into the African mine and was close to his wits end. He couldn't ask the king for help since the venture was unauthorized by the crown. Eli was cracking up laughing on the inside as she spoke about it all. "They actually fell for the lies hook, line & sinker"! He thought to himself. What a bunch of royal dumbasses! Before Lanora fell asleep from pleasurable exhaustion, Eli got dressed and removed one of her personalized blue garters from her leg saying, "This one is mine now! I want to see more colors on you in the future. The stockings & garters fit your new persona perfectly"! He added that the French make some very exotic corsets and lingerie. "I want to see you in them when we meet again"! She grinned with a naughty look and said, "Yes, my Master, as you command...anything you say"! He leaned down and planted a farewell kiss on her lips and told her he would see her again very soon.

It was raining as Eli stepped into his waiting carriage and headed back to the brig just after 2 am. When the coach arrived, he handed the soaked driver a 5-pound note and said, "That is for you my good man, and I'm sure you'll remember nothing of this fare"! As they both smiled the driver tipped his hat and said, "Absolutely me lord, I was never here". Noah and Wolf had the watch as Eli walked aboard. They could see their captain had a quite eventful evening as they walked into the cabin to discuss it all with the rest of the brothers who woke up for a detailed account of the royal events. Tohru fired up the stove and made them some hot coffee as they picked on some leftover bread and cheese from the feast the night before. When the palace Captain arrived around 7 am, they quickly loaded up the wagon with 12 cases of the Pantelleria wine. He handed Everwyn, the acting cargo officer, 500 pounds sterling and thanked him on behalf of the king.

A few hours later they sailed out of London into the English Channel on an overcast day in mid-September. During the 36-hour run the entire crew went over the second phase of the plan before docking in Bristol. Now that the De La Regla was widely known in the area it was particularly important to continue the charade in the home port of the Royal Shipping Lines Company. "No one is to leave the ship while we are in port and absolutely no one allowed aboard. I will meet with Mister Asshole alone and see what he has on his lecherous little mind", Eli stated as everyone agreed. He added that no provisions be brought aboard since the ship was well stocked and didn't need to take any unnecessary risks in a port they didn't trust.

Rain drenched the docks as they tied up in Bristol on September 16th and quickly posted the watch. Noah met with the harbor master to relay their orders to him and to send a message to Viscount Ervin that Count Maschione will be at his office within the hour. A coach was made available for the short ride to the Royal Shipping Line office in town. Dressed in his gray uniform, Eli was happily greeted by the pudgy owner as he arrived an hour later. They sat down in the large ornate office as Ervin spoke," Thank you for coming so soon sir, I wasn't expecting you to respond this fast. I would have had something special arranged for you". With a business look in his eye, Eli replied," That isn't necessary, you said you wanted to talk business so let us get down to it, I'm only in port for the day and my time is precious".

The stout man leaned back in his chair saying, "Very well, I like a man who is direct. I understand your island has recently uncovered some quality uncut diamonds". Eli reached into his jacket pocket and placed a small one on his desk saying, "You mean something like this"? Ervin's eyes lit up at the sight of the thumb nail sized gem. "Yes...yes that's what I'm talking about"! As his fat fingers twirled the stone around in his hand. "So, what is on your mind sir?" Ervin thought for a moment and said, "I'd like to personally invest in a possible mining venture there for a percentage of the yield". Eli pulled out a folded note and handed it to Ervin saying, "I anticipated that was what you had in mind. There you will see the estimated cost for equipment, manpower & materials needed as well as time factor", 50,000 pounds.

From the captured paperwork the brothers had gathered off of Ervin's ships he had a rough idea what was spent on the African mining disaster. Not counting the loss of ships, Ervin had spent around 35,000 pounds of his own money. In order to maintain his court status, he had been forced to dip into the company funds that was governed by the British crown. Embezzlement was a nasty word but that was exactly what he had done assisted by his equally lecherous accountant, Ervin II. They were in too deep by now to stop so it was imperative this deal was made as soon as possible. The problem was Ervin didn't have 50,000 pounds without totally liquidating the shipping line.

The viscount explained he didn't have that much on hand at the moment but could probably raise it in a few weeks or so. "I can give you 25,000 now and the rest within a month at most". Eli agreed on the condition payment be made in gold since it would be easier to fund the venture on the island. "I will have the papers drawn up immediately. When I return, please have the gold ready. I assume your bank here has the sufficient bars to complete our transaction". Ervin nodded as he stood to shake the count's hand before he left. Eli got back to the ship and had Darin carefully work up a set of forged papers that showed Viscount Ervin investment of 25,000 pounds and now owned 25% of all diamonds mined from Pantelleria Island as of September 16th, 1760. Signed & sealed by Count Ricardo Maschione, Viceroy to Pantelleria Island.

3 hours later he returned accompanied by his armed guards, Noah and Marino. Once Ervin put his signature and stamp on the documents, they carefully counted the fifteen 400-ounce gold bars and loaded it on the carriage to return to the ship. He handled a duplicate copy of the transaction to the overjoyed fat man and said he would return in roughly a month for the balance and a complete update on the progress. With everything loaded they wasted no time sailing out of Bristol for the short trip to the safety of Liberty. Sitting in their cabin the brothers marveled over the lie they pulled off as they gazed at the 15 gold bars, compliments of Viscount Dumbass. The bars were stamped at the bottom end with the British bank seal along with each one's troy ounce weight. Once they reached Liberty, Wolf would add the finishing touch to them.

The town's people greeted the brig as she quietly slipped into the dock around 2 am. The crew wasted no time changing her over to the regal looking Dutch "Sea Stallion". The hull was repainted in dark blue along the cannon line striping with beige trim top and bottom of it. The massive black stallion figurehead was mounded to her bow as they fixed the ornate painted name plate to the stern. 3 new stern lanterns were set in to replace the 2 older ones. The large Dutch crested main sail was fixed into place for that final touch before hoisting the elaborate silk coat of arms flag of their new Danish captain, Count Elijah Studman. With the town forge fired up to full capacity, Wolf heated up the cast iron stamp Darin had made and branded in the Dutch crest on all 15-gold bars. They spent the next few days in Liberty till everything was ready and the ship was reprovisioned for the 2 weeks plus voyage to Palermo to have a chat with King Ferdinand III of Sicily.

Dark of the moon on September 23rd they crept out of Liberty headed south into the Atlantic. With the stormy hurricane season coming to a close the brig dealt with heavy seas and trailing winds for the first

5 days till things calmed somewhat as they made their way into the Straits of Gibraltar. Course was altered due to some minor repairs needed to the rigging as they headed for Pantelleria. The quiet port was happy to see the Dutch royalty arrived as they unloaded needed supplies of rice, corn & wheat they had aboard to spare. Darin put together a set of phony documents to be sent off to Palermo on one of the larger fishing boats hired to take it. While they did repairs it gave ample time to let Ferdinand know about an unexpected regal visit within the week.

A day and a half later, Ferdinand received the papers and was informed of a magnificent brig clearly owned by Dutch royalty that was headed for Palermo to discuss some vital business that would be financially beneficial for both parties. They waited in port to ensure the message was delivered and accepted before sailing to the capital city of Sicily. Morning tide of October 10th the Sea Stallion majestically sailed off northeast for the 180 nautical mile trip to Palermo. Fair weather and a brisk tail wind found them docking in the busy port the following afternoon to a curious crowd gathered to have a firsthand look at Dutch royalty. The city fort saluted the vessel with a full 21-gun salute much to the delight of smartly uniformed crew including a now bearded Count Studman who was sporting his dark blue custom uniform trimmed in burnt orange and beige pipping.

With the port's best soldiers assigned as honor guard on the dock, the crew went through their well-rehearsed routine. The king's palace general saluted and informed the well-groomed count that he was honored to escort him to the royal castle, "King Ferdinand III is very anxious to meet you your grace". Eli thanked him as he boarded the coach joined by Noah, Marino, Wolf & Everwyn as a locked heavy chest was placed aboard. The streets were lined with cheering onlookers all the way to the castle entrance as Eli waved to the peasant crowd. Many in wore tattered clothing as a foreground to the small shops & businesses that looked somewhat beleaguered. It was what the brothers had expected from the tales they heard of the island country in desperate need of help to their declining economy. They were in a prime position now to pull off the most profitable lie yet.

As they made their way into the castle, Eli noticed the average décor of the king's surroundings in comparison to that of the elaborate one in England. But the 5 brothers knew it was still important to accord the king all the respect to his position. After the usual regal introductions Ferdinand said, "All of Sicily is pleased to have you here Count Studman... surprised but pleased. I understand you are here to discuss some business with me". Bowing Eli replied, "Yes, your majesty, but only at your personal convenience". Understanding his meaning, the king dismissed his royal entourage so they could speak privately. Wasting no time Eli got right to the point, "I am interested in Pantelleria Island your majesty. As you know the Netherlands is not a hostile nation, neither am I. I have explored all 32 square miles of the island and would like to make it my new home. With my financial support I know I can bring a better life to the people there while making a good life for myself and my men".

He could see the king was definitely interested, especially since Pantelleria wasn't bringing in much money for him. "It is true Pantelleria Island is one of my more spectacular islands under my rule. The export of its exquisite wine is a lucrative part of my revenue. What is it you have in mind Count"? Eli unlocked the chest his officers had carried in to reveal it filled with 15 shining gold bars. "This represents 26,500 British pounds sterling or 2.65 million liras". The brothers watched the king's eye light up with delight as he pondered the lucrative offer. Moments later he made a counteroffer that he would agree to, a 10-year contract for 3.5 million liras with the option for another 10 years at the same cost. It was evident to the brothers that Ferdinand was more than interested as Eli agreed with the stipulation that he retain all resource and mineral rights from the island extending out 50 nautical miles around.

Eli ordered is officers to head back to the ship and return with the 8,500 pounds in British gold coin to complete the transaction. "And have Darin work up the appropriate documents for King Ferdinand III & me to sign". They saluted and quickly left as Eli followed the king on a tour of his castle before sitting down to a quickly prepared meal. Within two hours they returned accompanied by Darin carrying the Studman stamp. As everything was carefully read; the 2 men signed & sealed the official contract making both very happy. Ferdinand knew he now had the money to start Sicily back on their economic recovery path if he didn't squander it first as his family had done repeatedly in the past. As for the brothers, they could hardly believe they now owned Pantelleria Island thanks in part to their shrewd young leader. The brig was reprovisioned along with needed supplies for the people of their new island as they sailed out the next morning.

The Sea Stallion quietly docked in her new home port around 3 pm the following day with everyone busy at their usual tasks. Eli instructed the town mayor to gather up the island folks for an important announcement. All the cargo was offloaded and kept on the dock till the town meeting was held the next morning as the word was spread. Eli instructed the mayor to prepare the festivities to be held at dock side of the Sea Stallion. The old Italian official was a bit confused but quickly obeyed Eli's order as everything was ready before daybreak. On the Bright Sunday morning, the bulk of the inhabitance had gathered up to appease their curiosity. Eli stood atop the gangway of the brig with eager ears awaiting him to speak, "I asked you all here to make an official announcement". He unrolled the royal scroll and read, "On this day October 14th, 1760, the Island of Pantelleria is now officially governed and owned by Viceroy Elijah Studman. Signed, King Ferdinand III, sovereign ruler of Sicily". The crowd was quiet, unsure of how this transfer of power affected them till Eli explained. "From this day forth, there will be No taxes collected on the island. Each business, large or small will retain 100% of its revenue. The Island treasury will be funded strictly by export trade from outside countries with 10% going into the island fund. Starting with all this cargo you see here, every bit of supplies my ships bring in is considered property of Pantelleria Island, thus free of charge". The crowd burst into a resounding uproar of cheers as Eli signaled the new flag of the island be hoisted, the coat of arms flag of Viceroy Studman.

The celebration went on throughout the entire day and well into the night. The entire crew was treated with the utmost respect and admiration from the mayor down to the most common worker. The following day they all were back at their usual tasks, a little hung over and a lot happier than before. Over the next few days, the brothers met with the various city officials to go over plans to properly oversee their island paradise. With the flag ship of Pantelleria fully stocked with wine, capers, olives, lemons and more they sailed out letting the people know they would return before Christmas. 6 crates of black coral and 100 pearls were also purchased at the agreed 50% wholesale price as their Viceroy generously deposited 100,000 liras in the island treasury. Everwyn charted a course for Bristol so Count Maschione could collect the second half of the gold bars before Ervin learned of the new owner of his fictious diamond mine.

CHAPTER 9

Black and White

Changing over to the De La Regla while at sea they returned to Bristol on November 1st in record breaking time thanks to a strong tail wind they picked up on the Atlantic route. Eli immediately heard the news of the death of King George II on October 25th as all of England still was in morning. The throne was taken over by his 22-year-old grandson George III. Wasting no time Eli met up with the viscount to express his condolences and take of some business. Ervin told him he had almost all of the second payment ready for him. The now clean-shaven count spoke up saying, "It seems you are short by 5 bars sir, our agreement was for 15 not 10", as he checked them carefully. The look on the fat man's face was one of desperation. Eli knew he had milked Ervin dry figuring he had sold off all he could and probably even mortgaged his estate to come up with the money so far. His only reply was, "I'm sorry sir I need more time, I know I can raise the balance. I am waiting for my main ship to arrive from the colonies with more than enough funds to cover the difference".

He went on to explain the Carrack had the British Crown appointed tax collector on board and is due to arrive within a week or so. Eli knew the ship all too well having seen it docked in Charleston several times. She carried 20 cannons along with a platoon of British troops to help safeguard the tax collections from Savannah to Boston. It would usually have a military escort while making the coastal run through the colonial ports but would make the Atlantic crossing solo with a final stop in Cork, Ireland before docking in Bristol. Eli told him he had pressing business in Antwerp and would be back for the rest of the gold in 7 days. They agreed as Eli had the 10 bars loaded in his coach and left to relay the information on to his brothers. They set sail that night to slip into Liberty under the cover of darkness.

Like all of the Royal Shipping Line vessels, Darin knew all too well they had a set route they would take going and coming from the new world. If the Carrack was on course, she should be approaching the southern tip of Ireland approximately 20 nautical miles of the coastline. The plan was to use the Ketch disguised as a British Naval ship and meet up with the Carrack before she ported in Cork. Hardy doctored up a half a dozen barrels of fresh water with his special ingrediencies. Darin drew up an official dispatch that proved a serious threat of Smallpox had hit Cork, possibly brought in from a few ships that had carried it from Boston or New York. Posing as British Naval doctors, Hardy and Everwyn would have the Carrack dump their remaining drinking water and replace it with the 6 barrels.

Meanwhile, Eli would sail the De La Regla to Antwerp with Darin, Tohru and his usual crew while the rest manned the Ketch. Before the sun came up Eli set sail as the rest stayed to get the Ketch ready. The following night the British Ketch snuck out of Liberty to hopefully meet up with their target. Following the course Darin laid out they sighted the Carrack 2 days later about 50 miles off the southern tip of Ireland just before dust. Closing within 500 yards they hailed the slow-moving ship, "Ahoy Royal Star, I'm Captain Hardy of his majesty's medical corps, I have vital information of a pending epidemic of Smallpox in the port of Cork. It is possible it came from Boston, and you may be carrying it as well. We have clean drinking water for your crew. It is imperative you dump your remaining water supply overboard". The reply came back quickly, "Thank you Captain Hardy, I will dump it immediately".

The Ketch crew and officers were all wearing protective cloth masks as they cautiously rowed the 6 barrels over to the halted Carrack in their long boat. As Hardy, Everwyn, Noah & Marino boarded they explained it was essential every man have a full ration of water before setting sail while the 4 doctors checked the captain and his crew for any signs of the spreading disease. When the last of the 82 crewmen had been given the water, their captain drank his ensuring the entire ship had been served. Moments later he joined them in a deep restful sleep. The brothers quickly went through the entire ship to make sure everyone was taken care of. Noah signaled the Ketch to come along side to complete their mission. Minutes later the 2 ships sat tied up together in the dark of night as they stripped the remaining cargo and supplies including the 20 cannons.

Marino and Noah gutted everything in the captain's cable including the chest containing over 8,000 pounds of crown gold coins from the taxes collected in the colonies. Every bit of paperwork including the ship's logbook was taken while the crew finished up loading the Ketch. They stripped down the still unconscious 82 and moved them all below in the empty cargo holes. With the deck hatches locked down everyone returned to the Ketch and cut loose the lines. The last to board was Hardy who had set a powder keg charge in the stern hole below the captain's cabin. As the Ketch drifted away, they hear the explosion and saw the ass end light up. Fire spread quickly below decks as the silent Carrack began to sink stern first. Sails set full they headed off slowly peering at the massive ship ablaze until the bow disappeared into the black waters of the Atlantic.

In Antwerp, Eli sold off the remaining uncut diamonds the brothers had in their treasury. Including the interest accumulated, Count Maschione now had 66,600 pounds sterling in his account. They left to sail to London to make an essential appearance and sell some cargo to the jeweler as well as off load some wine the young new king would enjoy. An hour or so after they docked, a representative of the king arrived at dockside to see if there was anything the count needed while in port. He had 12 cases of the rare vintage loaded on the royal carriage with a message to his majesty, "Please enjoy this as an early holiday gift from me your majesty". Using the coach put at his disposal Eli headed for jewelry shop to take care of business there.

The old craftsman was delighted to see his best supplier as they sat down to chat and enjoy some of the Pantelleria wine Eli brought for him. It seemed the jeweler's business was booming with the latest creations he had made for several of the ladies of court. Eli had a special request for him as he produced the large pink tear drop shaped pearl, he had hung on to until now. "I'd like this made into a simple choker with a color matching pink ribbon". The jeweler nodded quickly and said that it would be very easy to do. "No rush I will pick it up from you when I return again in a month or so".

Eventually they got down to business as Eli sold 4 of the 12 cases of black coral as well as 80 white pearls & 40 black ones to the elated man. The total came to 5,100 pounds as they headed to the London Crown bank to make the exchange. Eli requested he be paid in the bank's gold bars this time as 3 stamped bars were handed over. The 2 men departed with Eli heading back to his ship. A few hours later a courier arrived with a letter addressed to Count Maschione. It read, "My Lord and Master, I anxiously await you at my apartment if you can". Signed, your eternal servant, Lanora. He quickly wrote a reply for the familiar looking coachman that he would be there within an hour or so.

With young Elinore attending ladies' private school in London, her mother had the perfect excuse to maintain the secluded apartment there. Ervin II was content with having his wife and daughter out of his hair while he played about at their palatial home in Bristol. The only time the family came together was for occasional court functions at the palace or when the viscount called a gathering at his estate. The distance allowed Elinore to stay clear from amorous advances of her uncle Reginal who was itching to make their engagement official backed by the viscount and her own father. Even at this time in history, many royal families felt the need to arrange incestual marriages to keep the "royal blood" as pure as possible and maintain their name in sovereign line of rule.

Eli was met at the door by his carnal lass, clad in a blood red corset and stocking. Her golden garters reflecting off her milky white thighs and wearing a pair of gold heeled slippers. As he closed the door, she curtsied low before him and gracefully dropped to her knees with her head bowed down softly saying, "Welcome my sweet Master". He reached down to cup his hand on her chin and lifted her erotically painted face as she rose with his grip to savor a long desired wet kiss. Together they climbed the staircase to her bedroom where chilled champagne and caviar awaited them. She assumed her sensuous position on the satin sheeted bed as he opened the bottle and poured out two glasses of the sparkling wine. Once disrobed he climbed in next to his sultry wench for a night of pleasure.

Few words were spoken as their mouths stayed occupied with the enjoyment of each other's lusty bodies. Several minutes later Eli settled on his back amid the plush pillows as Lanora perched herself on her knees between his open legs as she slowly devoured him inch by inch with a mouth full of champagne as an added erotic touch. From the corner of his eye, he saw a shadow slowly move across the crack at the bottom of the closed bedroom door. His first instinct was to grab for his knife he kept close by. Lanora hearing to creek of the wooden floor, she quickly looked back over her shoulder then turned to her master whispering, "Relax my master, it's just my daughter Elinore. She is at that curious age and I told her she could watch... if that is already with you of course".

He thought it over and spoken in a commanding voice, "Elinore come in here"! A few seconds passed till the door slowly opened. The timid teenager crept in wearing a soft pink nightgown and nothing more as Eli could see through it from the light reflexing behind her. As she closed the door she innocently asked, "Are you sure it's alright"? Her mother, still on her knees with her master's erection in her hand nodded and said, "Yes dear, come in and make yourself comfortable". She settled down on the edge of the bed as her mother visually instructed her on the art of fellatio. Eventually the young student felt comfortable enough to disrobe as the 2 teachers took her though the basics of sex education. Lanora eventually explained to her master that the 2 ladies had spent private time discussing this erotic scenario in hopes it would eventually come to pass. Elinore was at the age she needed to take her first step toward knowing who she was and what she desired.

Deep into the night, Elinore was schooled about the pleasures of erotic sex that went far beyond the typical baby making fornication. A few hours later, the 3 relaxing together in pleasurable silence till the glowing young lass said, "I know one thing for sure now... there is no way Reginal could ever please me like this"! They burst into laughter in total agreement with the newest member of the sexual human race. The discussion turned to mother and daughter bantering back & forth on how to deal with the pressure being put on them about the pending engagement. Both the viscount and Ervin II were pushing to have it officially announced at the annual royal holiday ball in early December. Listening carefully, Eli chimed in, "I think I have a solution to your problem! It seems there are two obstacles that are keeping both of you from living your life as you see fit... both named Ervin"! The women nodded as Lanora added, "Precisely, but what can we do about it"? Elinore looking down ashamed said, "I know it's my father & grandfather, but I wish they we dead... they have made our life a living hell for as long as I can remember. The only time mommy & I are happy is when they are far from us like now". Agreeing with her tearful daughter, Lanora reached over to comfort her as she kissed her tears away. Seeing this sincere act of tenderness and emotion, Eli decided to trust the 2 beleaguered women.

"I have already put a plan into motion that will put a permanent end to them both, but I need your help to carry it out. If I put my trust in you, both of you must trust me without question". Both women now hung on every word their master uttered. He explained that merely killing them off wasn't enough to wipe out the name. It had to come from the king's decree to eliminate the title once and for all without involving either of them. As for Reginal, he had plans for him. The youngest son wasn't exactly the brightest candle in the family chandelier. He was given the menial job with the family company as official protocol liaison. His job was to send out letters to business associates while screening all incoming mail before it got to his father. He shared the office in Bristol with his older brother who kept the private account ledger book locked in his safe. It was true the elder was smart enough hold down the accounting position in the shipping line company, but his father was still hesitant to fully confide in him about certain things, like the investment in the Pantelleria resources and the failed diamond mine catastrophe in Africa. Eli had to be sure about his presumption and the hidden ledger book would tell the true tale. The plan was let the family think both mother & daughter was now in favor of the engagement announcement. This would relax things in the Ervin family minds. Lanora knew if the viscount and his 2 sons were eliminated the business and estates would go to her since Lady Winslow had passed away 3 years before.

Eli worked out the remaining details with his 2 nude cohorts before eventually getting dressed to leave. Sliding off one of Lanora's gold garters, he smiled and said, "My usual souvenir my slave bitch"! Elinore hopped out of bed and said, "Wait one second, I'll be right back", as she raced off to her bedroom. A minute later she stood at the doorway wearing only a pair of light pink garters on her blushing thighs. Eli motioned her in as she sat back down on the bed to allow him to remove the one of his choosing. "So, am I your slave bitch now too my master"? Looking at Lanora who was grinning proudly he answered the teen, "No... not yet! Consider me your erotic instructor and your mother is now your sex mistress. You are just starting your training"! As they all smiled & laughed knowing he wasn't far from the truth. During the short coach ride back to the ship, he reflected on the past hours and was confident he had acquired 2 new allies who would do anything he said, in or out of bed.

On the morning tide, they sailed out bound for Liberty to rejoin the brothers and see how they all faired on their mission. Following his instructions, mother & daughter prepared to journey by coach back to their home in Bristol and put the plan into motion. A late-night chill from an early winter rain covered the brig as she pulled into Liberty greeted by all. The ketch had already been unloaded with its cargo handed out to the town. 10 of the 20 captured cannons were now mounted on the deck of the Miss Fortune giving her the original 18 guns she had before the ship was taken. The entire crew sat down exchanging the details of both successful ventures as they planned the next move. Darin had some work ahead of him drawing up some official documents that should put another nail in the viscount's coffin. Wolf and Hardy had a little blacksmithing task ahead of them. Using one of the London Crown Bank gold bars as a pattern, they would melt down one a spare iron cannon and forge up 25 bars of phony gold using Hardy's matching fool's gold mixture. Darin was instructed to make replicas of the seal stamps on them in order they be clearly seen when carefully inspected. The rest prepared to sail back to Bristol for Eli's scheduled meeting with Ervin and finalize the Pantelleria charade.

Using the evening cover of darkness, the De La Regla sailed out to time their arrival around mid-morning as the winter breezes of early November were upon them. Once docked Eli Met up with the fat man at his office and immediately noticed a look of distress on his face. He explained that he didn't have the balance he owned at the moment. With a disappointed look the count said, "I think we need to renegotiate our agreement. Since you have contributed 25 gold bars already, I recommend a new contact be drawn up giving you 40% of the venture rather than the original 50%. The alternative is I will refund your entire investment and we part ways". Ervin immediately replied, "No, no… the 40% is more than fair sir. I greatly appreciate your generous patience and offer". Eli stood up and said he would have the revised contact drawn up for him to sign later that afternoon. "I'll need the old contact now to have my script alter it properly". Ervin quickly opened his hidden wall safe and handed it to the count as he left quickly. Eli took his waiting coach back to the brig and relaxed for a few hours since he already had the new document Darin had worked up in Liberty. This one stated, "As of November 9th, 1760, Viscount Ervin, of Royal Shipping Lines Company owns 40% of the natural land recourses mined from Pantelleria Island for the sum of 25 gold bars averaging 400 troy ounces per bar". Eli signed and seal stamped it, Count Ricardo Maschione. 3 hours later, Eli returned to a much happier man who had been celebrating with a liquid lunch. He greeted the count's return offering him a glass of wine that he had put a serious dent in already. Without carefully reading the new contract he quickly signed them both and locked away his copy in the safe as he turned and said, "I am so thrilled we finally got that done sir; this has turned out to be a very good day for me".

He went on to explain that while the count was gone, news of his son's engagement came in. "My youngest son Reginal and his new fiancé Elinore came in to bring me the great news. My elder son Ervin II and his lovely wife Lanora were with the happy couple to confirm it all". The count briefly smiled and said, "I guess congratulations are in order for you & your family. Please pass along my best wishes to them all". Obviously feeling the effects of the wine, the fat man invited the count to a celebration dinner he was having later that night at his estate. Eli paused a moment before replying, "I suppose I could attend it since I'm not scheduled to sail until tomorrow morning". Ervin was overjoyed and said he would have a coach pick him up at the docks later that evening. Eli walked out confident that his 2 ladies had completed the first step of their mission.

An hour coach ride had Eli showing up at the massive estate outside of Bristol in the small hamlet of Kingwood. He brought a case of his fine Pantelleria wine as a token gift for the invitation that everyone greatly appreciated to see. It was a small gathering of a dozen people, mostly family and a few close friends as they sat down to dine and chat mainly about the upcoming plans for the family arranged marriage. As was customary for events like this, it was agreed the official engagement announcement would be given at the palace annual Christmas ball scheduled for December 8th. The viscount extended a personal invitation to the count adding, "I sincerely hope you are able to attend, my family would deem it an honor sir". Eli nodded and said, "Thank you, I will do my best to find time for it". Before he left, Lanora managed to hand Eli a folded note without the others seeing it. On the coach ride back to his ship he opened it to find the combination to Ervin II safe in his office. The ladies accomplished the second part perfectly as the plan was falling into place.

At sunrise the De La Regla sailed off into the channel and arrived at dusk back at Liberty. The crew was delighted to hear they would lay over there while preparations were completed for the next step on the ladder of revenge. It took a few more days to get the phony gold bars produced and stored away on the brig. The crew split up to do some needed repairs on the ketch and brig while others helped out in the ever-growing village. Eli took a small crew in the De La Regla over to Cork to sell some of the remaining wine and have a new outfit made for the upcoming ball in London. Eli figured it was time for the count to make a change in his appearance with a trimmed moustache and an edged pointed jaw goatee to give that mature regal look.

While the crew enjoyed the relaxing fortnight in Liberty, it gave them a chance to tell the villagers about Pantelleria Island in detail. It seemed a few found it an intriguing place to relocate including Sage. He was content there but had that adventurous look in his eyes, as did a few others who pondered the thoughts of becoming fishermen. The brothers were already planning to move the ketch to their island paradise after the Christmas ball so there would be plenty of room aboard both ships for passengers. With some of them more acclimated to hotter climate being born in the humid regions of Western Africa, the thought of a warmer place to live added to their decision to leave Liberty. But they had plenty of time to decide since the voyage wasn't happening for another 10 days or so.

The full crew sailed back to Cork on December 2nd to pick up Eli's tailor-made outfits and exchange some supplies for Liberty. As the ship docked it seemed there was a small crowd gathered in the trading area. One of the Dutch East Indies ships was forced to port there due to some serious hull damage they had. The ship was coming from the African coast bound for the colonies to sell off its cargo of slaves when it encountered a freak storm off the French coast. Cork was the closest port to pull into for repairs so the captain decided to try and sell off whatever human cargo he could since over half had already perished on the journey. As Eli and some of the brothers approached the trading block, they quickly noticed the bulk of the slaves were young females, mostly in their teens. The local bidders seemed more interested in the stronger black men for their labor use.

Eli quickly gathered the brothers up and decided to throw their hat in the bidding ring considering they were being sold off for about 10 pounds each. It took no time for the crowd to see the regal dressed young man was buying up the black lassies. When all was said and done, the brothers escorted 16 females back to the brig as Everwyn was instructed to pay the auctioneer the total sum of 120 pounds. Abel was standing at attention at the gangway with an amazed look in his eyes at the cargo coming aboard. Eli commanded, "Boatswain, please take these ladies below... clean them up and get them some decent things to wear. Doctor Hardy please look after them... and get those fucking shackles off them immediately. Mister Tohru feed them please". The women who could understand what their new owner was saying were astounded and quickly interpreted his commands to the rest.

Once below decks, Abel explained to the new passengers the situation, "You all are safe now this is a freedom ship so just relax and let us take care of you". 16 deep sighs of relief came out almost in unison as they were tended to. Eli and Noah headed back to town to finalize their cargo trade and eventually head to the tailor shop. One of the Irish dock workers overheard Eli's orders. As he walked past him Eli heard the worker mutter, "fuckn' nigger lover"! He turned silently and got face to face with the loudmouth and replied, "You have a big mouth for such a little asshole"! The Irishman reached for his knife at his side but before he could pull it from its scabbard the quick handed captain stopped it with one hand as his other was wrapped around the insolent man's throat and was squeezing the breath out of him. One of the town guards saw this and raced over saying, "Is there a problem me Lord"? Eli replied, "Yes corporal, it seems this man needs a serious lesson in manners". As Eli stared deep into the trembling work's eyes and said, "Unless you demand satisfaction in which I will gladly accommodate you"! The chocking man shook his head no as the soldier grabbed him up and said, "I'll take care of this now me Lord, sorry for the inconvenience". As 2 other guards arrived to escort him to jail. Those who witnessed the brief scuffle parted the ways as Eli and Noah proceeded to complete their business in the Irish port.

They sailed out the next morning with 16 passengers cleaned up, fed and resting comfortably to make the return to Liberty. The crew had already felt a deep admiration for their captain, but the brothers noticed a bright gleam in every man's eyes now. They long since had their freedom and were well paid and taken care of. What had transpired in Cork had every man feeling a true sense of pride & loyalty knowing they would die for their gallant captain. It was the binding tie that would bring them all together as one no matter what the future would bring.

Back in Liberty the new arrivals were housed and properly clothed. The girls were amazed at the village of free black inhabitants and how well everyone was living. Darin went to work drawing up freedom papers for each of them while Eli handed over 220 pounds of profit to the town treasury for the goods sold in Cork. With the first fall of snow coating the village the girls were comfortably set up in one of the newly built barns till better housing was made available. Eli gave his crew the choice of staying in Liberty or traveling to London for the 2 days stay since it wasn't necessary for a full crew for the holiday joy ride there. Abel spoke up for them with him and 15 others deciding to take the trip as he jokingly said, "Who knows Captain, we might get treated to another royal feast"! Those staying said they would help out the newcomers all they could. As for the brothers they elected to make the return to merry Ole London town and "Make a serious dent in the taverns and brothels" as Hardy so eloquently put it.

Decked out in her most regal look the De La Regla arrived in snowy London on December 7th to its usual royal greeting. Eli wasted no time to head to his jeweler to do some last-minute trading for the remaining black coral and pearls they still had aboard and pick up the pink pearl choker. Delighted to see the count again the old craftsman sat down to share a bottle of delicious wine Eli brought with him along with 3 more bottles as an early Christmas gift for the old man. He had crafted the pink pearl jewel so that it could slide off easily since he added an array of various colored satin choker to the order. About a half hour into their chat & cheer the door to the shop opened. Eli turned to see a ravishing beauty clad in a rich fur lined floor length coat. It was Lady Belinda Winslow who was there to pick up a lavish necklace the jeweler had created for her. Delightfully stunned at sight of the count she immediately curtsied saying, "Oh your grace this is truly an unexpected pleasure to see you again". Eli quickly approached her and took her gloved hand and kissed it as he helped her up saying, "Oh no my Lady the pleasure is all mine. Please come join us for a glass of wine".

She hesitated at first saying, "I hope I am not interrupting anything I just wanted to pick up my necklace for the ball tomorrow night". The men both eased her mind that she was more than welcome to join them while the jeweler retrieved her creation. The 3 sat for a brief toast as she inquired, "Count I do hope you will be attending the ball". Eli smiled and told her, "I am looking forward to it my lady and I sincerely hope your dance card isn't filled this time... We are long overdue for that dance you promised me". He winked and gave the blushing woman a devilish grin. She gazed into his sparkling eyes and said in a sultry voice, "My dance card is yours my Lord", as she winked back. Moments later, with her business completed there she politely bid them a fond farewell and left. The old man saw the chemistry spark between the two and slyly remarked, "In the many years I have known her, that's the first time I've seen her smile that way since her husband died".

As Eli was recounting the 4,900 in pound notes from the exchange with the jeweler, his mind was calculating the following night's festivities. If Lanora & Elinore did as they were instructed to do, he could concentrate on an enjoyable campaign with a stunning widow. From what he could surmise about Lady Belinda, she wasn't the type to idly flirt without her desiring more in return. Add to the fact that the lecherous Ervin II would be thoroughly pissed off if Count Maschione swooped in and snagged his long-desired prey right out from under his turned-up aristocratic nose. On the coach ride back to the brig he sat and snickered murmuring to himself, "Yep, I think I'll see how far I can push the little bastard... this should be fun"!

Prior to returning to the ship, he made a stop at the dock side tavern & brothel to take care of the party for his brothers. He handed the bar owner and the madam 200 pounds each and told them to take good care of his crew when they arrive later that evening. He figured that should more than pay for a couple of fun filled nights for everyone. He added one more thing, "My crewmen are Tunisians, free men...not black slaves! They are to be treated with the same respect you would give any other sailor! I hope we understand one another perfectly". They both completely agreed with the highly respected count and assured him that both the tavern & brothel will be at their disposal.

Before boarding the gangway Eli spoke to the sergeant major who was in charge of honor guard posted dockside. "My officers & crew will be paying a visit to the "Ale n Tail" establishment while we are in port. Please see to it they are not disturbed"! As Eli briefly smiled at the grinning soldier who saluted and replied, "Yes me Lord I will see to it personally"! Eli told him to contact the palace quartermaster and have him come to the ship at his earliest convenance to pick up a dozen cases of wine he was gifting for the royal ball. The count snuck a 20-pound note in the jacket pocket of the burly sergeant and whispered, "When you and your men are off duty enjoy a round or two on me...Happy Christmas Sergeant Major"! "And the same to you your grace... thank you very much".

Once aboard he gathered the entire crew below deck and told them everything was arranged and paid for. "I suggest you all work out a rotating shift making sure there is a sober enough watch aboard at all times"! With everyone laughing. When the grateful Thank You's subsided Eli informed them he was staying aboard for the night to help out till the ball the follow evening. Noah slapped him on the back laughing and said, "You get your rest captain, you're gonna need it for tomorrow night"! To ensure everything went smooth, the brothers decided to split up and take half the crew with them to party in town while the other half had the watch till relieved. Before they disbursed Eli handed each crewman 50 pounds and gave every brother 100 pounds and simply said to them, "Call it an early Christmas gift".

About an hour later, the coach arrived with the quartermaster to have the 12 cases of wine loaded up and taken back to the palace to be chilled. He asked Noah, who had the watch, how many were aboard. Noah replied, "We have 41 officers and crew including the count". He knew not to divulge the real amount aboard just to be safe. The officer said the palace kitchen will prepare a dinner to be delivered for the entire crew within a few hours. "Please thank Count Maschione for the generous gift, I know the king will be especially delighted". Noah replied, "I will tell the count personally and please pass along the De La Regla's thanks to his majesty for the dinner as well as the entire kitchen staff".

The following day, with the entire crew well fed and well pleasured, they ventured into town to do some shopping, always keeping close to the docks per the orders of their captain. Late that afternoon a messenger arrived with a letter addressed to Count Ricardo Maschione from Lady Belinda. Eli strolled the deck as he read, "I look forward to our meeting tonight with great anticipation, sincerely yours, Belinda". Enclosed was a copy of her dance card with only one name on it, Ricardo. Eli stopped and looked at the messenger waiting on the dock. He walked down and quickly wrote a reply, "My dance card has but one name as well, a ravishing beauty named Belinda, graciously yours, Ricardo". He handed it to the courier who sped off to delivery it.

As he began to dress that evening, he stared at the captured portrait of raven-haired goddess hanging inside his clothes closet. The new outfit was custom made to entice Belinda in particular. A flowing black silk ruffled shirt topped off by his gold double headed eagle medallion around his neck attached to a red & grey stripped ribbon. His tight form fitting black pants had a wide red & grey stripe running down the sides that blended into his knee-high shiny leather boots. Around his waist was a wide blood red sash accompanied by a black leather belt to secure his shining custom sword and scabbard. The open waist jacket was deep red velvet trimmed in black piping and a cascading row of silver buttons down each side. His well-trimmed moustache and sharp-edged jaw goatee set perfectly with his long flowing hair pulled back neatly in a ponytail that went down past his shoulder blades.

Just before he put on his floor length black cloak there was a knock on his door. Noah entered along with the rest of his brothers including Abel. "Captain, you look splendid, but there is something missing", Noah slyly said. Eli knew they were up to something, and it probably was no good by the smiles on their faces. "Ok, let's hear it. What the hell are you guys up to now"? They snapped to attend as Darin unrolled the scroll in his hands and read it, "For conspicuous gallantry against our enemy we are honored to present you with The Order of the Double Cross"!

Noah stepped forward with the decoration Darin designed and Wolf, Tohru & Hardy created. It was a pearl white cross of Malta inside another gold one. At the center was hand painted the golden double headed eagle. It was attached to a 3-point ribbon stripped vertically in red and grey. He pinned it on Eli's jacket as they all saluted. Abel spoke up from the ranks proudly saying, "I speak for the entire crew Captain when I say we will follow you to hell and back"! Marino opened up a hidden compartment in Eli's cabinet to reveal 4 painted British flags with the initials RSLC (Royal Shipping Lines Company) inside 3 of them, the other one read BRN (British Royal Navy). "As we take more, I'll gladly add to our score Captain", as they all burst into laughter. "Thank you, my brothers, I am deeply honored but I couldn't have pulled off the double cross without each one of you sneaky sons of bitches"!

The palace carriage was waiting as the elegantly dressed count climbed aboard and headed to the holiday ball. The palace was teaming with festive attired members of the court and their guests. Eli told the driver to take his time as he soaked in the atmosphere and the light sprinkling of snow falling from the chilly night air. When he saw the long line of carriages slowly disappear from the entrance, he told the coachman to proceed. As they stopped, he handed him a 5-pound note and said, Happy Christmas go have a few on me". "Oh, thank you me lord and a Happy Christmas to you as well". Like a regal peacock, Eli strutted in and handed his cloak to the palace attendant. Adjusting himself carefully he walked in as if he owned the place.

The royal herald bellowed out, "Presenting his grace, Count Ricardo Maschione of Pantelleria"! Heads turned as a round of applause echoed through the ballroom. One of the first to greet him was the viscount who was happy to see him accept the invitation. Behind him was Reginal with his fiancé' Elinore at his side. Before they could speak Eli politely kissed her hand as she curtsied while he watched out of the corner of his eye, the buffoon's attempt to do a half ass bow with a drink in his hand. "May I express my sincere congratulations to you both". Elinore softly replied, "Thank you your grace, we are honored to have you here". All the idiot could muster out was, "Yes welcome sir". It was obvious that he and his father were already deep into the liquid celebration.

As they turned away, up stepped Ervin II and Lanora clad in a low-cut emerald, green gown and flashing a matching emerald and gold necklace that bounced off her full cleavage. Ervin II was touting a half empty champagne glass as he casually said, "Good to see you again sir... let me present my wife Lady Lanora". She was still at full curtsy when Eli took her gloved hand and kissed it royally and replied, "Ah yes Lord Ervin is it? And the always radiant Lady Lanora. A pleasure to see you all again". Smiling politely, she spoke, "Always an honor to see you your grace". Eli turned away curiously to allow some of the others waiting to express their best wishes to the happy couple.

Surrounded by admirers and hopeful suiters emerged the ravishing goddess dressed in a deep red velveteen gown trimmed in sparkling silver sequins and white fur. Her midnight black hair cascading over her bare shoulders and down her back. As their eyes locked in from across the room and slowly approached one another, he could see the elaborate black pearl and coral necklace gracing her V neck dress that adorned those blossoming full breasts. As they came closer, others could see just how perfectly they matched up in their chosen attire. Eli stopped and regally bowed in time with her majestic curtsy as she extended her hand tightly covered in her elbow length black satin gloves. His black wrist glove cupped in hers as he slowly kissed it while his thumb hidden inside her palm circled ever so slowly and sensuously. She looked up at him smiling as they winked slyly at one another.

"Lady Belinda words cannot describe the splendor you bring to such a stunning gown. Then again, I believe you could bring life to a burlap sack with all your nature beauty". They both chuckled as she rose to speak, "And may I say Count Ricardo your outfit puts everyone else to shame. But with your looks & physique I'd imagine you could make peasant rags look regal". He extended his right arm as she happily clasped it as they slowly strolled over to share a glass of holiday punch and chat. She leaned over and whispered, "You realize that every single lady here is absolutely green with envy of me right now... I love it". He leaned down replying, "Yep, but I'm loving the fact that every eligible bachelor here would kill to be in my boots right now. And the night is just getting started too".

Several minutes later the young king made his entrance to kick off the festivities. The announcement came from the herald of the royal betrothal of Reginal and Elinore moments later as they were presented to the king for his official approval. Eli watched intently at the face of new monarch as the engaged duo approached him. Eli saw a look of indifference in King George's eyes as if he was granting amnesty to a dying cow. He tried his best to show pleasure in the decision but like his dead grandfather it seemed he could care less by putting on a decent showing of happiness for the betrothed pair. As the King proclaimed their engagement official, Eli could feel Belinda's hand grip his forearm tight in a disagreeing cringe. All this noted now in his mind as it was time to discover all he could about Belinda.

As they took the floor, others watched the chemistry of their perfectly synchronized moves. It was almost second nature for them as they glided together in harmony while they gazed, smiled and became better acquainted with each other's lives. Eli quickly got his condolences out of the way about her loss as she thanked him and asked about Pantelleria Island. As they chatted Eli kept a watchful eye on the Ervin clan without Belinda noticing. He asked about her lineage knowing already how she was related in court.

He wanted to see and hear her personal reaction to being associated with the Ervin family. "Benjamin was first cousin to the late Lady Winslow, Viscount Ervin's wife. I'm second cousin on my father's side of the family. My parents died when I was 8 so I became a ward of the royal court. Like young Elinore, my marriage was arranged when I was 14 and we were married for 8 years before he passed away".

Eli stopped her saying, "I'm sorry Belinda I didn't mean to bring up the sadness of your past". She gazed into his deep hazel eyes and said, "no... no... it's quite alright, for the first time in years I feel comfortable talking about it. Maybe this is just what I needed, someone I can relax with and confide in". She smiled as he grinned back and told her to go on then. "Even though he was at sea most of the time I honestly felt I could learn to truly love him. We tried several times to have a baby, but the doctors eventually came to the conclusion I was incapable of it. When word came that he had died I went into morning because it was the traditional thing to do. It gave me time to think and grow inside. To see if I could discover my true self and identity. I suppose I was blessed with good looks for a reason, but I'll be damned if I know what they are", as they both laughed.

Soaking in every word and emotional inflection, Eli said knowingly, "Ask yourself this... have you ever truly felt love, deep sincere love"? She searched down to give him an honest answer then timidly said, "No! Honestly no I don't believe I ever have. For so long I have been trained and pushed to think and feel as others want me to. It's just been in the past year or so I have begun to act on my own and do as I see fit". She paused to smirk and say that it came out at first when she was angered and shoved into an emotional corner. Eli asked, "From a suiter who went too far"? She laughed sarcastically replying, "Definitely not a suiter I would desire chasing me". "Then I'd assume an older married man you find repulsive". She had that amazed look in her eyes saying, "How did you know?" He smiled and simply joked, "Lucky guess".

"Ricardo, you do know who it is, don't you"! Eli explained that he watched her the last time he was at court. He saw how she reaction to one man in particular who was there acting like a drunken idiot. She finally spoke, "Yes, my cousin by marriage, Ervin II. The thought of him makes my skin crawl with disgust. And how poor Lanora puts up with him is beyond me. Now sweet little Elinore is going to be saddled with that simpleton Reginal". This is exactly what Eli was wanting to hear from her lips. When the waltz ended, they walked arm in arm to get a glass of wine. "I got something I want you to try, it's a special vintage of sweet wine I brought for the ball from Pantelleria. I think you'll enjoy it, especially chilled". At the bar the count request 2 chilled glasses of the Pantelleria wine. The bartender said, "Right away me Lord". Once served they toasted as she slowly savored it. "Oh my God this is fabulous Ricardo. It's so sweet and easy on the pallet. It's like drinking in sweet clean air, I love it".

Belinda asked if he had a chance to view the palace yet. Eli said, "Not yet but I would like that very much". She smiled sweetly, took up his arm again and said, "Then let me give you the Royal tour me Lord... Free of charge", laughing happily. As they strolled away from the rest Eli eventually returned to the subject of the Ervin family asking, "So why does the king tolerate them? It's obvious, even to an outsider like myself that they don't fit in with true royalty, viscount included". Belinda answered back with one simple word, "Money! The viscount has made a lot of money over the years for King George through the shipping lines. But you're right, I've noticed lately he has become more disgruntled with the family for some unforeseen reason. If it was left up to me, I would oust the drunken lot into the channel. Well except for Lanora and Elinore of course". They laughed it off as Eli dropped the subject. He found out what he wanted to know and more.

They eventually returned to the main ballroom to dance and mingle with other friends of Belinda. Before the festivities ended an intoxicated Lord Ervin walked up to the armed couple and said, "How about a dance with me cousin"? Before she could reply the count stepped in and politely said, "Oh, so sorry Lord Ervin we are in the middle of a very deep conversation, maybe some other time"! Belinda tried her best to not burst out laughing and added, "Yes cousin, please forgive me we were just about to debate the ramifications of colonial independent control in comparison to the European economic expansion and how it effects the existing overall format". Dazed & confused the mindless drunk just waved his hand and staggered away. The two couldn't hold it any longer as they burst into laughter with Eli muttering under his breath, "God, what a dumbass"! Belinda barely heard it added, "Yep"!

As the ball ended Eli walked Belinda to her waiting carriage. She asked in a sincere tone, "So when will I see you again"? He explained he would be sailing out on the morning tide for Pantelleria to spend Christmas there. "You know you have an open invitation for the wedding in January, I will personally see to it you're put in the list... preferably as my escort if you like"? As he helped her into her coach he replied, "Belinda, I wouldn't have it any other way. It would be an honor & privilege to be your escort my sweet goddess". He leaned inside the coach and softly kissed her full moist lips as she cupped her hand around to gently grasp the back of his head. "And before I sail tomorrow, I'll send you a few bottles of that wine you like so much". She quickly wrote down the address as they said good night and wished one another a very Happy Christmas.

They caught the morning tide and set sail for Liberty to prepare for a fortnight voyage to Pantelleria Island and the holiday festival there. Once docked the crew immediately went to work to change over the brig to the Sea Stallion. The ketch was already transformed to the Dutch Studman colors and fully loaded with more than amply provisions. The 16 newcomers were looking much better having been cared for by the entire village. Sage was in charge of seeing who wanted to make the trip to the island paradise as he handed the list to Eli. It was comprised of 10 villagers including Sage, 6 men and 3 women. As for the 16 girls they all agreed to relocate to the much warmer climate to start a new and better life, jokingly saying they might open a brothel there if there wasn't one yet.

Wishing everyone a Happy Christmas the 2 ships sailed out on the chilly night of December 11th bound for the warmth of Pantelleria. They evenly split the crew with Noah in command of Miss Fortune and Eli at the helm of the Sea Stallion. Once they cleared the English Channel and hit the open warm waters of the Atlantic it was smooth sailing all the way into the Straits of Gibraltar. The passengers spent the bulk of their time on deck basking in the delightful weather as they watched in awe when the 2 ships docked in beautiful sunny Pantelleria on Christmas Eve morning. The entire town turned out to happily greet the Viceroy and his crew as the echoes of "Buon Natale" could be heard from miles around. There was a massive 20-foot-tall Christmas tree constructed and adorned with colorful decorations. Since there were no real evergreen trees on the island the town built one out of wood and painted it a brilliant shade holiday green.

Once the passengers left the ships, they began offloading tons of needed cargo and supplies. Among them was a surprise for the town, almost 2 dozen live boars and turkeys to be penned for breeding and eventual eating. The people of Pantelleria had been busy themselves with several new stone buildings appearing around the dock area. One of them was a hotel specifically built to house the crew while they were in port, free of charge of course. A fully operational blacksmith forge was setup including an enlarge furnish much to the delighted Wolf and Tohru. With all the growth the carpenter shop was expanded to almost double in size including the shipyard as well. Sage knew he had come to the right place as he would fit in perfectly there.

The crew noticed some stone construction at the mouth of the horseshoe shaped harbor entrance when they sailed in. The mayor smiled and said, "We figured our new Viceroy would need a proper place to reside, so we are building a castle for him. And when he is at sea it can double as the island fortress to help scare off the riff raff"! As everyone got a good laugh from the stout old gent. He went on to say the city council was seriously considering building a house of pleasure, but they wanted to check with the Viceroy first. Eli looked over at the female passengers and said, "Ladies it seems you will have your brothel as soon as it's built". He turned to the smiling mayor and said, "You better tell the tailor shop to get ready for some serious business". Eli assured him on his next trip he will bring in plenty of cloth, especially since linen was plentiful in Tunis only 70 miles away.

Everyone got settled in by late afternoon to relax and enjoy the Christmas festivities and put aside any work for the next few days. Eli tried his best to clear his mind for at least one day but he kept thinking about a mission that span over 8 years since he was 11. He was so close now he could taste the revenge every time he swallowed. He could smell it with every breath he took. His eyes tried desperately to focus on the Christmas colors of red and green, but all he saw was retribution in plain old black and white.

CHAPTER 10

Eli's Coming

The island was back to normal a few days later as preparations were made for the Sea Stallion to head back to sea. Miss Fortune was moved to the soft cove inside the harbor and moored there allowing any incoming ships to dock easily. Eli would be sailing with his full crew of 40 men & 8 officers who were seasoned and ready for anything that may come their way. Before they left the hull was repainted and figurehead changed back to the De La Regla colors leaving only the name plate and sails that they would easily swap out while at sea. The crew noticed their captain was in a constant state of quiet resolve and a smoldering look about him. It was something Noah had not seen since he was that young boy who crushed his first victim's head open over 8 years before.

December 29th, 1760, they left out of the calm deep blue harbor to head back to Liberty. During the 2-week voyage everyone went over the plan repeatedly till it was burned into their brain. The culmination date was January 18th, 1761, the wedding day of Reginal and Elinore in Bristol. But in Eli's mind it would "Death Day" for one man in particular. The trip went without a hitch as they pulled into Liberty 15 days later under an overcast night sky. The De La Regla was quickly provisioned the following day and ready to sail again. Everwyn, Darin & Hardy would stay in Liberty until it was time to travel by horseback to Bristol dressed as British Royal Officers.

The night of January 16th they sailed out to quietly arrive in Bristol before daylight the following morning. The wedding was to be held at the city church on the far side of town. Usually, a royal ceremony like this one was done at the Royal Chapel in London but since the king didn't feel compelled to attend Ervin decided to have it there in town. Later that night when the shipping company was locked up Tohru snuck in undetected and retrieved Ervin II ledger book from his safe using the combination Lanora had gotten a month earlier. Then he picked the lock and entered the viscount's office to retrieve the document marked "VBR" that was secured in a secret compartment in his desk Lanora had heard about long ago. He handed them to the 3 British Royal Officers waiting outside in the darkness as they quickly went their separate ways as planned. Lanora's job now was to keep her husband occupied till it was time to get ready for the wedding at 11 am the next morning.

That was made a lot easier as he and his father, along with several other men were throwing Reginal a bachelor party at the viscount's estate where they would sleep off the aftereffects till morning. The viscount's servants were instructed clean up the mess, including the whores, and prepare the estate for the reception before 1 pm when the guests would start arriving. Lanora told 4 of her male servants to fetch her husband and the bride groom before daybreak no matter what condition they were in so they would have ample time to clean up and change before traveling to the church 10 miles away.

The guests began arriving slowly due to the unexpected heavy downfall of freezing snow and sleet. The male members of the Ervin family didn't feel the frigid effect since the three were carrying a hangover from the debauchery the night before. Eventually most made it to the church including Eli who was waiting in his coach for Belinda to show up to properly escort her in. Dress in his grey uniform with the crimson trim he emerged from the coach as he saw Belinda arrive. She was in a regal flowing light pink gown and wearing a fur lined full length coat to help brace the cold. When she saw her elegant escort, she immediately tossed the coat back into her carriage knowing she now had something much better to keep her warm. He surprisingly kissed both her blushing cheeks in true European fashion and said, "Now pink really becomes you ma lady, it's wonderful to see you again". She returned the European greeting and replied, "After that unexpected greeting I'm certain I'm pink all over by now. Unexpected but definitely welcomed", she whispered in his ear as she took his arm and entered the church.

As they walk down the aisle she leaned in and softly said, "By the way, you look exceptionally dashing ma lord. I'm thrilled you could make it". Once seated in their reserved pew they silently got comfortable while the rest of the guests found their seats. Eli was admiring the soft white sheer laced top of her gown that started around her throat and cascaded in a stunning effect across her blushing cleavage. He leaned down and whispered in her ear, "I see you're not wearing any jewelry today". She softly replied back, "I adore this dress so much but none of my necklaces seem to go well with it". Eli looked into her sparkling blue eyes and gave her a devilish grin suggesting, "What about a simple pearl drop choker? Maybe something like this"!

Reaching into his jacket pocket he pulled out the silk pink choker that had the thumb nail size iridescent pink pearl attached to it. Belinda's jaw dropped, unable to utter a word as her eyes glistened in the reflection of the unique tear drop shaped jewel of the sea. All she could do was quietly stutter till she eventually composed herself as Eli watched her mouth silently say, "Oh My God"! He gave her a smartass grin and whispered, "Listen, if Ya don't like it just say so I'll find Ya something else"! She giggled and elbowed his ribs as she finally was able to speak, "I have never seen anything as beautiful as that in my entire life, I love it". She looked about knowing all too well they were in church surrounded by royalty then she let herself go, "Oh the hell with it... put it on me now"! She turned her back to Eli as he meticulously tied it around her neck to a perfect fit. He leaned down and whispered in her ear, "Thank God you decided to wear your hair up otherwise I would have been here all day tying this on you"! As he kissed her ear lobe while she turned back around. Blushing the color of her new accessory she threw care to the wind and quickly kissed cheek then nestled back into place snuggling closer to her escort.

Throughout the entire ceremony he marveled at her constantly fiddling with her gift, like a child with a brand-new toy. Every now and then she would repeatedly sneak in a whispered "Thank you" and clutch his arm tighter. He even caught her occasionally bouncing up & down on her heels with delight. Eli only wanted to please her; he wasn't expecting Belinda to take such a broad leap out of her emotional shell. Yet he was equally delighted she did, it was long overdue. With the vows said the priest pronounced them man and wife as they walked down the aisle to the waiting carriage that would take them to the reception. When Eli and Belinda exited the church, he put her in and signaled his coachman to follow as he rode with his little pink lady to the Ervin estate.

She wasted no time digging in her handbag and pulled out a small mirror to admire her radiant gift. Before Eli could properly close the coach door, she pounced on him with a kiss she had been craving to give him for over an hour. She draped a thick warm blanket over their lap and snuggled in for the hour-long ride to the reception. Throughout the trip she asked about the pearl and where it came from as well as assuming the London jeweler crafted it for him. Belinda paused when she came to the realization, she had totally missed the entire wedding ceremony. "I was so caught up with this fabulous gift you surprised me with I completely forgot about wedding". Eli cupped her hand and said, "I know, I was hoping you would". She looked at him with a question mark covering her face as he explained, "you told me at the ball that the bulk of your life had been spent listening to others. Never having the chance to think for yourself and follow your own instincts. In church just now, you cut some of those ties and acted the way you wanted to. All I did was give you a gentle nudge to get Ya started".

They finally arrived at the estate just about the time the snow slowed up to a light flurry along with the rest of the invited guests to help celebrate the newlyweds' happy day. After everyone paid their respects through the long reception line it was down to the usual cake cutting and all the rest of the semi boring traditions associated with this type of celebration. Through it all Belinda never left Eli's side and every chance she had to brag to everyone about her rare gift with childlike glee. There was one person in particular she made a point of show it off to. Ervin II was finishing off his second "hair of the dog" drink when her & Eli walked up to the bar for a glass of champagne. As if to rub his red nose in it she boasted, "Did you see the wonderful gift the Count gave me Ervin", as she pointed at the pearl choker. Trying his best to focus his still blood shot eyes all he uttered was, "Oh yes nice". He quickly cut a disgruntled leer at Eli and walked away as the 2 just snickered under their breath.

At 3 pm a British officer arrived looking a lot like Darin. He waited at the door instructing the servant he had a letter addressed personally for the viscount. Moments later Ervin walked up as Darin saluted and said, "Please forgive the intrusion your grace this letter is for you". Ervin opened it to read, "It is imperative you meet with me tonight at 9 pm sharp at your office and come alone. This is a matter of "Royal" importance. Signed, King George III ". His eyes lit up as he looked back at the awaiting officer who silently nodded and took back the letter and ripped it up saying, "I was never here your grace, understand"? Ervin nodded in agreement as Darin saluted again and left.

Eli pulled out his pocket watch and noticed the time as he gazed out the large front window seeing a soldier riding away. Thinking to himself, "Step one done". He peered about the room seeing all three Ervin men still there and drinking as anticipated. From the usual chat in the room, he knew the couple would be honeymooning in London at the Palace Hotel. Traveling there by coach it would take them at least 8 hours or more depending on the weather since the trip was almost 120 miles by land. Lanora had already told her husband she was staying in Bristol at their home for a few days before she headed back to London. If Ervin II was going to do any fooling around with one of his paid whores, he would have to do it elsewhere.

Milling about was Hardy in his British Royal Captain's uniform well disguised with a full beard and eye patch. For about an hour he had been casually chatting with the viscount and Ervin II mostly about the "sexy young lassies" at the reception. A subject both enjoyed telling tales about. When the timing was right, and both had enough liquor in them Hardy started the verbal contest by weaving a story of how he bedded his first virgin when she was only 15. She was the daughter of an Irish innkeeper who owed him money, so he took his daughter in partial exchange. The 3 men laughed as Ervin II thought for a second and gloated about how he lost his virginity when he was 15 to a 16-year-old tight little Welch virgin. "As good looking as she was, it surprised me someone hadn't busted her open sooner". The viscount snickered and toasted his son saying, "Yeah, I remember that little red headed bitch. She was our house maid at the time. I should have gotten some of that too before she left. Didn't Reginal bed her too"? Ervin II chuckled saying, "Yeah, he did but I ruined her first"! Hardy forced a laugh out knowing once he told Eli that would be the end of the Ervin assholes.

The boastful chatting eventually ended as the 3 went their separate ways to mingle with the other guests. Hardy caught Eli's attention and signaled him to have a private talk. He politely excused himself whispering to Belinda that he would be right back. She smiled and understood as Eli made his way to Hardy who was in the barren back hallway. The talk was quick but shockingly informative. He turned to Hardy and said, "Ok we still go as planned". Hardy patted his shoulder and said, "You got it boss". When he returned to his gorgeous companion, he leaned down kissing her cheek and whispered, "How about we get the hell out of here and get better acquainted"? As he softly nibbled her ear lobe. Looking into her gleaming eyes she replied, "I thought you'd never ask... let's go"!

Several minutes later the newlyweds departed for their long journey to London as the reception was now winding down with almost everyone leaving before it got too late. It seemed Ervin II was going to stay there and arrange for a play toy to join him once Lanora and everyone left. Aboard the coach she told the driver to take her back to her hotel. Belinda had checked into the Bristol Palace Hotel a block from the main harbor. Eli told the coachman to stop at the docks first as he turned to his luscious companion and said he had something to get off the ship for them. By the time they reach the wharf it was already getting dark and overcast with snow coming down again. Softly grasping her cheeks with one hand, he kissed her and said, "Don't go anywhere my Venus, I'll be but a moment". She sat there grinning from ear to ear as she whispered, "Venus... I like that"! Eli quickly returned wearing his long black duster coat and black 3-point leather hat.

Once inside he pulled out 2 cold bottles of her favorite wine as she smiled saying, "Now that's my kind of coat! You got any more surprised under there my sexy Adonis"? Quickly picking up on the nickname he grinned devilishly and replied, "I guess you'll just have to wait and see for yourself Venus"! When the coach stopped Eli handed the driver a 10-pound note and thanked him while Belinda said, "that will be all for tonight thank you". Tipping his snow-covered hat, he graciously thanked them both and said, "Have a wonderful evening me Lord & Lady". She laughed as the rushed inside saying, "I plan on it"! When they reached the reception deck Belinda requested a champagne bucket and a plate of their best hors d' oeuvres be sent up to the princess suite. Laughing and giggling the entire way up the staircase to the second floor.

Inside was a spacious sitting room with a fireplace that needed stoking. Taking off his hat and coat she saw he was wearing only his black silk ruffed shirt, black tight pants and boots. Dazzled by his look she walked to the bedroom door and said, "Get that fire going baby while I get comfortable myself, I'll be right back", as she winked and blew him a kiss. In no time he had the fire blazing again as a knock on the door came with their request. He tipped the steward a half a crown and walked out to the balcony to gather up some fresh fallen snow off the rail and filled the bucket with it to ice down the wine. As he was finishing up the bedroom door opened. Perched and seductively posed stood his Venus wearing a floor length sheer black negligee. See through enough for Eli to notice she was wearing nothing more than a pair of black stocking secured at the top of her thighs with black sequined garters and a pair of petite black heeled bedroom slippers.

Eli stood several steps away from his erotic goddess and spoke, "Now unpin your hair". She pulled them out as the long raven cascades fell softly down. "Now shake your head"! She swung it back and forth till her bangs crossed over her eyes so she could barely see through. He walked up to her and brushed them away enough to let those blue bedroom eyes appear. Firmly cupping his hands to the back of her neck that still had the pink choker around it, he leaned down and kissed her full ruby red lips. Pressing them open with his tongue they engulfed one another's mouth in moist wet ecstasy as she wrapped her arms around his neck and hung on for dear life. With his shirt undone to his belly he could feel the impression of her puffy pink nipples against his skin.

Belinda had much more than just an exquisite face and stunning silky hair. She had a tight firm disciplined body at the age of 25. Since she was unable to give birth, every inch of her was smooth perfection. For over three years, since her husband died, no one had come close to laying a hand on her statues frame. Eli standing well over 6 feet tall, he had to literally pickup her 5-foot self to kiss her, which she adored him doing. He picked her up further as she instinctively wrapped her legs around his waist as they entered the huge bedroom. Approaching the large satin sheeted bed that was already turned down, he suddenly Dropped her on it till she bounced in delightful surprise. He pointed at her and commanded, "You! Wait there I'll be right back"! She mock saluted and said, "Yes Sir"!

He returned with the wine and 2 tall, chilled glasses and poured them a drink. Staying on the bed she popped up on her knees with a saucy impish grin and torn open the rest of his close shirt. She then stretched up to undo his pony tall as his dark brown hair fell about his neck and face. They clinked glasses as she pierced her impassion eyes into his and softly said, "To a night I hope we both will never forget". They drank it down then put the empty glasses on the night table. Still in her sexy upright kneeling position she firmly pushed him back and commanded, "OK Adonis...Strip"! As she leaned back to take in the show. Once he had his boots off the remains of his shirt fell to the floor and then finally his tight pants that was already showing his erection.

From their pressed body's while they were still clothed, she knew he was gifted but she had no idea just how thick and massive he really was until now. He stepped up to the edge of the bed as she took off her slippers and stood up. Slowly she untied the neat bow from around her waist and let the sheer gown fall on its own. His face was perfectly parallel with her firm budding breasts and turned up nipples as he gently cupped and savored one and then the other. Her pink puffy nipples melted in his warm wet mouth as her moans erotically echoed through the room. Slowly he moved into the bed as she softly laid back to begin a night of body shattering passion. From cunnilingus to fellatio and back again, they explored their bodies in a wild delirious fashion till she climbed up & mounted her stallion and rode him with everything she had. That night, Belinda let every inhabitation she ever had go and never looked back once.

Eli got up and poured them another round as Belinda laid on her back embedded in her plush pillows with a dazed look of absolute exhausted ecstasy. He grabbed up his pocket watch from his pants without her seeing and checked the time, it was almost 8:30 pm. He picked up the tray of hors d' oeuvres as they began to feed one another the delicious appetizers. When they had their fill, she snuggled into his bare chest softly saying, "I am so relaxed baby, I haven't felt like this since..." He looked down and saw she fell fast asleep in mid-sentence. Quickly remembering where he was in bed he got up and dressed. Hardy's potion he slipped in her glass worked perfectly figuring she would be out for at least a few hours. More than enough time for step two.

He closed the door of the bedroom as he walked over to the balcony in the dark sitting room and carefully climbed down the iron lattes work to the back street below. Keeping out of sight he made his way to his destination with time to spare. Meanwhile the viscount arrived at his office anxious to discovery what his majesty had in mind for him. Checking his watch, he saw he had time for a drink or two to calm his nerves. As he gulped down his second shot of scotch the town clock chimed out 9 times signifying the royal arrival. Looking up from his deck, the office door opened as 3 armed British Royal Officers walked in. "Viscount Ervin, I presume"? The fat man staggered up from his chair and replied, "Yes sir I am please come in gentlemen and have a seat". They close the door and approached him as the officer in the middle spoke.

"I am Colonel Smyth of his majesty's Royal Guard; this is Captain Harden, and this is Major Karlson. You are under arrest for numerous counts of embezzlement and high treason". The colonel placed the arrest document on his desk stamped and signed by the king. Ervin sat there speechless as he looked briefly at his arrest warrant before the colonel picked it up and put it back in his jacket. "I... I... I don't know what to say except I'm innocent, I swear I am". The colonel pointed to the hand painted mural of the world map on the wall behind his desk and told him to please open it. Disguised in the painted map was a false panel that hid his safe. Without hesitation he stumbled up and quickly did as he was told. "Take your seat please Mister Ervin" as the captain inspected the contents. From his jacket he pulled out the ledger book from Ervin II along with the VBR document and put it with the rest of the various confidential items that were inside and placed it all on the desk in front of the stunned bastard.

Ervin's eyes widened when he saw the ledger among everything else. He knew the transactions written in there could cost him his life. He also knew with him gone his backstabbing son would take over as owner of the company, not to mention his estate. Looking through the assorted papers the colonel picked up the ledger book and began to thumb through it. It only took a few moments as he snapped it closed with a loud crack and gave the petrified man a deathly stare. Then he picked up the VBR paper that contained a list of over 2 dozen names and locations of members of the so-called Viscount Bandit Raiders including the code words to gather them up. "Just as we suspected! You have been dealing in illegal & unauthorized action for years! Not to mention the tens of thousands of embezzled tax money collected in Wales, Scotland, Ireland, and the new world"! The colonel snapped his fingers as the captain walked to the door and signaled. Seconds later 4 more soldiers walked in escorting Ervin II who was handcuffed from behind.

The fat man started to get up and lung at his turncoat son when he was halted at the point of a rapidly produced pistol from the major who told him, "Sit down Mister! Move once more and I'll spread your fucking brains everywhere"! The shackled son was still half drunk when they kidnapped him while he was still in bed with one of his whores. The servants at the estate had long since finished they work and left, thus leaving the place empty except for the two in bed. She still laid there with a mini ball shot through her head and a ransom note that read, "We have your son, he is still alive, For Now! We demand 50,000 pounds in gold in exchange for him! We will be in touch when you have the money"!

The 4 soldiers pushed him down in a chair in front of the desk so father and son could clearly see each other. The colonel put the ledger book in Ervin II face and asked, "Is this your handwriting"? Looking at the book then back into his father's raging eyes he meekly said, "No". Ervin yelled, "He's Lying, that's his book not mine, check the handwriting colonel, I'm left-handed he's Not"! The son sobered up enough to realize his father had him as he said, "You lousy Bastard! After all I've done for you, this is how you repay me"? Eli had heard enough as he was listening from the closed door and walked in. Only the 2 Ervins looked up to see who was coming in as Eli slowly approached with a smoldering look in his heated eyes as he muttered "Step 3"!

Without hesitation he dropped the phony Italian accent and spoke, "Well... well... well... what have we here gentlemen? Is this another party? I do hope I'm not intruding". Seeing the befuddled look on the face of the Ervin's at the clear and natural English accent, Eli continued. "Oh, I'm sorry, I suppose you're wondering what happened to Count Maschione. I decided to let him stay in bed with his latest conquest, the Lady Belinda Winslow who he just fucked till she passed out"! He walked up behind Ervin II and patted him on the back and added, "Just like I thoroughly ravaged and screwed Lady Lanora and the young innocent Elinore. Oh, by the way, dear old Reginal ain't getting a virgin tonight, I saw to that"! As he slapped the back of her daddy's head. From his coat pocket he pulled out 3 garters and dangled them in front of his face. "Just so you know I wasn't telling a story the blue and gold ones came off of your wife's sultry thighs. Did you know she has this cute little heart shaped birth mark on her left butt cheek? It's rather becoming, especially when I have her down on all fours slamming that ass hard till, she explodes. But I'm sure you knew that, Junior! You don't mind if I call you junior, do you"? As he slapped the side of his head even harder.

"Oh yeah, this dainty little pink garter is your sweet daughter's. Actually, Lanora and I both slide it off her semi pure thigh". He grabbed the back of his hair hard and continued, "See Junior, Ya missed out on a fun 3some all this time. But I guess Ya had more fun with your diseased ridden street walking sluts". Eli looked at the soldiers and said, "I'll bet your pecker must look like it's been run through a meat grinder by now Junior". Eli let go of junior's hair and turned to the fat man and said, "I'm sorry Viscount Ervin, please allow me to introduce these find gentlemen here. The Sargent is Wolf Schutze my expert gunnery officer. Next to him is Corporal Fabrice Naviree, my Ingenius Shipwright. Next to him is Corporal Marino Tiburon, my prolific chief carpenter. Captain Harden is in actuality Hardy McKay, my multi-talented ship's doctor. This major is really Darin Cavety, you may recognize the name when he was harbor master in Charleston, he's now my brilliant artist, forger and mapmaker. Oh yes, Colonel Smyth you have to meet. He is really Everwyn Morwer. You might not remember but a few years back you screwed him out of the flute his uncle owned before he died. And the big burry Sargent Major is actually Noah Studman, my long trusted first mate and a man who has been like a father to me"!

"There is one other I wished you could meet, Tohru a genius in the kitchen when he's not at his best attributes of stealth and lock picking. He is unable to be with us tonight, he is far too busy insuring the safe kidnapping of the happy bride groom, with a little help from his new wife and mother-in-law"! Eli took a breath and pulled out his old journal and proceeded. "That leave just me viscount, or maybe I should officially call you Grandpa now. My name is Eli Griffin. My birth mother was Elizabeth Griffin, daughter of the late Nicholas and Maybelle Griffin of Pyle, Wales". He pulled out his knife and threw it hard into the desk as it wavered back and forth in front of dear old Grandpa Ervin. "I'm sure you don't recognize this blade; it was taken off the dead body of my true grandfather shorty after you ordered the entire family murdered by your so-called bandit raiders. You remember Horace McLeary, one of your paid assassins from Scotland'. He could see Ervin was thinking clear enough to remember it all as Eli continued his trip down dark memory lane.

"It's a shame you never had a chance to meet his wife, Colleen. There was never a sweeter person in the world, and I am so proud to call her mother since she stepped up to raise me right, along with Noah. But then you did know of her since you sent another assassin to Charleston to kill her. No worries, Grandpa I took good care of Fahen personally. I cracked his fucking skull open with an iron skillet, and I was only 11 years old at the time"! As Eli and his brothers burst out laughing. "Just to keep the records straight, she died from injuries in a hurricane. That brings me back to my birth mother Junior, or maybe I can call you daddy now"! As Eli turned his satanic glare at the terrified bastard.

"Yes, Hardy told me all about the bragging contest you 3 got into this afternoon. How you and your retarded little brother took turns raping her. And how dear old Grandpa encourage it too. But then I guess perverted sickness like that runs in your inbred family. Maybe that's why I'm the survivor of twins or maybe it was because my mother Elizabeth was forced to give birth at sea since she was impelled to flee to the new world. Nevertheless, she died a few hours later giving me life. And the only will and testament is this tatter journey her and Colleen left for me along with this knife that I cherish"! As he pulled it out of the scared desk and put it back in his scabbard.

He pulled out a scroll and put it in front of Ervin. "This is your will Grandpa, I took the liberty to draw it up for you. It states that in the event of your death everything you own will go to your eldest son. If and when he passes away it goes to the dumbass Reginal. And when he's gone Lady Winslow takes over. Sign it Grandpa and maybe I'll let you all live"! Ervin glanced it over and signed it with a trembling left-handed scrawl. "Stamp it now"! He reached in his desk draw and pulled out the family seal and stamped it. What he didn't notice was the date on the will, June 6th, 1756. Eli picked it up and looked to see if everything was in order before placing it in the open safe. He nodded at his brothers as they stepped out for a moment only to return with 25 bars of the phony gold and carefully stacked them in the safe. "You see grandpa I can be generous when I want to be. In fact, let's you and me have a toast to it". Eli picked the bottle of scotch and grabbed a couple of glasses off the shelf.

He placed them on the desk and quickly poured out two generous portions. He could see the fat man's hesitation at the prospect of some kind of trick till Eli gulped his down. Relieved and in desperate need of a drink he finished it off quickly. Eli turned and said, "I'm sorry daddy, I completely forgot about you, I'll bet you'd like a drink too". As he helped him up from his chair Eli caught a whiff of urine noticing the chair seat was wet. "Awe, did you piss your pants again? Here let me help you with that DADDY"! Noah and Wolf quickly grabbed his arms a pulled him back. Eli whipped out his pistol and made dead aim at his face. Junior closed his eyes and cringed till he heard a single click. The yellow urine was now dripping down his pant leg and puddling on the floor. As he slowly relaxed and opened his eyes, he heard Eli say, "Opps that one didn't work".

Before he realized it and could react again, he saw the barrel of a second pistol fire hitting it's aimed mark with pinpoint accuracy. He screamed out in excruciating agony looking down to see a widening stain of blood mix with his piss. He glanced up at the face of Satan himself as Eli's voice smoldered out, "You won't need that pecker anymore Daddy, or your balls. You've fucked with them for the last time". He put his pistols back in his shoulder holsters and walked up to the castrated bastard and told Noah and Wolf to shake him. They did until his severed genitals drop to the floor. "Sit him down"! Eli bent down and scoop the remains up in one hand a walked up behind. "There's only one place they belong now... and may you rot in hell with them you fucking bastard"! He shoved the handful into the son of a bitch's mouth and forced it closed until he choked to death.

Ervin was paralyzed sitting there witnessing it all. Eli turned and gave him the same satanic look as the fat man's face began to cringe in growing pain. "I'll bet your wondering about now what's become of your mentally defective boy. Well, he's probably dead by now too, and it seems he passed away from the same cause as his big brother. Choking to death on his useless crotch. If I know Tohru he took as much pleasure slicing them off as I did blasting his brother's all to hell". Eli could see the fat man's face turning red as he gripped his disgusting obese belly. Before he lost it all Eli leaned in and asked, "Any last words old man... now's the time?" He struggled for the final bit of strength and barely said, "you said I could live if I signed my will". Eli slyly grinned and said, "I Lied! But take solace in the fact that everything now goes to your daughter in law and granddaughter who are forever my personal sluts since they proudly call me Master! Go rot in hell with your sons' old man"! Seconds later he flopped forward on his desk echoing out his last breath.

Eli looked over at Everwyn and said, "Ok he's all yours now". Eli pulled him back into his chair, so he was sitting upright as Everwyn put a clean shot between his eyes. They carefully put back everything that was in the safe except for the ledger and the VBR list that they kept. The desk was cleared of the 2 glasses including the one Eli managed to slip the clear liquid poison in while he was taking them off the shelf with his back to everyone. They locked up the safe tight and before leaving an anonymous note was left on the desk reading, "We have Lady Winslow and daughter Elinore. If you want to see them alive again bring 50,000 pounds before nightfall to the red door cottage, 5 kilometers due east of Wick on the London Road". It was dated January 19th, 1761. Eli grabbed the dagger in the desk and posted the note with it in the same hole he threw his blade in. Undetected they all snuck out and one by one made it back to the ship wearing their long black coats. Eli cleaned his hands up in a nearby snowbank before climbing up to the balcony to return to his still sleeping Belinda. He stoked up the fireplace then stripped and got back into bed as he left it 90 minutes before and drifted off to sleep as well.

As for Tohru, he accomplished his mission to the letter. Before the coach left the estate, he stowed away in the rear baggage compartment after all the luggage was loaded and secured. When they reached the milestone east of Wick, he climbed up and strangled the driver and brought the coach to a halt. Dressed in his black ninja clothes and masked he waited till Reginal stepped out to see why they stopped. Coming up from behind Tohru chopped him in the back of the neck knocking him unconscious long enough drag him into snow covered woods and immediately tied his hands behind his back and gagged him. Using his razor-sharp dagger, he sliced off the bride groom's pathetic genitals as the idiot briefly screamed into his gag and passed out. Tohru replaced the gag with the bloody mass and suffocated him till he choked to dead. Wiping off the excess in the snow he returned to the coach, looked inside to see if Elinore was ok, nodded to her and drove the coach to the red door cottage.

Lanora showed up on horseback about 30 minutes later and Tohru quickly tied them up comfortably but secure enough to fool anyone. Still wearing his mask, he assured them they would be discovered by early afternoon or before. He stoked the fireplace enough to make sure they would be kept warm adding a few logs near their feet so they could kick them in if needed. Hitching the horse to the back of the coach he drove off eastward for a mile then stopped and unhitched his ride. With the dead driver still sitting in his spot Tohru slapped the team as the coach sped away. He went on to finish the arranged mission and eventually made his way back to the ship undetected.

At midnight Belinda slowly woke to the sounds of the city clock chiming and the town crier bellowing out, "Twelve o'clock and all is well"! As she focused her heavy eyes, she saw her Adonus right where he was hours before she drifted off. Eli was in that light state of somnambulance and opened his eyes with the silky feel of Belinda's naked body warm against his. "Seems we both passed out Darling", she quietly said as she leaned up and kissed him completely awake. "Frankly I'm surprise I'm still alive after what you did to me... you sexy beast! I have never climaxed that much before even when I'm pleasuring myself". She quickly giggled blushing, "Oopsie... did I just say that out loud". Eli stretched out his long muscular arms and said smiling, "How does it feel to be free my sexy Venus? Free to say what you feel and finally be yourself". "It feels like a ton of bricks has been lifted off me... and I have you to thank for helping to remove them too". She hopped up and straddled his belly and asked in a coy manner, "Baby, can I ask you a question"? Eli nodded yes. "Would you please spend the night with me"?

He gave her a stern look, then reached up and rolled her pink nipples between his fingers and replied, "Only if I can play with these some more"! In a high pitched little girly voice she answered, "Oh Ta but I get to play with this some more too"! She reached around and firmly gripped his growing shaft. Looking intently at his smiling face she remarked, "With everything happening I failed to mention how much I love your new look", as she ran her long fingernail across his moustache then outlined the sharp ends of his goatee. "Kinda makes you look a little like the devil himself. I like it"! Leaning in to playfully tongue the edged patch of hair below his lower lip. "Funny you should mention it baby. After some close lengthy inspection, I noticed you shave and trim your sweet little "Venus Trap"! Belinda glanced down between her spread legs and giggled saying, "Yep. I started it a few years back. I got sick and tired of getting my fingers tangled up whenever I was feeling a bit amorous. Oh my God, I still can't believe I'm telling you all this. You really are the Devil"! With them both laughing as he rolled her over on their side and intertwined in passion.

After a heated second round of erotic exploration, they drifted off to sleep once more until they both awoke to the loud clamoring in the streets. It was just past 6 am when the cries rang out about the tragedy of the Ervin family. Quickly putting on his pants and Belinda throwing on a robe they opened the glass doors and walked out on the balcony. People were rushing about passing on the terrible news as Soldiers on foot and horseback raced around securing the city entrances. Eli got the attention of one of the villagers below asking what was happening. The man loudly proclaimed that Viscount Ervin and his son had been killed by bandits. And it's rumored they kidnapped Lady Winslow and her daughter. Eli tossed down a gold sovereign to the man and told him to go to his ship in port, "I'm Count Maschione. Tell my first mate Commander Noah to send a squad of my best men to safeguard Lady Belinda here at the hotel... and hurry"! "Yes, your grace", as he raced off.

Within a few minutes Noah, Marino & Wolf arrived dressed in the appropriate uniforms along with Abel and a dozen of the largest crewmen fully armed. They posted guards around the hotel perimeter with Abel at the door of the suite. Meanwhile Fabrice setup an armed guard on the dock alongside the De La Regla with Everwyn commanding a second line of defense on deck as every crewman was armed and ready. Eli kissed Belinda and told her he would be back as soon as possible, "Your safe baby my men have orders to shot anyone attempting to enter". She replied, "Thank you darling hurry back and please be safe". Eli opened the door and told Abel to post a man on the balcony, "Shoot the first bastard who tries to come in"! Abel snapped to attention and said, "Aye Captain they gotta get through me first"!

Eli hurried to the ship to change and make sure all was secured aboard. Once he changed into his uniform, he raced off accompanied by Darin & Hardy. They ran across one of the British officers commanding a squad of foot soldiers. The Lieutenant halted his troops then saluted saying, "Are you ok your grace? I was ordered to secure the area around your vessel". Eli nodded, "I'm fine I have already done that and setup a guard around the hotel where Lady Belinda Winslow is. Bring your troops with me we are going to the shipping company". "At your command your grace", as they double timed it to the office to secure and investigate.

The Lieutenant posted his men around the building as Eli, Darin & Hardy entered to be met by the magistrate and the captain of the guard who bowed & saluted. "I came as soon as I heard the news. I have already placed personal guard at the hotel where Lady Belinda Winslow is staying. I came to see what else I can do'. They thanked the count as everyone proceeded into the gruesome remains of the office. "This is my ship's Doctor First Lieutenant McKay and Quartermaster Cavety". They slowly looked about to size up the situation as well as look for any clues. The magistrate pointed out the ransom note as the captain wondered why the 2 men were so brutally murdered. Darin eventually walked over to closely exam the mural. Tracing his hand around the thin seem he noticed an indentation on the map around the town of Kingwood and pressed in. The door popped open revealing the hidden safe that was locked and untouched. Deducing the culprits didn't know about it and tortured the 2 in hopes they would speak. "How brave and gallant they were", uttered the captain as everyone nodded in agreement.

"The important thing now is the safe return of Lady Lanora and Lady Elinore", stated the count. The captain said he had a garrison of troops ready to march immediately to the location. Eli paused a moment and said, "No captain they will be expecting just that and will kill the women before you get close. May I suggest an alternative plan"? "Please do your grace", said the intrigued magistrate. "My officers & crew are trained for a mission like this. I have an excellent tracker as well as my Tunisian crewmen are expert marksmen and stealth fighters. Let me take in a squad of my best men with your garrison in reserve as a flanking decoy. We will retrieve the ladies unharmed I guarantee it"! The townsmen agreed fully as the plan was set into motion.

But the captain was unaware this was the plan all along. Months before when Tohru grabbed up the ledger book, he also had the KBR list. Using her personal messenger in London, Lanora dispatched him to contact the leader of the raiders in Scotland about a very profitable mission. The letter was composed by the ambidextrous Darin who signed and stamped it, Viscount Ervin. They were to secretly gather just outside of Wick on the night of January 18th, 1761, and await further instructions from Lady Lanora personally. Their mission was to eliminate Count Maschione who was led to believe the 2 women were held captive in the red door cottage.

Arriving by horseback, Lanora met up with the 20 men of the VBR at the prearranged spot 2 kilometers west of the cottage. She told them a small man all dressed in black & masked will show them were to position themselves for the ambush. She handed the leader 2,000 pounds in bank notes and rode off. Shortly after Tohru secured the women inside the men arrived as he showed them the setup position on the wooded bluff 50 yards across from the cottage and wait until morning when the count would arrive. For 2,000 pounds they would happily camp in the cold night for several hours.

Eli gathered up Tohru and a dozen of his best marksmen as they boarded a covered wagon and headed east toward Wick about 5 miles away. The captain had already moved his assembled garrison on the march as the wagon passed them at the halfway point. About 1,000 from their target the unloaded and quietly worked their way through the woods till they came up behind the line of shivering bandits. Eli silently snuck around the right flank while Tohru moved to the left. When they were both in position, Eli signaled his squad to open fire on their selected targets. From 25 yards away it was a turkey shoot as the first volley took out the12 bandits in the middle. Leaping up from the flanks the flashing blades of Eli & Tohru sliced open the 8 men left. He signaled the squad to join them as to insured they were all dead using the thrusts of their razor-sharp bayonets. Eli found the leader and relieved him of the letter and the 2,000 pounds as he said to his crew, "Great job men please feel free to take whatever Ya like, the day is yours"!

Hearing the shots, the captain hurried the garrison up the road and moments later saw the devastation the count's elite crew had made. They opened the cottage door together to happily see the two women unharmed as they quickly untied them. "Oh my God thank you so much captain you saved us just in time. We thought everyone had given up on us". He tipped his hat and replied, "Lady Winslow all the thanks must go to Count Maschione and his men, they single handedly eliminated the vermin". Elinore replied, "Count my mother & I are forever in your debt as is our entire family". Eli looked at the captain and said, "I think you should tell them Captain". Acting out the part to perfection the two women looked at the officer curiously and said, "Tell us what"? "Lady Lanora... Lady Elinore It is with deep regret I must inform you both of the tragic loss of Viscount Ervin and both of your husbands. Please take comfort in the fact that they died gallantly protecting the honor of your family and the crown".

Once a coach was brought up to carry the women back to Bristol, the Captain pulled the count aside and informed him they recovered the dismembered body of Lord Reginal. "It wasn't a pretty sight either, seemed he met his fate in the same ugly way his brother did". Eli quietly suggested the way all 3 died should be kept a secret from everyone. "I completely agree your grace, they will be buried in London with honors. And again, thank you... all England is forever in your debt. My report to King George III will tell of the heroic action by you and your gallant crew. I'd be honored to shake your hand"! Eli pulled off his blood-stained glove and firmly shook hands saying, "It would be my pleasure Captain". Before the coach carrying the 2 ladies away Eli opened the door and whispered, "I believe you dropped this Lady Lanora", smiling slyly as he handed her the 2,000 pounds. They all grinned as he closed the door of the coach and told the driver to safely take them away.

He gathered up his crew who were still being saluted by the garrison and boarded the wagon for the ride back to their ship. Sitting up front with Tohru who was driving, he lit a match and set fire to the letter he took off the dead bandit leader and the 2 watched it turn to ashes. He patted his brother's back and said, "You know, for a worthless cook you ain't half bad". He smiled and replied, "Yeah, and for a scrawny little bastard I guess you'll due". By the time they got back to town the entire city had turned out to welcome the Heroes of Bristol. The captain took the advice and had the 3 Ervin men quickly boxed up in sealed coffins and taken to London. Once the mess was cleaned up a day later at the estate, Lanora and Elinore returned with an armed escort to begin taking up residence in their new home.

As for Belinda, she was thrilled to see her Adonis return unharmed as she waved to him from the front balcony of the hotel. The ship's guard at the hotel was relieved and replace with a full squad of British troops and remained there until she left for London to attend the funeral within the week. As Eli returned to his ship, the British guard had replaced his crew while the town people on the dock cheered each one of them. He saw a newfound respect for his crew being handed out. The villagers looked past the color of their skin for once and admired them as men, not slaves. Even if it was for a brief moment, he thought, it was well worth it. Eli quickly cleaned up and changed to return to his awaiting Venus to enjoy a delicious lunch, compliments of the hotel as the clock rung out 12 noon.

When the preparations for the funeral had been finalized to occur on Sunday January 25th, 1761, it was overshadowed by the announcement of King George III's selection of his queen, Charlotte of Mecklenburg, much to the delight of her first cousin Lady Belinda. Belinda's deceased mother was

Charlotte's aunt and held the title of Duchess by blood relation. Thus, she now would be given the title as well by British law in accordance with the crown. But that wouldn't happen until September when the king planned to marry her. So, it seemed the early announcement was far more important than the Ervin triple funeral in the eyes of the Royal Court. Most were well aware of the less than regal characteristics from the 3 men, especially the viscount. They were elated to hear that Lanora and Elinore were safe since they commanded more respect than their dead male counterparts.

The De La Regla sailed into London harbor to a tumultuous welcome and a full 21-gun salute a day before the scheduled funeral. He was met at the gangway by the Captain of the Palace Royal Guard who immediately saluted the count and handed him an invitation reading, "Your presents are respectfully requested at the palace of King George III on January 26th, 1761, for an award ceremony in your honor". Signed King George III, ruler of England and Ireland. "My garrison is honored to be at your disposal your grace and anything you or your crew may want is yours, compliments of the King". Eli thanked him as he pointed to Darin standing behind him and said, "My Quartermaster has a list of supplies & provisions for my ship". The captain saluted again and added, "Your entire crew will be taken care of and treated with the utmost respect by the people of London".

Before he left, he handed a sealed letter to him and quietly said, "I was told to personally hand this to you your grace", as he smiled and proceeded to fill the list Darin gave him. Noah leaned forward, speaking for the crew whispered, "Another love letter Captain"? As they all snickered. Eli turned around and muttered, "Shut up you sons of bitches", with everyone laughing under their breath. Eli continued to chuckle as he walked back aboard to his cabin to read the note. "I will have warrant put out for your immediate arrest if you don't join me for dinner this evening. The charge: Theft of one black garter! Signed, Lady Venus, p.s... My coach will pick you up at 6 pm sharp". He burst out laughing and opened his cabinet to speak to her portrait, "Lady you are one crazy bitch"!

Wearing his blood red open shirt, black pants & booted he put on his hat and black duster coat and boarded the coach for the short 3-mile ride to her palatial home in Peckham. She greeted him at the door dawned in a form fitting red sparkling gown. Around her neck was a matching red choker with her tear drop pink pearl attached to it. They kissed and embraced as she escorted him in. "It's so wonderful to see you again my Adonis". "I figured I better show up on time before you called the law on me", as he took off his hat and coat to displace the stolen item, he was wearing around his right bicep. "I knew it you rotten theft"! Laughing as he picked her up and kissed her passionately with her arms locked around his neck. "And just so you know little girl, Ya ain't getting it back. I earned it the hard way"! She said in a naughty voice, "A very Hard way too"! He pulled back the slit on the right side of her gown and looked down saying, "And don't be surprised in the morning you're missing a red garter too"! She gazed in his eyes and sincerely said, "Nobody does it better... baby you're the best"!

The following afternoon they attended the funeral amidst a sparce crowd all dressed in traditional black including the black vale widows. As Eli looked about, seeing emotionless faces from the court members and guests. Thankfully both of the widow's vales we thick enough to hide the careless looks they carried. The ceremony was brief with it all over in less than an hour. Eli forced himself not to bust out laughing when the priest read the eulogy, "We commend the spirit of these 3 noble men to the ground remembering they gave their lives honorably for King and Country". As he muttered to himself, "Ashes to ashes... dust to dust you worthless bastards. Enjoying rotting in hell"!